The

Also by Gerrard Cowan

Gerrard Cowan is the author of The Machinery Trilogy, the story of a world whose leaders are chosen by a machine – until the machine breaks.

He lives in Ireland with his wife Sarah and their children. His first known work was a collection of poems on monsters, written for Halloween when he was eight; it is sadly lost to civilisation. When he isn't writing strange fantasy books he works as a freelance journalist. He can be found at gerrardcowan.com, at facebook.com/gerrardcowanauthor and @GerrardCowan on Twitter.

Praise For The Machinery Trilogy

'The story is part apocalypse, part mystery and entirely captivating. If you're looking for a new voice in fantasy whose writing is going to get you thinking, then look no further'
The Eloquent Page

'if you enjoy epic fantasy with a little sci-fi thrown in, I highly suggest you grab a copy and prepare for a wild ride'
Mom With a Reading Problem

'Every so often you come across a book that really hits the spot. For me, *The Machinery* was just such a book ... The degree of abstractness and the disjunct one only normally experiences in dream creates an underlying mood that put me in mind of Mervyn Peake'
Graeme K. Talboys, author of the Shadow in the Storm series

The Strategist

GERRARD COWAN

The Machinery Trilogy

Harper*Voyager*
An imprint of HarperCollins*Publishers* Ltd
1 London Bridge Street
London SE1 9GF

www.harpervoyagerbooks.co.uk

This Paperback Original 2018

First published in Great Britain in ebook format by Harper*Voyager* 2017

A catalogue record for this book
is available from the British Library

ISBN: 978-0-00-816022-7

Typeset in Sabon by Palimpsest Book Production Limited,
Falkirk, Stirlingshire

Automatically produced by Atomik ePublisher from Easypress

A
re
i
ph

For my parents, Marie and Ronnie, and my sister, Rosaleen

Chapter One

'What is the Machinery?' the man asked.

There was silence for a moment, and then a great sigh, somewhere far away.

The man opened his eyes, to a black, starless expanse. He was alone, held up by invisible strings: a puppet in the abyss.

The man flexed his fingers. He reached up to his face, felt the stubble, and confirmed he was what he had always been: Charls Brandione. A physical being. *Not a nothing.*

He looked into the dark, and searched for her.

The Dust Queen.

'Ask me another question,' she said.

It was strange, that voice of hers: three people speaking at once, and one voice from three mouths. He sensed she was impatient, and the thought sent a spasm of laughter through him. How could *he* hold such power over *her*?

He turned his head, focused on another stretch of darkness. She had taken him here before, many times. What was this place? It was a void, yet there was something there, in the darkness: a deep intelligence, like that of the Queen, but older even than her, its thoughts stretching across age after age. He could feel it. He could hear the whispers of its great-

1

ness. There was a conflict within this unknowable mind; he could taste it.

The darkness changed. Three sets of unblinking eyes appeared before him.

'Ask me another question.' The eyes narrowed. He could ignore her no longer. But only one question ever came to mind. It was a question she would not answer, but it mattered more than anything else. Everything was tied up with it: the old world and whatever had taken its place; the rules they lived by, all their fears and dreams.

'What is the Machinery?'

The eyes blinked.

He was back in his tent.

No: not tent. He had been in many tents before, in the wars. *The wars, the wars, the endless wars, now a bloody dream.* This was a great hall, a monstrosity of flowing silk, dyed into violent shades of red and gold. In the centre stood a magnificent table, covered with maps of the Machinery knew where and bowls of fruit in a riot of colours. Candles burned on thick iron stands, and a gigantic bed dominated one wall. Along another was a series of wooden shelves, groaning with incomprehensible books. Brandione sat at a gleaming mahogany desk, the knobs on its drawers shaped into likenesses of his own face. In a corner was a bust of the Queen, or rather three busts growing from one base, staring at him with wicked intent.

Wayward was standing before him, smiling his usual smile. Tonight he wore a velvet coat of dark purple; shreds of cloth of the same colour were threaded through the braids of his hair.

Brandione turned his gaze to the entrance, a flapping

segment of parchment. Outside, the sand was cold and blue in the moonlight. There was a desert, there. Was it the Wite? He did not know. *Questions, Wayward, and the tent. That's all there is. Questions, Wayward, and the tent.*

'You were gone for a long time,' Wayward said.

His accent was familiar to Brandione, echoing with the heavy cadences of the South. *My old home, in an old land.* But it could not be so, for Wayward was surely an ancient thing. *Perhaps he alters his voice to put his companions at ease.*

Brandione shrugged. 'No longer than usual.' He looked down at the desk, and saw that his hands were intertwined. There was a small scar on his thumb from some unknown wound. For a moment he was jolted back to reality, to his old self: the commander of the armies of the Overland. But those days were gone, now. He was no longer a General. *What are you, then?*

'You are the soldier and the scholar,' Wayward whispered.

Brandione met the courtier's eye. Wayward had been there from the beginning. The General had been taken prisoner, accused of murdering the Strategist and three Tacticians, and sent to the Prison. He suppressed a bubble of laughter. *I fought to declare my innocence. But in the end, it didn't matter. I was always going in the same direction: to her.*

He had met her in the Prison of the Doubters, in a tower in the sun. She had formed before his eyes, taking her shape from mounds of sand, coalescing into three beings: three women with one voice. He tried to picture her, in his mind, but the image was broken, incomplete, a thing of red and black and grey and white, a thing of glass crowns, a thing of mighty thrones. *The Dust Queen.*

She had been expecting him. *The Last Doubter*, she called

him. *A soldier and a scholar.* She had enveloped him, shown him things he could not comprehend, strange things from other places, abandoned cities and broken fortresses. He saw the Strategist, in shadows and towers: the *new* Strategist, the one that had been prophesied. She had taken the form of a girl he recognised, a girl he had searched for long ago, in that strange museum ...

The Queen always told him to ask a question, and threw him back here, to Wayward, when he asked the same one, over and over and over again.

Wayward. *What is he?* A guide, on this journey. The man who led him through the Queen. The one who steered him in the right direction.

'Did you ask her the same question again?' the courtier asked. There was an edge of impatience in his voice.

Brandione looked away for a moment. Outside, in the desert, a person had appeared. It was a man, but it was not a man. It was a creature, formed of sand, wearing a yellow cloak, holding a glass spear. He was one of the Queen's soldiers, a member of the army Brandione had seen in the Prison of the Doubters. Her army, for him to command, she had said: his army of dust.

There was a gust of dry wind, and the soldier disappeared.

Brandione turned his attention again to Wayward. He nodded at the courtier, who frowned back.

'What is the Machinery?' Wayward asked. There was mockery in his words. He turned from the desk, and made his way to a golden sofa, throwing himself down and spreading out his lengthy frame. 'She will not answer that question. Do you know why?'

'No.'

Wayward sighed. 'It is not a good question. It is too ...

precise. The Queen is old indeed. She thinks in ...' Wayward screwed his eyebrows together, and clicked his tongue in his mouth. 'How to describe it? How to describe eternity?' He smiled. 'She thinks in *great, sweeping, movements*.' He accompanied each word with a swing of an elegant arm. 'Her thoughts are the circuits of the stars. Her wishes are the birth of mountains. She is the sun, hmm? She is the moon.'

Wayward cast a glance at Brandione, who did not attempt to hide his incomprehension. The courtier giggled.

'I am ... what is the word? I am *pretentious*.' He giggled. 'I'm young, you know, very young, compared to the others. I have to make up for it by appearing knowledgeable.' He grinned.

Brandione nodded. 'Tell me in small words. I'm just a soldier.'

Wayward grimaced and raised a finger. 'And a scholar. A soldier and a scholar. The Last Doubter: a man the Queen saw long ago.' He waved his hands above his head, as if scrabbling there for the right words. 'The Queen will only answer what she wants to answer, or what is proper for her to answer. However, she does *want* to answer. The more specific your question, the more precise you are, the less chance there is that she will respond. But if you are nice and general, then she will speak to you, for she can twist your question as she wishes. Hmm?'

Brandione nodded. 'I think I understand.'

Wayward nodded. 'Good. I am not surprised. For you are not just a soldier. You are a soldier ...'

The tent began to fade away before Wayward could finish.

He was back in the blackness.

'Question.'

The voice filled the void, the word echoing into the blackness. The eyes were no longer to be seen.

The one-time General searched for a question. There was something pathetic about him, this ridiculous animal, suspended in a world of higher beings, scrabbling around in his fleshy brain for something to say. In his days as a scholar – the days before soldiering, the days before the end of the world – he had read about ancient cultures. They were hives of ignorance, he had been taught, where people saw gods in the trees and the rivers. In some of the old stories, these people had met with their gods, conversed with them as equals, and even tricked them. Here he was, now, playing that same role. He was no different to the savages who walked the Plateau in the days before the Machinery.

But we were never any different, were we? The thought burst to life like a black weed. *What was the Operator, if not a god? What was the Machinery?*

Her eyes were before him again, no longer angry but hungry, waiting for him to speak. *A god, and her mortal.* But there were no tricks to be played here. Not with her.

Nice and general.

He opened his mouth, and the eyes widened.

'What comes next?' he asked.

The eyes widened. The darkness around them was slowly replaced with the outlines of three faces, and in a heartbeat she was before him, shining in her glory. She had taken a youthful appearance, her hair falling in golden curls, her cheeks rosy and unblemished. She wore three silver dresses, lengthy garments of a gleaming material, shining with the light of the stars and studded with tiny black stones. She grinned at him with three red mouths. She seemed more substantial than usual, though streams of dust fell away from the tips of her fingers.

She was beautiful, but she faded from his mind as soon as he turned away from her, like the memories she showed him. He closed his eyes and the image of her vanished, with only the outline remaining, only the sense of her. But when he opened them again, she was there, more terrifying and radiant and impossible than before.

'That,' the Dust Queen said, 'is a good question.'

Smiles broke out across her three youthful faces, and she raised her hands. The dust at the edge of her fingers began to flow more quickly, falling away into the ether. In a moment she had disintegrated into sand. It swirled forward, encircling Brandione, and he heard her voice in his own mind.

A game.

He opened his eyes, and the darkness had gone.

They were on a beach, of sorts, but unlike any the former General had ever seen. The sand beneath his feet was black, and the sun in the dark sky was blood red. The water of the sea beyond crashed rhythmically against the shore, over and over, like the movements of a machine. The air here was cold, and still, and deadening.

'Where are we?'

The Queen was by his side. She seemed smaller, somehow.

'The Old Place,' she said. 'The Underland. Two of the names it has been given, over the long years.' One of her figures knelt down, and scooped up some of the black sand in a hand. She lifted the sand up, and shared it with the other two. All of them held it in the air, and allowed it to drop from their fingers.

'Why is the sand black?' Brandione asked.

A moment passed, before the Dust Queen answered.

'It is not truly sand,' she said. 'It is a memory. Or more than one, perhaps, fused together, and residing here in the Old Place.'

'Sand is not black. And the sun is not red.'

The Dust Queen raised her eyebrows. 'Have you seen all sand, my Last Doubter? Have you seen every beach since the beginning of the world?' She pointed her three right hands at the burning orb above. 'Have you witnessed every age of that star? Do you know what it was in its youth?'

Brandione shook his head.

'No,' said the Queen. 'But the Old Place does.' She sighed. 'Do you know what it is?'

'The home of the Machinery.'

The Queen laughed. 'Yes, yes.' She pinched three forefingers and three thumbs tightly together, and raised them to her eyes. 'But only for a sliver of its lifespan: the most recent moments in its long years.'

Brandione blinked, and suddenly the three bodies surrounded him, her faces inches from his own.

'Everything in this place is a memory,' she said. She gestured at the beach around them. 'Memories have power, because humanity was made to die, to burn in beauty and flutter out, in wave after glorious wave.' She pointed to the sea. 'The creator hated that: how could he not, when he would live forever?'

'The creator?' He thought of the endless chasm, and the intelligence he had felt there, that sense of conflict.

She ignored him.

'He wanted something to remain: something of each of

them, something that would not die. He took mortal memories, and gave them power to make them last forever, so he would always have them to play with.' She smiled. 'It was his great mistake. The immortal power he placed in memories grew beyond even his control. Something new emerged: a thing that could rival even him.' She glanced around, with a blend of love and fear in her eyes. 'This place.'

She sighed. The three young women flickered into something else: old creatures, balding and stooped, their skin lined and fragile. But the moment passed, and the young Dust Queen returned, staring sadly at the sands.

Brandione looked from this creature of three bodies, to the red sun, then down to the black sand at his feet. Thoughts of the past appeared in his mind, unbidden memories rushing through him in a flood. He thought of his days in the College, and then the army. He looked back on his unrelenting ascent to the top of the Overland's military hierarchy, his role as Strategist Kane's senior advisor, and all the things that once seemed weighty in his mind. He was a man of many parts, someone had once told him. He was ambitious, but not boastful: popular with those above and below him, but not a craver of adulation. He had seemed a quiet and modest man, but, in truth, he revelled in his complexity. They never saw him coming, because they did not know what to make of him. *A soldier and a scholar.*

He looked to his left, and for a moment he caught a glimpse of a figure from his past: Provost Hone, the head of the College. The old man was standing far away, beside a towering black dune. He smiled, and Brandione was reminded of all the love he had been shown by men like that, all the counsel they had given him, all the ways they had lifted him up, and propelled him to glory.

But Hone began to fade away, until only his smile was left, hanging ludicrously in the air. It disappeared, and Brandione was reminded that the past was dead, and he was here now, with a three-bodied creature from ancient times, on a beach from a memory, and that none of the things he had accomplished mattered any more.

'Memories,' the Queen said. She shook her three heads.

Something new had appeared at the Queen's side. It was a table, a circular thing formed of a dark green stone, surrounded by great wooden chairs that seemed to have grown straight out of the sand. Brandione approached it, and looked upon its surface. A vortex of shapes and symbols twisted before him, dancing across the stone, laughing at his ignorance in an ancient and unknowable tongue.

Five figurines had been spread across the table's surface. They were formed of different materials – wood, glass, stone – but they each were shaped into a person. He went through them, one after the other, lifting them up and examining them carefully. One of them was oddly familiar, though he could not think why: a plump woman, wearing a Watcher's mask that had been formed into the face of a cat. Another figurine meant nothing to him: a young girl, slight, but displaying a kind of defiant bravery. The girl held a parchment, on which tiny letters had been written. Brandione held it to his eye and read the meaningless words: *House of Thonn.*

'I saw that girl, long ago,' the Dust Queen whispered. 'She is not a citizen of your Overland. She has never set foot on your Plateau. But she will help to reshape your world. She will fall, and she will rise again. The Fallen Girl.'

Brandione studied the figurine for a moment longer, then placed her back on the table, near the plump woman. He knew the other figurines only too well. He lifted one of them, formed of painted glass: a youngish man with narrow features, his hair painted a garish yellow. His hands were steepled, the tips of his fingers resting at the base of his chin. He wore an aquamarine cloak.

Brandione glanced at the Queen, whose eyes sparkled at him.

'This is Aranfal,' he said. 'A Watcher of the Overland.' He sighed. 'A torturer, like all the rest of them. But he was the worst.' He raised the figurine to his eye. 'In the ... olden times, he took me on a journey to a museum in the Far Below. Him and Squatstout.' The thought of the little man sent a shudder through him.

The Queen laughed. 'Squatstout!'

Brandione looked up at her. 'Yes. He's an assistant to the Watchers. Do you know him?'

The Dust Queen shook her three heads. 'He is not an assistant to the Watchers. He is a thing of the oldest ages. He is a creature of the shadows, though he longs for the light. He is a glory of the world.'

'He is like you?'

The Queen favoured him with three faint smiles.

Brandione placed Aranfal back on the table, and lifted another figurine. The marble was formed into the shape of a fat man, clad in a shawl. He was bald, and even in this form, a heavy sadness clouded his eyes.

'Canning,' Brandione said, placing the last Expansion Tactician back into his place upon the swirling board. 'He was always a good man, though he was weak.'

'A strange man,' the Queen said. 'He is complex, though

11

he sees no good in himself. He has been suppressed by others, through his life; the higher he climbed, the worse it all became.'

'He was not a bad person,' Brandione said, 'but he was not a good Tactician.'

Three sets of shoulders shrugged. 'He was Selected by the Machinery. You all followed it blindly, yet you loathed one of its choices.'

Brandione nodded. 'Perhaps. But it's too late now. We will never know what he could have achieved.'

The Queen laughed. 'Never know? The game has not even begun, Brandione.' She pointed one of her fingers at the last figurine. 'Pick that one up.'

Brandione lifted the final piece, and held it before him.

'I know this man better than all the others,' he said. 'Or perhaps I only thought I did.'

The figure of Brandione was carved of wood. It showed the one-time General as he once had been, clad in his leather armour, upright and proud. He thought of himself now, still wearing the rags of a prisoner. *Am I still a General, with my army of dust?* No. The old Brandione was dead; he had died with the Overland. They all had. He began to long for this person, and for all the things he had worn, all the things he had been, when he was Charls Brandione, leader of the Overland's armies, at the right hand of the Strategist …

The Dust Queen coughed. The rags disappeared, and his armour returned. A handcannon hung from his left side, and a sword from the other. He nodded at her, but his mind was elsewhere.

'Question,' she said.

His mind swirled with possibilities. He could ask her about

this game, perhaps. He could ask her what his role was to be in the future. But strangely, these did not seem to matter.

He turned back to the board. 'What are you?'

He wondered if the question was too specific. But then the Dust Queen smiled.

Chapter Two

'Canning.'

The last Tactician in the Overland sat on a wooden stool, wearing only a ragged smock. He was thin, these days. He lifted his head and glanced at Aranfal, before turning once more to the dirt.

'Tactician Canning,' the Watcher said. He wasn't supposed to use that title. Not any more. But he couldn't help himself.

Free Canning, if you can. That's what Jandell had said. The one we called the Operator, before we knew there was more than one.

The prisoner forced his head up and looked at Aranfal again, his eyes dull in the candlelight. He was attempting to control himself. *The greatness of the spirit.* How many times had Aranfal seen that, here, in the Bowels of the See House?

But never like this. Canning is braver than he looks.

'Water. Please.'

Aranfal walked out into the corridor, scanning it quickly. Operator Shirkra would not like it if she knew he was helping Canning. *She wouldn't like it at all.*

He crouched down, and pulled a stone up from the floor. Inside the hole was a wooden cup of water, hidden on another

14

visit. The liquid looked rancid, but Canning wouldn't mind. *It might keep him alive. And he still wants to live, though only the Machinery knows why.*

The Watcher returned to the cell, and lifted the cup to Canning's lips. The former Tactician drank greedily, dirty water slopping across his cheeks. He gave Aranfal a hopeful look when he had finished. The Watcher had seen that look many times, too, down here. For a moment, memories crowded his vision: the broken rubble of his past.

'There is no more,' Aranfal said. 'It wouldn't do you any good, anyway. You shouldn't have too much, in your state.'

Canning nodded. His head fell forward, and it seemed for a moment that he might have fallen asleep. Before long, however, he hacked out a cough, and looked up again at the Watcher.

'You're helping me. Why?'

Because Jandell asked me to, in the ruins of the Circus. But it wasn't Aranfal who bowed to the Operator, back then. Aranfal would have nodded, before running as far as he could. No: Aranfal was fading away, and Aran Fal was returning. That was the boy who went to the See House all those years ago: the boy whose names were forced together by Brightling herself. Not perfect, not by a long shot. *But a man who helps another man in the Bowels of the See House.*

He studied Canning again. There was something different about the former Tactician, something that had changed fundamentally. The Watcher struggled for the word. *Toughness, perhaps?* Was he changing, too? Did the end of the Machinery do something to them all – free them to become themselves?

'Because you're not allowed to die,' he said.

'Ah.' Canning nodded. 'Shirkra. She likes having me here.

She likes to hurt me.'

Aranfal shrugged. 'That's part of it, I suppose. But nothing happens without the Strategist's say so. Not any more. That's why you're alive.'

Canning snorted. 'Why would she want to keep me alive?' *Why indeed?*

'I cannot begin to fathom …' He thought, for a moment, of the new power in the Overland. He had not seen her since the Selection; no one had. Still, her presence was everywhere, a purple smoke that clogged the lungs and stung the eyes. 'Perhaps she thinks you will help her.'

'How could I help her?'

Aranfal squinted at Canning. They had had this conversation many times, here in the darkness of the Bowels, but Canning never seemed to remember. *What has happened to him? Has Shirkra rummaged about in his mind a little too much?* Aranfal had seen what the female Operator could do. She played with a person's memories, and she twisted them until they bled. *But no. More than that.* She took *power* from them. It reminded him of a story he had read, long ago, as a child in the North: a story about ancient magic, of gods that toyed with men and women, stole from them and abused them, but who always were defeated, in the end, tricked by the same ploys they used against their victims. *Were those just stories, or were they history?* He smiled at his own hopefulness: Aranfal laughing at Aran Fal.

'The Strategist only cares about one thing,' Aranfal said. He looked into the corners, as if she might be hiding there, the thing that had once been Katrina Paprissi. *She would not like me talking about her. Or perhaps she would. How would I know?* He sighed. What did it matter, anyway? He never knew how things worked in this new world.

16

'The Strategist only cares about the Machinery. That's all. She's not been here; she's been searching for it. Perhaps she thinks you can help her find it.'

Canning coughed a laugh. 'Me? I thought she was the One, whatever that means? She thinks *I* could help *her*? Not even Brightling knew where the Machinery was. No one knows, apart from the Operator, and sometimes not even him, if the stories are to be believed. Doesn't she think I would have said something by now, to get myself away from her ... her ...'

'Shirkra,' Aranfal said, glancing again at the shadows of the cell.

'Yes. Her *Shirkra*.' Canning trembled, and his head lolled forward again. He lifted it with great effort, making a grunting noise.

'I don't know what the Strategist thinks,' Aranfal said with a shrug. 'I'm just guessing. Maybe she likes the way you smell. How would I know? We never see her.'

Canning's face broke into a dark smile. 'Then who rules the Overland? Shirkra?'

Aranfal shrugged again. He was being too free with his words. *What does it matter? Shirkra will kill him soon anyway. Whether the Strategist wills it or not, Shirkra will kill this man ...*

'No one rules the Overland. The Watchers do what Shirkra wants, but I'm not sure you could call it ruling. I don't know what the people are doing. I don't know how they run their lives.' *By running away, if they have any sense.*

'They look after themselves now,' Canning said. 'As it should be. We would have been better off all along, without these gods and their machines.'

For a moment, the Watcher was surprised. *Is that how*

we all think of them now? As gods? But his attention was soon diverted by a noise in the corridor outside: a gate being opened, far away.

'She's coming again.' There was a tremor in Canning's voice. 'The woman in the white mask.'

Footsteps came to them, delicate feet padding across cold stone.

'Have you seen what she does to me, Aranfal? Have you been here, when she … I can't remember. I can't remember seeing you here.'

The Watcher did not respond. It was too late, now. Shirkra was among them.

She was the same as always, a thin woman in a green dress, curls of red hair flowing behind her mask, that weird thing that approximated her own face and seemed to shift between expressions. It was strange; the Watcher had seen her many times since the events of the Circus, but he could never quite hold a steady image of her in his mind's eye. To leave her side was to wake from a nightmare; there was always a sense of something vast, terrible, and untouchable, fading into nothingness.

In Mother's absence, she had emerged as the dominant force in the See House, and in the Centre at large. Her reign was strange and volatile: she would lock herself away for days, and then appear, ordering the Watchers to burn every second house on an unfortunate street, or poison the wells of an almshouse, or swap the stones in a cemetery. It was chaos. But then, so was she.

Still, it was clear she worked within certain boundaries that Mother had laid down. This was agony for her; she took out her anger on Canning, and the other unfortunates she held in the Bowels.

Aranfal, though, had become something of a favourite of the woman in the white mask. It was not a comfortable place to be; sometimes he would have traded places with Canning.

'Watcher Aranfal!' she cried, clapping her hands. 'What a *delight*! You have been avoiding me, hmm? You have. I know you have.'

She went to him and reached out a hand, brushing a tendril of blond hair from his cheek.

'Why don't you love me, Aranfal? I love *you*.'

'Thank you, my lady.'

'Am I wrong, my Aranfal? Do you love me? Tell me. Please. Tell me if you love me, or if you don't. I can withstand the blow, Aranfal! I am so old, you must realise. I have seen so many come and go, and very few of them loved me, no, very few indeed.' She sighed. 'Tell me. Do you love me, or not?'

The Watcher stretched out a smile. 'I love you, of course, Operator. I love you more than the stars.'

'More than the stars!' Shirkra clapped her hands together and spun on her heel, her green dress billowing through the cell. 'That is good, that is good!' She halted, and the eyes behind the mask suddenly narrowed. 'You will not look at another, will you, Aranfal? I should take your eyes, perhaps, and hide them in my little cupboard, and then you will never look at anyone else, for it will be beyond you, hmm?'

Aranfal bowed. 'As you wish, madam.'

The Operator's shriek of laughter echoed off the stone walls. 'As I wish, indeed! Someone who cares for my wishes, hmm? Mother won't let me do *anything*, you know. All she worries about is the Machinery! "No fun until we find its remains! Work before play!" Who would have thought that victory would be so *boring*?'

The Operator walked towards the one-time Tactician, who moaned as she approached. His eyes flickered, and he looked once more to the floor.

She raised a finger, and began to play with a memory.

They were in some kind of a harbour. Before them was a wall, and below that the grey sea. The cobblestones reeked of fish, rotting before them, dead eyes staring up into nothing. Canning was there, a more youthful version, with a woman at his side. She was younger than him, much younger, barely older than eighteen. The girl reached out to Canning and struck him, before climbing the wall, and falling, down to the sea below.

They were back in the cell. There was a dull glow of reddish light, fading into nothing.

The former Tactician wheezed, and blood fell from his lips. *How does she make them bleed?* 'It did not happen like that ... I know it did not ... you have twisted it.'

Shirkra laughed. 'No one is ever right about memories, not even the people who own them. What does it matter, anyway? They are so much more than ... mere records.'

She leaned forward, and kissed Canning on the forehead. He flinched, but was too weak to move away.

Shirkra laughed. 'Memories are strange things, you know. They are not just images in the mind.' She reached out and touched a black wall. 'This See House of yours – there are memories in the stones.'

'When will you kill him?'

Canning caught Aranfal's gaze for the briefest of moments,

and the Watcher saw a spark there: the light of life. But it quickly expired, and the former Tactician's head slumped forward once more.

Shirkra hesitated. 'Kill him?' The shadows in the cell grew longer. 'That would be a kindness. I am not cruel, you know. I like my games, but I am not cruel. Still – I cannot kill him – no, I cannot.'

'Why not?' Aranfal stepped towards her. 'You are the Mother of Chaos. Who can stop you from doing *anything*?'

Shirkra snatched her mask from her face. She giggled like a young girl, her hand held before her little mouth. 'You seek to trick me into bringing his death, Aranfal! You think it would be a kindness, hmm? I see through your tricks. If I kill him, you know, I will be in *such trouble,* because Mother loves him, hmm? She thinks she sees something in this creature, though what it is, I cannot tell.'

She turned upon Canning.

'But then again – trouble. Hmm. What would happen if I got in trouble? *Real* trouble? Would it not be a bit ... *fun* to get in trouble with Mother? I haven't been in trouble with Mother for *ages*, you know. I've been so good all this time. It's nice when you get in trouble with Mother. It shows she *cares*, ha ha ha ha ha!'

Aranfal laughed, though he did not know why. *The longer you serve her, the more you become her. Everything is a cloud of nothing, and only laughter breaks it.*

'We should do it together, Aranfal!' Shirkra was beside him, wearing her mask once again.

Chaos is making a plan, making it forever, abiding by it, building the rules, and then twisting in a new direction, a different way, hmm, without knowing where it will take—

She held his hand in hers. 'Imagine, both of us getting

into trouble with Mother! And Jandell would be so angry, too, wherever he may be – you told him you would look after Canning, hmm? I don't need any powers to know that, ha ha. I know what he's like. "Oh, promise me, Aranfal, promise me, hmm, won't you look after my little child, who withers in the den of the vipers, hmm?"'

Aranfal looked to Canning. *It's true, it's true, she knows you so well.*

Children.

Another voice, from nowhere and everywhere.

The Strategist.

Come to me.

Aranfal was in the Underhall.

This was the largest room in the See House, as far as anyone knew, a vast cavern of damp stone, broken portraits, and rotten wooden furniture. It was said to be the dining hall of ancient Tacticians, before they grew tired of feasting in the Bowels. But no one came here, now.

Shirkra was at the back of the hall, her ear pressed against a wooden door that festered with mould. She was no longer wearing her mask. She called Aranfal to her, and beckoned him to do the same.

A thin, reedy sound came from beyond.

'Music,' he said. He looked at Shirkra, who nodded once, and giggled.

'Why are we here?' the Watcher asked. 'How did we get here?'

Shirkra grinned at him. 'Mother has summoned us. Didn't you hear her?'

Aranfal nodded. 'Yes.'

'One must come promptly when summoned by Mother.'

She tapped the side of her head. 'It's stupid to do anything else. Mother is very patient, you know, very patient, but it's not good to test her, oh no, not good at all.'

The Watcher was afraid. He was Aran Fal.

'Have you met Mother before, Aranfal, hmm?'

'No. At least, not in her new guise.'

'Ah. You knew her host.' Shirkra giggled. 'It will be so lovely to see you together! I love both of you so much!'

They walked through the door, and found themselves in a corridor. There were torches along the walls, burning in that strange flame of Strategist purple. As they went, a light grew before them, a tempest in the same colour.

The environment began to change. The corridor faded away, and the air became wet and cool. New sounds inter-mingled with the strange music: the movement of leaves in the breeze, a dappling of water on rocks, weird chirps and chirrups of animals.

'Where are we?' Aranfal asked. 'It feels like we've gone outside. How can that be?'

Shirkra tutted. 'Your questions are born of the Overland. We are not in the Overland, my Aranfal.'

Aranfal looked up and saw a bright moon, a perfectly smooth and circular body that radiated a cold intensity.

'That was not here before,' he said. 'What is this place?'

'A memory. Many memories. Woven together, made more beautiful than before, oh yes.'

They came to a garden. Aranfal saw a wide, dark pond up ahead, its surface a perfect reflection of that unnatural moon, its waters utterly still. Black plants surrounded the pond, tall things with dark, glossy leaves and pale, pink flowers. Animal sounds could be heard in the dark, but there was no sign of bird or beast.

Sitting on a rock and staring into the pond was the Strategist. Katrina Paprissi. The One. Mother. *Always Mother, always call her Mother.* She was dressed in her purple rags, her pale skin exposed to the moonlight, her black hair tied tightly back with an ivory pin. She held in her hands a long, thin, wooden instrument: the source of the strange music. It was a lament. It told a story of a time long gone, though no one sang along to it.

At her side was a mask: the face of a white rat.

Mother cast a glance in their direction, and removed the pipe from her lips. The music died slowly, echoing through the garden. The Strategist tilted her head very slightly, and placed the tip of her tongue on her upper lip, as if tasting something there.

Aranfal bowed to her.

'The Machinery is broken,' the Strategist said. Her words had hints of Katrina, but there was something more besides, as if several speakers were talking at once in voices from the past.

Aranfal hesitated. 'Yes, Strategist.'

Mother did not seem to register his words. 'The Machinery is broken. It must be. It Selected me, and gave me such powers. But Ruin has still not come. There is more work ahead of me.' She sighed. 'I must find what remains of the Machinery. I must shatter it into a million pieces. Only then will Ruin come.' She placed the instrument to her lips once more, and music filled the garden. After a while she removed the pipe. 'Ruin is waiting for me.' She looked directly at Aranfal. Her gaze penetrated him. 'Do you know who I am?'

'Mother,' Aranfal whispered.

The Strategist nodded. 'I am Mother.' She looked at Shirkra. 'You sought to disobey your mother.'

Shirkra shook her head. 'No. No. I would not have killed him. I think I would not have.'

'You think, but you do not know. You are not the Mother of Chaos. That is the wrong name for you. You are a child of Chaos, and nothing more.'

Shirkra sighed. 'I am a child. I am a child. I cannot tell what I will do.'

Mother called her daughter to her side, and made her sit on the rock. 'You stayed with me during many long years. You are more than Chaos. You are ... light.'

Shirkra grinned.

'Torturer.'

Aranfal snapped to attention. Their eyes met again, and all the world was purple.

'I am glad you have come.' Something flickered in her eyes; for a moment, the Watcher saw himself standing before the gates of the See House, long ago. *Before Aran Fal became Aranfal.*

'Shirkra,' Mother said, looking away from the Watcher. 'When was the last time we played a game? *The* game?'

Shirkra's eyes narrowed. 'You know when, Mother. Long ago. Before the Machinery.'

Mother nodded. 'It is time for another.'

There was a long silence. Shirkra remained utterly still for a long while, before leaping to her feet.

'Another game?' she hissed. 'We swore we would never play again. And we are *busy*!'

Mother nodded. She lifted her instrument to her lips again, and played a low, solemn tune. When it was finished, she raised her hand in the air. A ball of dark flame appeared there; Aranfal saw things in the darkness, memories that were not his own.

'The Dust Queen demands it,' Mother whispered.

She threw the flame to the ground, and it burst into the forms of three identical women.

They were hard to look upon, unnatural creatures, formed of a substance somewhere between sand and dust, fine and flowing and *alive*. They were tall and thin, their limbs weird and long, their eyes dark, the skin of their faces in constant flux, grey like the sand from which they had formed. They wore crowns upon their heads, made of glass, though even these seemed to change, flickering with a strange light. Their dresses shimmered in a thousand colours, dancing around them like cat's tails.

Dust, dust, dust.

As Aranfal looked upon these women, a realisation dawned. These were not three women at all, but *one*, a singular creature. The Watcher had seen many strange things since the fall of Northern Blown, but here was something new. Here was something beyond even Mother. He was utterly insignificant as he stood before this thing of three parts. He felt compelled by her, madly attracted; he wanted to throw himself into her and become a particle, a speck of dust, flowing with her, within her, and she within him.

Mother coughed, and the women disappeared.

'She has spoken to me in the night,' Mother said. 'She wants to play a game. A last game, before Ruin comes.'

Shirkra made a strange sound. A *growl*. 'We cannot trust her. She betrayed us before. She helped Jandell build the Machinery. It is a trick.'

Mother sighed. 'Her motivations cannot be understood. But we will play.'

Shirkra stomped a foot. 'Mother! Why must we always dance to her tune? Say no! Tell her we don't have time for games!' She bent down, and touched the Strategist's shoulder. 'You could resist her, you know. Your powers are growing again.'

Mother smiled. 'There is no resisting her. Not until Ruin comes. And Ruin will not come, until we find the Machinery. Do you understand?'

Shirkra shook her head. For a moment, she was nothing more than a child, her eyes wide and innocent. 'What are the prizes?' she whispered.

'If we play with her, she says she will take us to the Machinery after the game: no matter who wins.'

'It is a trick, Mother! She sees some advantage in this. It cannot be otherwise.'

Mother shrugged. 'Either way, we will play the game. If we refuse, she could simply compel us. And how long would it take us to find the Machinery without her guidance? I do not want to wait on Ruin for a moment longer than is necessary. If we accept, she will take us to whatever remains of the Machinery, and I will bring Ruin. We will accept.'

'Do you think she is telling the truth?'

Mother nodded. 'I have known her for longer than almost any of us. We will play the game, and she will show us the Machinery. Why? That, I do not know. Perhaps she *wants* Ruin to come. She saw it, before any of us. They were her words, were they not? *Ruin will come with the One.*'

Aranfal gasped.

'Ruin will destroy her,' Shirkra said.

Mother narrowed her eyes in thought. 'Yes. But I believe she knows that. I think she wants to die. I think she wishes to play a last game, before death comes.'

Shirkra threw herself down, and placed her head in her mother's lap. 'Very well,' she said.

Mother stroked her daughter's head. 'I know this is a struggle for you,' she said. 'All of this – all that we have done, just to survive.' She smiled. 'You know where you have to go, now. You know whom you must seek.'

'Yes, Mother.'

'Take him with you,' the Strategist said, pointing at Aranfal. 'We should keep him safe. I think he will be useful to us in the game.' She nodded to herself. 'Yes. So useful. So safe.'

Shirkra grinned at Aranfal, and the Watcher sighed.

Chapter Three

'I am dead,' Brightling said.

She was sitting on the deck of Jandell's ship, legs crossed, smoking her pipe, and staring out at the bleak grey waters of the world beyond the Plateau. From time to time she picked at a bowl of dates, or sipped at a glass bottle of some red spirit the Operator had procured. He stood beside her, his head bowed.

'That is a strange thing to say,' Jandell said. 'I can see you, sitting there, breathing in smoke, eating and drinking, and talking to me, telling me that you are dead.'

Brightling flicked a date into her dead mouth. 'Whatever I thought I was is now gone forever.' She nodded. 'We all believe we know who we are. We look in the mirror, and think the truth stares back at us. It is a lie, though; it can be changed. I saw it happen in the past. I *made* it happen. A new creature, in the original shell. Aran Fal becomes Aranfal.'

She sucked on her pipe, and exhaled a dancing circle.

'But the Machinery saw the *real* truth. It looked beyond the mirror. It knew who we really were.'

Jandell grunted. 'Aran Fal and Aranfal. Those names sound

29

almost the same.'

'The two men are very different.'

The Operator nodded. 'And what about you? Who is the real Brightling?'

She looked up at him. He had grown younger on their journey, at least in appearance: black hair now fell from his skull; the lines in his face had faded away, and there was a new light in his eyes. But he still wore that terrible cloak, and the faces within glared at her, smiled at her, licked their lips and laughed at her.

'I was made for the Machinery, and now it is gone.'

'You were the greatest person on the Plateau.'

Brightling shrugged. *The greatest person on the Plateau.* She thought of all the things she had done in her efforts to impress the Machinery and wreck the hopes of others. She thought of Canning, of the humiliations she had poured on him. It had all seemed so clear, once: so fair. The Operator loved her; he had told her so himself. She could do *anything* with his backing. She could ruin her enemies, in their own minds, and in the eye of the Machinery. She could expose them. She could stage plays to display their weaknesses to Overland and Underland alike. That world she believed in was at an end. The Strategist was broken, the Tacticians were broken, and the Machinery was broken. *All of it, all of it, all of it, was always going to break.*

She shrugged. 'It didn't matter. I was supposed to be a Watcher, but I was blind. I blinded myself. I didn't see what was happening to the Machinery.'

Jandell laughed. 'That guilt is mine, not yours. I created it. I spoke with it. I turned my eyes from the truth.'

'The truth of Katrina Paprissi. But that was my error, more than yours, Operator.'

'She was important to you,' he said. 'She was a daughter to you.'

Brightling turned once more to the waters.

It had been months since Brightling had joined Jandell on his ship, in the far North of the Plateau. She had never been on one before, yet even she could tell it was no ordinary vessel. When she looked out upon the waves she could see them rolling wildly, slamming and whirling in a great grey storm. But this had no impact upon the black ship, which seemed to float above the water, ignoring all its motions.

In the mornings, she would see him on deck, his cloak blowing in the wind, the faces wailing in their prison.

He had told her, in the beginning, where they were going: to the home of Squatstout, the little creature who had followed Aranfal around the Overland, all that time ago. But he said nothing more about it; he only stared at the ocean.

The ship had no crew.

They spent their evenings in the galley, a kind of kitchen below deck. He would speak to her, as she ate the food he conjured from only he knew where. He told her of strange things, of cities long gone and wars among the Operators. He told her of dreams that lasted millennia, of the birth of stars and the fall of civilisations.

When she thought back on these conversations, the memories turned to dust.

'You are happy now, Operator,' she said one evening. They sat opposite one another at a rough-hewn table. He watched her, with a smile, as she plucked at fruit and cheese.

'I am not happy,' he said after a moment. 'I am ... relieved.

31

A weight has been lifted from me. I no longer hide from the truth.'

'Ruin will come with the One.'

Jandell closed his eyes.

'Prophecies are strange things, and this one was spoken by the strangest of all creatures. Who knows the truth of it? Who knows when Ruin will come, and what it will mean to us all? Perhaps she does not know herself.'

'Who is this woman? Shirkra?'

Jandell smiled. 'No. Shirkra is nothing but madness: twisted and deformed. The one who made the Promise ...' He stood from the table and walked to a shelf on the wall, where there was a small wooden box. He opened it, lifted something out, and returned to the table, placing the item between them. It was a statue, perhaps as tall as Brightling's hand, depicting three women: identical creatures, wearing crowns of glass and dresses as white as ivory.

'The Dust Queen,' Jandell said. 'Oldest of us all. I could not have made the Machinery without her. She looked into it, when we had finished, and she saw those words: *Ruin will come with the One.*'

'Who is she?' Brightling asked. She stared at the statue, and for the briefest of moments, the edges of the figures seemed to fall away, as if they were formed of dust. 'Where is she now?'

'I do not know.' Jandell took the statue back to its box, and returned to the table. 'I wish I did, now that ...' He let the sentence die.

In a swift movement he snatched up a fork and pronged a grape, thrusting it at Brightling, like a child trying to please a favoured aunt. The Watcher plucked it from the blade, and crushed it in her mouth.

32

'This food is very old, so old,' said Jandell.

'It can't be. It's delicious.'

'It is only as old as the memory itself, which is as fresh to me now as when it was made, back then, so long ago.'

'The food is a memory?' She lit her pipe and blew a ring of smoke into the air. The Operator watched it dance. 'How can I taste a memory?'

Jandell laughed again. 'Why shouldn't a memory be real? Memories are what we live for, my family and I. Memories are our power. We can bring a memory back to life; we can twist different ones together, to create something else. It is our ... *magic*. Yes, that is what they called it once.'

He put out his hand, and opened his palm. In the middle of it was a small flame, a flickering tongue of red fire.

'What is this?' she whispered.

Jandell laughed. 'This is nothing. This is just a little trinket.' He leaned towards her. 'Touch it.'

Brightling hesitated. 'It will burn me.'

Jandell shook his head, and she did not hesitate again. She plunged her hand into the fire, and felt only coldness.

'What kind of flame is this?'

Jandell smiled. 'A thing of memory.'

'You remember a cold fire?'

He shook his head. 'No. There is more than one memory at work here. My people can mix them together like paints on a palette. And they are not my memories; they are the memories of humanity. There is no Jandell, in truth. I was born in the pool of human memory that you call the Underland, long, long ago. My family and I are creatures of memory.'

As Brightling looked upon the flame, without thinking, she shifted her hands underneath her cloak, and felt it: her

33

mask. An image appeared in her mind's eye. She was a young Watcher, sitting at her desk. The Operator appeared behind her, and she did not react. It was as if this was simply to be expected. She turned to him, and he handed her something: her mask.

She felt it, now, and she lifted it out. It had taken the form of an old man, his features flashing with anger. Without knowing why she did it, Brightling put the mask on her face, for the first time in an age. Wearing it was painful; she could feel it weighing on her, tugging at the core of her being. She turned to Jandell, and for a moment he looked like his old self, ancient and weak. The flame spluttered in his hand, and suddenly went out. He lifted his other hand to his eyes, and she realised he was in pain.

She snatched the mask from her face and placed it on the table. Jandell was young again, though his palm was still empty. He gave her a weak smile. *I have hurt him. The mask has hurt him.*

'What is this thing?' Brightling whispered. She looked at her mask, which had formed into the face of a young woman, placid and plain.

'Memories are what we live for,' Jandell said, 'because memories are life itself.' He nodded at the dark mask. 'That is the opposite of life. It is all that remains of our old enemy: a thing called the Absence. A creature that wished only to destroy memory, and all of memory's children, and life itself. The masks your Watchers wear are formed of the Old Place, and give them a little sliver of its power: the power of memory. Your mask senses memories, but only to destroy them.'

'When I have worn it, sometimes ... I have felt I could strip out a person's soul.'

Jandell did not respond. Brightling took the mask in her hand, and hid it away again.

'Was Katrina a memory, Operator?'

Jandell sighed.

'There is no Katrina any more. She is subsumed by the One. My people ...'

He stared at her, unblinking. 'This body is not mine; I took it long ago, because it suits me. I feel whole when I am within its memories. I warp it now, as I wish, but I did not create it. It is the same with Katrina; whatever she once was has now gone, replaced by a creature of memory. My mother.'

Brightling ran a finger along her mask. 'If she is a creature of memory, Operator – then I could use my mask—'

Jandell silenced her with a finger. 'You could not stand against her. And neither could that mask – remember, the Absence was defeated. That is only a shard of it, a piece of its corpse, and it would be defeated again.'

Brightling nodded, but she was unconvinced. A fantasy took life in her febrile imagination, and she grasped her mask. *One day, I will destroy the thing that has possessed her, and I will bring Katrina back.*

'Look ahead,' said Jandell.

Brightling pulled her black cloak around her and walked to the deck. The Operator had given her the garment, along with several pairs of trousers and shirts. She had no idea where the clothes had come from, but she was glad of them. *Perhaps they are memories, too.*

'What is it?'

'It is land, Amyllia.'

She squinted, and could just make out a patch of darkness, rising up from the water far in the distance.

'Is it where Squatstout lives, Operator?'

'Yes. My brother.' The Operator sighed.

He turned to face her.

'We will be there in a day.'

Brightling knew, when she woke, that something had changed.

She climbed from her bed hesitantly, and made her way to the deck. Jandell was already there. 'It will grow larger, as you watch,' he said. His back was turned to her.

The Watcher looked ahead. The island seemed no closer than it had the day before. However, as she looked, it appeared to lurch forward, forcing its way into view.

It was as if a mountain had been plucked from its home and dropped into the water, far from where it was supposed to be. There was nothing else in view, nothing but this black rock that reached from the sea to the sky: a balled fist, where the See House was a claw.

'Our destination,' Jandell said. Something had changed once again in the Operator. He still appeared young, but the lightness and vitality of the previous days had vanished. He was weaker, to the Watcher's eye.

'This is not a good place,' Brightling said, sucking on her pipe and blowing pale smoke into the still air. 'I am afraid of it.'

The Operator nodded.

'Have you been here before, Jandell?'

'No. I never had the inclination. I wish now that I had.'

'Why?'

The Operator shrugged. 'To see what sort of creature Squatstout has become.'

'Squatstout knows we are here,' Jandell said.

Brightling looked up from the deck of the ship. The cliff was a vast, dark wall, as impenetrable as the battlements of Northern Blown. Far above them, lined along the edge, she could make out people holding torches in the night. In the middle was a lumpen creature in a peasant's shawl. *Squatstout.*

'This seems a lovely place,' said Brightling. 'Operator, have you seen these?'

There were corpses in the water. They had not been there for long, by the look of them. She thought of the Bony Shore, and the things that Katrina found there, long ago. Brightling had told the girl they were just rocks. *Perhaps they came from this place.*

Jandell glanced at the bodies in the waves, before turning his attention back to the island. 'There is an inlet here.'

Brightling studied the shore, and saw nothing but black stone. But the boat, guided by some invisible force, threaded its way through the boulders until the rocks hung over their heads and to their sides.

They had entered a cave, and she could see nothing.

'Operator ...'

There was a jolt, and the ship shuddered violently to a stop.

'Do not be concerned,' said Jandell. 'They will find us soon.'

There came a noise of footsteps, and the cave filled with light. Brightling saw that the ship had run up onto the ground, on a patch of land mercifully free of jagged rocks.

They were in a giant chamber, carved from the very centre of the island. People were milling around, carrying their torches. Directly below, at the front of the ship, stood Squatstout. This was not the cringing servant Brightling remembered, but a lord, his posture erect, his eyes cool and watchful. Was this really the same creature that had once followed Aranfal around the Centre? He seemed tauter, somehow. He was still the same small, fat man, but there was an edge to him, now.

'I knew you would come here, Jandell,' Squatstout said with a smile. 'I always knew you would come.'

'Impressive. I only found out recently myself,' Jandell replied.

'Indeed. You left it a very long time, a very long time, which some would construe as rude, though not I. I have watched you, and I know you have been most busy.'

Jandell bowed.

'But I am being so rude!' Squatstout cried. 'These are my companions, and my loyal servants,' he said, gesturing behind him. 'I call them my Guards.'

There were about a dozen Guards. Their faces were hidden behind gleaming masks, from which hung long, silver beaks, giving them the appearance of monstrous, metallic birds. They all wore chainmail under short green cloaks, and on their heads were wide-brimmed hats. Some held pikes.

Beyond this group were others, maybe a hundred of them, people with pale faces and curious eyes.

'Come, join me for dinner,' said Squatstout. There was a hissing quality to his voice that Brightling had not appreciated before. 'We have a great deal to discuss, but I would not – I would *not* – have you go hungry in my home.'

As they clambered down from the ship, a bell began to ring.

Squatstout took them to a stone staircase embedded in the wall and leading into the heart of the island. The staircase was narrow, its stones slick with damp. The torches of Squatstout's companions illuminated the way. On and on it went, through rock and mud, up into the island.

Brightling was sandwiched between several of the strange, beaked Guards. As she looked at their pikes, she thought of the bodies in the water. She felt under her cloak, and brushed a finger across her handcannon.

There was a commotion ahead, and the group came to a halt. Peering into the torchlight, Brightling saw one of the Guards huddled together with Squatstout, muttering incomprehensible words. His beak was painted a dull gold, and he seemed to hold a senior position, judging from the way the others kept their distance. Squatstout gestured at a section of the cave wall, and the Guard touched it with a gloved hand. The wall fell away, and the group marched through.

The bell kept ringing as they climbed, steadily, in the dark.

'The bell rings only in my Keep,' said Squatstout. 'But soon, it will ring across the island.'

'Welcome to my throne room, Jandell,' said Squatstout, 'where I have thought of you for ten thousand years.'

The room was circular, its floors and walls formed of heavy dark stones. Dawn was creeping through the windows, bringing with it a grey light. Brightling's attention was seized by the throne itself, which sat on a slightly elevated platform in the centre of the room. It was made of wood, and had been warped and twisted into an 'A' shape.

The Guards fanned out. The one with the gold beak assumed a position directly behind the throne, a long wooden stick held firmly in his grasp. The other people, the pale-faced inhabitants of the island, were now nowhere to be seen.

Squatstout skipped to his throne and jumped into the air,

thumping his backside down hard on the wood. He immediately locked his gaze on Brightling, who did not flinch. The lord of the island held out his hands, the palms facing outwards.

'Tactician, I would like to say how sorry I am. I enjoyed the time I spent in the See House with that lovely man, Aranfal. I hope you don't feel I tricked you.'

Brightling bowed, judging that silence was the wisest option.

'I like to keep an eye on things, you must understand, and the Watchers of the Overland were very accommodating. I thought that perhaps I would be able to find the One among your number, as the Machinery spluttered to its end. My people like to live within mortals, you see. We *worship* you, in a strange way, and we love to be one with you. Isn't that right, Jandell?'

Jandell did not respond.

Squatstout giggled. 'She may have taken a host, I thought, and not yet revealed herself. I had a hunch it would be a Watcher: someone near the beating heart of power in your land. In the end, she did not need my help. But I was right, wasn't I? I knew where she'd be hiding, though I did not find her.'

Brightling did not react. Squatstout smiled, then whistled through his teeth and rolled his eyes.

'You are a hard woman to apologise to! Anyway, never mind. In truth, I didn't really do anything wrong, did I? All I did was watch. Well, yes, I could have told you who I really was. Or rather, *what* I really was, for I told you my true name, did I not? But no: omitting the truth is just as bad as lying, as I'm sure the Bleak Jandell here would agree. But at the end of it all, you are here, now, in my home, and

I aim to be a gracious host.'

Squatstout clicked his fingers. Several Guards exited by a door at the side, and came back hauling a long wooden table. Others appeared with piles of food on silver platters.

'We have much to eat here,' said Squatstout, 'if you enjoy fish and seabirds.'

The Guards placed three wooden chairs behind the table. Brightling sat, but Jandell remained on his feet, watching Squatstout with a steady expression before walking towards the throne.

'What do you call this place?' he asked.

The Guard with the golden beak visibly tensed, and laid a hand upon his master's throne.

Squatstout raised a hand. 'All is well, Protector, my darling,' he said. He cocked his head and grinned at Jandell. 'This is the Habitation, Jandell. I am surprised you never learned that, over these long years.'

'And he is the Autocrat,' said the Guard known as the Protector. It was a deep voice, leathery, old. 'You would do well to respect him.'

Squatstout – the Autocrat – gave a tinkling laugh. 'Protector, you do not know whom you address. This is Jandell. He is one of the oldest of our kind, though he does not look it, does he? You grow younger in appearance, Jandell. The breaking of the Machinery has lifted a weight off you, hmm? The things Jandell could do … well, I have seen them all too often. Is that not right, Jandell?'

Jandell did not react. Brightling reached under her cloak, and placed her hand on the hilt of her blade. Strange, they had not taken her weapons. Perhaps they had no fear of them in this place.

The bell rang again.

41

'Squatstout, listen to me,' Jandell said. 'I need your assistance. Where has Mother been, all these years? Are there mortals there? People who helped her? Perhaps they know something that can help us.'

Squatstout laughed, harsher now than before.

'Help you do what?'

'Stop Ruin. She has not found the Machinery: Ruin cannot come, until she does.'

'Stop Ruin? No one and nothing can stop Ruin, not even the Dust Queen herself. The Strategist will find the Machinery in the end, and Ruin will come with the One. You think you see the truth now, Jandell. But you are arrogant if you think you can halt the inevitable.'

Jandell sighed. 'You call yourself Autocrat again, then.'

Squatstout shrugged.

'That is a name from a different time,' continued Jandell. 'It is strange to hear it.'

The Autocrat gave a fierce nod. He seemed exasperated.

'It was a different time, so different! We were happy then, Jandell! All of us! Operator!' He spat out the last word like a curse.

And then the room fell away.

Brightling was standing on hard, bare ground, surrounded by a throng of people. They were a sorry sight, a ragged horde, thin arms held aloft.

A red sun burned in a red sky, and red sand blew across red soil. The rags the people wore were red, and so was their skin, as if they had spent centuries cooking under the sun. Before them was a crystal platform, on which sat five red thrones. On those thrones, wearing crowns of red, sat five beings.

Brightling recognised three of them straight away. In the centre was Jandell, the young version, black hair framing his narrow face. He wore a cloak, but it was not the one she knew; there were no faces in the red material.

To Jandell's left was Squatstout, who leaned forward to whisper something in the Operator's ear. To his right sat the woman in the white mask, the one who had emerged from the Underland with Katrina, in the ruins of the Circus – Shirkra, Jandell had called her. The mask was nowhere to be seen, but the skin of her face was almost as bleached and flawless, and her green eyes now glinted red.

Brightling did not recognise the last two. They sat apart from the other three, holding hands: identical black twins, a boy and a girl, watching the goings-on with a savage glee.

Jandell stood from his throne, his cloak sweeping into the air. Squatstout laughed and clapped his hands.

In the distance, a bell rang.

Jandell pointed into the crowd, to a thin woman holding a baby. She clutched the child to her dusty bosom, hoping, perhaps, that Jandell was pointing somewhere else.

But he was not.

Hands grasped at the woman and her child, pushing her forward to the red thrones. A sense of dumb foreboding settled in the pit of Brightling's stomach. *Why are you afraid? You've seen worse.* But there was something different, here, from the cruelties she had witnessed – that she had perpetrated – as a Watcher of the Overland. This was the dumb malice of a child toying with an insect: cruelty for its own sake. She looked to Jandell, to the real Jandell; he had averted his eyes.

The boy and girl leapt from their thrones and skipped to the side of the platform. The boy tapped the woman on the forehead. She looked into his eyes, and seemed to somehow deflate.

'Delicious,' the boy said, and his companions laughed.

The girl prised the baby from the woman's arms, and danced around the platform with it as it squalled. She threw it in the air and caught it; she seemed certain to drop it several times, but somehow held on, grasping it by an arm or a leg as it cried. The mother did not protest; she melted away into the rabble, arms hanging by her side, no longer concerned by anything.

'Bring the child here,' said Jandell.

A moan ran through the crowd.

The girl stopped dead and looked at Jandell. She seemed to hesitate.

'Girl, bring that to me.'

Jandell's voice was different. It was colder.

The girl did not hesitate this time. She bowed as she approached Jandell, the baby held before her.

He took the child. Squatstout threw his head back and laughed, a sound that echoed across the barren plain like that bell that came from nowhere and everywhere.

Jandell held the child in his arms, cradling it like it was his own. Then he thrust it in the air, gripped tightly in both his hands. His eyes burned, and he looked upon its small face with a fury until the child hung limp. The boy and the girl ran to Jandell, staring up at him with devotion. Squatstout clapped, and Shirkra looked on impassively.

The real Jandell turned to the real Squatstout.

'Why did you take me here?'

They were back in the Autocrat's throne room.

'You seemed to enjoy it, Autocrat Jandell.'

'No, Squatstout, do not call me that.'

Squatstout sighed. 'Very well, Operator, jester, innkeeper, whatever you call yourself these days. You did not seem to mind.'

'I did not want to go.'

The Autocrat laughed. 'So you say, yet you came anyway. You remember how it used to be, don't you? It was better, then.'

'No. It got better, later.'

Squatstout grinned. 'Ah! That little world you built, all of us such friends. But it was never going to last, was it? You always just believe what you *want* to believe.' He sighed. 'And now look at us. Pathetic.' He seemed to have a new idea. 'You said you did not want to go, Operator?'

Jandell nodded.

'Why did you go, then, if you did not want to? You are not so weak, are you?'

The Operator looked at the floor, and the Protector chuckled. *Oh, do not laugh at the Operator.*

Squatstout leapt up from his throne. 'It has been ten thousand years, brother. You mean to tell me that in all this time, you have allowed your powers to wilt? We feared you so much, all of us, hiding away until the Machinery broke. And yet you had turned to ... *this*.' He gestured at the Operator. 'All those fresh new memories, in that land, all those memories you could have taken!'

'It is a poor way to grow powerful: stealing the memories of mortals.'

Squatstout thumped his chest with a balled fist. 'Don't you think I know that, my brother? But it is who we are, and we cannot deny that, never, never, never!' He laughed. 'And how dare you talk of theft, hmm – you who stole a boy from his home!'

A picture of Alexander Paprissi appeared in Brightling's memory. A picture of a boy, with his family: a family that was ruined. She looked to the Operator, whose eyes were closed. She could not feel angry with him.

'He did that for the greater good,' she said. She had not meant to speak.

Squatstout spat on the ground. 'There is his greater good. He has been like this for too long, Brightling – when his brothers and sisters hurt mortals, we are creatures of unspeakable cruelty. When he does it, it's all about the greater good.' He sighed. 'But it doesn't matter. What matters is the state he is in.' He focused again on the Operator. 'You could have made a deal with them, hmm, a little arrangement, like it used to be? "You give me some of your memories and I'll help you with my lovely powers". Hmm?'

'No. I wanted them to go their own way.'

'Their own way! How could they go their own way, after you made that ... that *thing*? The Machinery!'

Jandell did not respond.

Squatstout turned to Brightling. 'I don't know which is worse: that the Bleak Jandell should allow himself to rot, or that you people should let such a weakling lord it over you!'

'That is not true. The Machinery is the master of the Overland.'

'Ah, the mistress of the See House, deigning to share her thoughts with us once again,' said Squatstout. 'Once my mistress, even, oh yes. And now you are a ... what? A simple Watcher?'

'Yes.'

Squatstout laughed. 'You did not watch well enough, it seems. Mother lived with you! She hid away, inside one that you loved as your own!'

He laughed, and Brightling's expression tightened. The Autocrat clapped his hands quickly, as he had done in that red country, and Jandell was thrown onto his back. The cloak flew from his body, faces shrieking, and fell at Squatstout's feet. Jandell was naked apart from a black rag.

There was joy in Squatstout's eyes. He raised a hand and the cloak flew to the wall, where it spread across the cold stone, a tapestry of agonised faces.

'I never thought such a day would come.' He clapped his hands again, and black chains sprouted from the stone floor, curling their way around Jandell and binding him tightly, before throwing him against the wall, with his cloak. The Operator closed his eyes, and did not make a sound.

Squatstout turned to Brightling. 'You, Watcher, did you think that such a day would come?'

Brightling shook her head.

'No, I'm sure you didn't. You will witness much, now, that you never expected to see.'

Squatstout snapped his fingers.

'Guards, take Brightling to some comfortable quarters. And remove her weapons.'

Brightling's heart sank.

'You didn't think they were a secret, did you, Brightling?' Squatstout smiled. 'Nothing is a secret to me on my island. Oh, but you can keep your mask. Aranfal told me about it, hmm. I want us to examine it later, together.' He smiled. 'I want to know your ... *relationship* with that thing.'

Two of the beaked creatures lifted Brightling from the table, each grasping one of her arms. A third snatched her weapons from their hiding places.

'I will visit you soon, Tactician,' said Squatstout. He turned

Gerrard Cowan

to the Operator on the wall. 'You once had such talents, Jandell. Such talents. I will be intrigued to look upon this mask you wrought. It will remind me of older times.'

Somewhere, a bell rang.

Chapter Four

The house was large, and echoed all around.

Drayn crept along a corridor. Engravings leered at her from the walls, images of ancestors long dead, spurring her on. Candles burned down to the very stumps. A spider made the mistake of crossing her path, and went away forever.

'I know you are here, wherever you are,' she whispered, leaping at the shadows. 'I will find you, and Unchoose you, and that will be the end of you!'

But there was no sign of Cranwyl. Where could the wretch be, by Lord Squatstout's foot?

On she went, the courageous girl, unafraid of the noises in the dark, or not too afraid at any rate. She heard a creaking noise behind. She swung round, ready to lay waste to her challenger. No one was there. Yet still the noise came. Drayn concentrated.

There was silence for a moment, and then a cough.

It was from the library!

She was about to charge forward when she got a hold of herself. Cranwyl was no fool; it would do no good to reveal herself too quickly. Perhaps that was even what he wanted. She gathered her thoughts, calmed her heart, and padded along the corridor.

Never have I caught you, Cranwyl, wretch of all wretches. Tonight the tables will turn. Tonight you will find yourself Unchosen, by me!

She reached the door. To her left, in the corner of her eye, she could just make out old Fyndir, founder of the House of Thonn, engraved upon one of the many walls he built, all those years ago, when the Autocrat had just come to the Habitation. *Wish me well, Fyndir!*

The girl reached out, and grasped the door handle. She pushed down, very gently, knowing that Cranwyl's hearing was second to none. She was almost there, down it went, down it went, and then – clunk.

The door was locked.

She pushed again, just to make sure it was not simply stiff, but no, there was no way in. *Could Cranwyl have heard me coming, and locked the door?* That had to be it; all was not lost. She simply had to find a way in—

There came a tap at Drayn's shoulder, and the blood stopped coursing through her miserable veins. She turned, defeated again. There he was, in the mask, the beak almost reaching to Drayn's own nose.

'Cranwyl,' she sighed, 'you are cheating. That is the only way!'

The masked monster laughed. *The temerity of it!*

'I don't cheat, not ever, lady,' Cranwyl said.

Drayn could sense the smirk beneath the beak. *The effrontery!* 'I just do my best. But it's not very hard. You're easy to throw off the scent, you know, very easy.'

Drayn exhaled and dropped to the ground, bum thumping on the floor.

'But I heard you in the library.'

'No, you didn't. You thought you heard something, but it wasn't me. I might have had a hand in it, though.'

'How?'

'Well, I know all the creaks and cracks of this house, you see. I can make it speak for me, just by tickling it in the right place.'

He removed his mask. After all these years, it still surprised Drayn how young he was, with his smooth skin and bushy brown hair and sneaky, bright little eyes. He could not have been more than, what, thirty? He had been working since before she was born; he had started working when he was her age, he said. *Fancy that!*

'You are too good,' she said. 'You're as good as the real beaks. You're not a beak, are you?' She laughed, secretly hoping that he was. *That would be great fun.*

Cranwyl returned the laugh. 'If I was one of them, I'd be in Lord Squatstout's Keep right now, not sat here, that's for bloody sure.'

He looked up to a shelf on the wall, where an old clock ticked.

'Come,' he said, the laughter gone from his voice. 'Your mother will be expecting you.'

Drayn had dressed in her finery, as she always did when dining with her mother. It did nothing for her mood, or for Mother's.

'Did you know, girl, that there are rats in the yard?'

Mother shot a hard glance in her daughter's direction, as if Drayn had herself introduced the vermin.

I suppose I did bring that baby thingermewhatsit into the outer barn, but that isn't necessarily connected, is it?

'No, my lady, I did not know.' Sometimes she used a

different voice when she spoke to Mother. More proper. She hated herself for it. 'But I will work to rid the property of them, with the assistance of Cranwyl, if it so pleases you.'

Mother shook her head. 'You are not a rat catcher. I will speak with Cranwyl in the morning.'

I could absolutely be a rat catcher, if I wanted. Anyway, I could help Cranwyl catch rats, that's for sure. He definitely wouldn't mind.

'Eat your food.'

Mother was wearing her black dress tonight. It looked good on her, with her grey hair. Drayn thought so, anyway. She'd never say it, though.

Drayn turned to her plate. Some kind of seabird looked back at her, its stewed eyes swimming in its head.

'I'm not hungry,' she said, hoping Mother would let her leave and knowing that would never happen.

'Eat.'

Drayn turned the bird over, so she could at least avoid making eye contact. She hacked off a piece of pale meat and looked to the walls. More old people, looking down at her. No doubt they had to eat this muck in their day as well.

When she was about halfway through the bird she put down her knife and fork, hoping the remains would be swept away before Mother could notice. Sure enough, a shadowy figure came out of the darkness and lifted the plate, muttering something as he went. This was a house of mutters and shadows, all right.

Drayn had a question on her mind, and was in no mood to mutter. She looked at Mother, carefully weighing her options. Was she in a good mood? Was she ever in a good mood? Who knew?

'Mother.' Never Mum – always Mother.

The lady in the black dress looked up from her bird, whose beak she was about to inhale.

'Yes?'

'I heard that something happened after the Choosing.'

'Really? I wasn't there.'

Mother was lying – she had been there, after Drayn had gone home, and she knew what had happened. The head of the House of Thonn always knew what was happening on the Habitation.

'They say there was something that came from the sea.'

'Who say?'

'They.'

'They say a lot.'

'Is it true?'

Mother sighed. 'You would find out, anyway, I have no doubt. Yes, something came. It was very strange. A black ship, far bigger than a fishing boat. It came from across the Endless Ocean.'

'That cannot be.'

'That is what we all thought, too. But it was there. And yes, I was there, and yes, I did see it.'

'What was it?' Drayn's eyes were wide.

Mother shook her head, and shrugged, as if the question didn't matter. Drayn hated when she did that.

'No one knows,' Mother said. 'It all happened very quickly. The Choosing had actually just finished when the thing appeared.'

'What was on it?' Drayn's voice was now a whisper.

Mother gave her a curious look.

'You will not tell your friends?'

Drayn shook her head. She only had one friend, anyway.

'I did not see them myself, but they say there were two

creatures.'

Drayn swallowed. 'What kind of creatures?'

'A woman. And another ... being.'

Drayn nodded. *This can only mean one thing.* 'Another Autocrat!'

'Yes.'

'What do they want?'

Mother tutted. 'How am I supposed to know? I am sure it's nothing to worry about.'

'Thank you, Mother.'

But Drayn thought there *was* something to worry about. Creatures did not just appear from the sea, not ever in all of history, apart from Lord Squatstout himself, may he live forever. She could tell that Mother felt the same way.

'You're always getting me in trouble with your mother,' Cranwyl said. 'When's it going to stop?'

'When we catch the black cat. Not before then.'

Drayn brushed a branch from her face. She lifted the torch higher, careful to avoid the trees. The last thing they needed was to set fire to the woods. That would definitely get Mother going.

She pointed the light towards an outcrop of brown boulders.

'That's where I last saw her,' she said.

'Or him.'

'That's where I last saw him, her, it, whatever. She was looking at me with her red eyes, and she seemed hungry.'

'So we are here to catch a hungry cat beast?'

Drayn nodded. 'We can easily take her, you and I.' She put a reassuring hand on Cranwyl's shoulder. 'It's just a cat. No match for us, definitely not.'

'I thought you said it was a very big cat.'

'Well, yeah, but still. No match for us.'

There was a creaking behind the boulders.

'You know what that sounded like to me?' asked Cranwyl.

'A large cat.'

'No. A baby thingermewhatsit.'

Drayn tutted at Cranwyl. Seizing the initiative, she crept behind the nearest tree and slinked her way towards the boulders. She put her hand in her bag and removed the net, planning to throw it over the beast once she had run it through with her stick. She had sharpened it specially for the occasion.

Cranwyl stayed where he was, the coward.

Round she went, until she was mere feet from the lair of the monster. She raised the stick aloft – actually, it was more of a spear, she had decided – and, with a murderous roar, leapt into the fray, thrusting her weapon before her.

When the bloodlust had subsided she threw the spear to the ground, triumphant, and opened her eyes, expecting to see the lifeless body of the creature that had tormented her, or at least walked in front of her the other day. She was surprised, then, to find a large pile of sticks, broken and shattered in her frenzy.

'It seems there was no beast, after all.'

Cranwyl was at her side, looking superior, the swine.

'Not on this occasion, I grant you that,' Drayn conceded. 'But it *was* there.'

'Of course it was. I have no reason to doubt you.'

'Cranwyl, it was there.'

'If you say it was there, I must accept that it was there.'

'Cranwyl.'

'What?'

'I hate you.'

'Thank you.'

It was two o'clock in the morning by the time Drayn and Cranwyl returned to the house. They entered through one of the gates at the back, in case Mother was keeping watch. But that was very unlikely; she was always asleep before midnight. To be certain, Drayn stole a glance at the windows upstairs. All was darkness.

The girl and her servant went into the kitchen, where they threw themselves into rough wooden chairs. Drayn kicked off her muddied boots; Cranwyl immediately picked them up and began to scrub.

'Mother says there were two creatures on the boat,' Drayn said, her voice barely above a whisper. She had wanted to talk to Cranwyl about this all night, but something held her tongue. She did not know what.

Cranwyl looked up. He looked so afraid, sometimes.

'What kind of creatures?'

Drayn beckoned him closer. Cranwyl gently shifted his chair forward and leaned in.

'Well, she says that one of them was a normal person. But the other one was like ...'

She did not need to go further. Cranwyl sucked in a sharp breath.

'Another Autocrat! Now that is something. I wonder: are they related?'

Drayn rolled her eyes. 'Who cares? I'm wondering what it all means, that's what I'm wondering.'

'Oh. Yes, well, me too.'

Drayn leapt to her feet. She found a loaf of bread to the side, and ripped off a chunk. She offered some to Cranwyl,

56

but he shook his head, so she tore into it with gusto.

'I wonder when we'll hear anything about it?' she asked, spitting crumbs on the floor.

'Soon, I imagine,' Cranwyl replied. 'The lord likes to keep everyone informed of things like this. He is a kind and merciful leader.'

Just then, as if in answer, a bell rang.

Drayn dropped her bread.

'Run,' said Cranwyl.

The girl was gone in a flash, shooting up the stairs as quickly and quietly as she could. She felt her way into her room, changed into her nightdress, and threw her dirty clothes under the bed.

The bell rang again, from nowhere and everywhere, all at the same time.

Mother came in, carrying a candle. She had been quicker than Drayn expected. She crossed the room and sat at her daughter's side.

'The bell has rung,' she said. 'It has rung out from Lord Squatstout's Keep, and everyone can hear it now.'

Drayn pretended as if she had just woken up, yawning and rubbing her eyes.

'Really? But there was a Choosing just the other day.'

'Yes. The lord is preparing another. Perhaps he wants to show the newcomers how we do things here.'

Drayn gave a little cough. 'I am afraid,' she said. She meant it, though she hadn't meant to say it.

'Don't be,' said Mother, as warm as she had ever been. 'The good lord would never allow you to fall, unless he *knows* you are the one to be Chosen. I am sure of it.'

Why does she speak such nonsense? I'm not stupid.

Mother stood to leave. 'Get some rest. The assembly is

at dawn.'

'I will.'

'And Drayn,' said Mother, reaching under the bed and lifting a muddied slipper. 'Don't go out again at night.'

Damn.

'Yes, Mother.'

Chapter Five

Canning had never had ambitions.

No – that was not quite true. He had them, all right. But they were quiet, dreamy things: not the burning desires of so many of his fellow citizens. All he had ever wanted was to immerse himself in the mundane: to live a humble life, a quiet existence, far away from the Centre and the Fortress, from Brightling and her schemes.

But there was no escaping the Machinery.

And where had it taken him, this dream he never wanted? The Bowels of the See House. They had found him after the Selection, and taken him away. His memory of those events was broken. He had seen a creature dressed in purple rags, standing tall, that *thing* in the white mask by her side. The new Strategist was a girl he once knew: Katrina Paprissi, the last of her name.

But no longer. That girl was gone now.

It was a very different type of Selection. There were none of the usual trappings: no parchment from the Operator, no phalanx of Watchers spreading from the Circus in a black arc, scouring the land for the chosen ones. There had been a flame, but a *person* had emerged, if she could be called a person.

He had fallen over somewhere, he remembered. He was always falling over. Feet had trampled him into the dirt. When he managed to snatch glances at his surroundings, he saw people charging towards the new Strategist, holding their arms out. There was something about them; they were possessed, like in the stories about the old gods. Canning forced his way to his feet to get a better view, but it was too late; there were too many bodies in the way. He grabbed a man by the shoulder, without knowing why. Human contact, perhaps? The man turned and stared *through* the Tactician; his eyes were stagnant pools.

Whatever was driving these people to the Strategist had not affected him, he realised. Hope grew. He could sneak away: run to the West, perhaps, and hide himself in a vineyard or a tobacco farm or a mine. But then he felt a cold hand at his own shoulder, and turned to face a Watcher.

He had been here, in this room, this cell, for as long as he could remember. Was there ever a time before this cell? He had new memories, now, things he was certain had never occurred, or at least not to him. He had been to a city of dark spires, where people plucked out their eyes, just to avoid looking at her, the woman in the white mask. He had seen a temple, a place of wisdom, reduced to ashes by the power of her mind, its inhabitants throwing themselves into the flame to escape her gaze.

Her name was Shirkra.

She had brought all this before him when she visited. She had penetrated him, used him, tormented him with visions. No, not visions. *Memories.*

She was here again, now. *How long has she been here?*

'You're wondering why I am hurting you,' she said, her

voice free of emotion.

Canning nodded.

The Operator – for that was what she was, she had told him so herself – shrugged her narrow shoulders, and giggled. Her red hair bounced in curls. She was the most beautiful thing he had ever seen.

'It's not your fault, really, I suppose. You didn't mean to be Selected. You are unlucky, so unlucky, to have been Selected when you were. Mother told me to kill you all, long ago. I didn't get you all, though, did I? The white-haired woman is gone, and you're still alive. But it doesn't matter, does it? Perhaps it never mattered – perhaps she made me do those things, just to *distract* me! To keep me out of the way, me and my Chaos! But still, we have you, and she doesn't want to kill you now. That means I can play with you forever. What fun!'

Sometimes, Aranfal was there, too. Canning did not resent the Watcher. It was not his fault everything had come to this. It was all her.

Aranfal gave him cups of water.

'When will this end?' he asked her one night. He was unsure if he had spoken, or simply *thought* the question; it did not seem to matter with her.

'It does not have to end, so it may never end,' she said. 'It might be good to make you into a story. Yes, everyone would know what you suffered, oh yes, down here, at my hand, and then they would never seek to place themselves against Mother.'

'I did not place myself against her.'

'Hmm, perhaps, perhaps. But the Machinery Selected you,

and that is the same thing.'

She raised her arms, and took him back to the day he was Selected.

The Watchers had come early in the morning. Strange, but he had already known what they wanted. He had known when he woke. His room was a hovel, tucked into the back of a shop, stinking of fish, like everything else, with one dirty window facing out onto the lane. It had been grey, and cold, as it always was. He was thinner then, before all the lonely gluttony of the Centre, and as he stood from the bed he wrapped his smock tightly around his bones. He looked out the window; a girl with a stick in her hand was staring back. She pointed it at him, and ran away. He never did find out who she was.

He left the hovel with a sense of dread. He knew, of course, that a new Tactician had been Selected. He had begged the Machinery to leave him alone. He hated the idea of being Selected, which meant he probably would be. Things always went like that for him.

He quickly exited the lane and joined the main street, planning to go to the market as usual. He hoped this feeling was misplaced, or that they would not find him. But he did not make it very far. As soon as he turned onto the street, they were on top of him: the Watchers. He remembered it so clearly. There were three of them, narrow creatures, all wearing eagle masks. One of them held a parchment. He scoured it quickly, and then approached Canning.

'You are Canning, the market trader,' he said in a thin voice.

Canning wondered how they had known where to find him, though he later learned much that was strange about the Watchers.

'I am,' he replied, feeling a fool.

The Watchers fell to their knees, arms raised towards Canning, and with one voice began their spiel about the Machinery and how it had Selected him in its glory. But he was not paying attention. He was looking to the edge of the gathering crowd, where a young woman was standing. Her face was torn with misery.

'Stand,' he told the Watchers. It was the single occasion he ever summoned the courage to issue orders to these people. 'When must I go?'

'You are a Tactician,' said one, though she seemed utterly unconvinced. 'You may stay or go as you please.'

The first Watcher came forward again. 'But of course, your people need you to lead them into Expansion – to conquer the very Plateau itself!'

The new Tactician nodded. 'I will need one day,' he said.

When the Watchers had gone, Canning moved into the ogling crowd. 'All of you, leave,' he said.

'You're enjoying dishing out commands,' said Annya, the only one to stay behind.

'I am not. I want to stay here.'

'You can't. You've been Selected. You're going to leave me behind.'

She gave him that look of hers, then, such a strange look, wounded and piercing at once, a trembling defiance. And she turned and ran from him.

He chased her all the way to the dock, where they stood before that hateful wall. She had done this many times before. She was half mad, he had been told. Half-mad Annya. But he never thought she would really do it. No, he never thought that.

When she turned to face him, she was crying.

'You have ruined my life,' she said. There was no emotion in her voice.

'Annya.' He reached out a hand to her, but she knocked it away. 'I didn't mean for this to happen. How could I have meant for this to happen? The Machinery Selected *me*. It wasn't the other way around.'

Annya walked to him, so their faces almost touched. 'They say it only picks those that want to be picked. That's what my father said.'

'Believe me, it is not true.'

She snorted.

'You can come with me,' he said, lamely.

'Tacticians aren't allowed wives.'

'It could be a secret.'

In an instant she struck him. He raised his hand to his stinging face.

'And then I can be your ... what, whore? Up there in your pyramid, hidden away like a secret?'

'I didn't mean it like that.'

Something changed, then. The anger seemed to leave her. 'I can't do that,' she said.

Canning nodded. And then, as if it was the simplest act in the world, the love of his life climbed onto the wall, and threw her young body into the sea.

He never understood why she did it. Sometimes he thought it was an accident; perhaps she only meant to scare him, and had taken a tumble. But no. She had jumped. *Half-mad Annya.*

This was the memory the Operator brought before him, more than any other. When he asked her why she did it, she just shrugged.

She brought other memories, too: things that happened after he was Selected, and some that occurred long before. They were all twisted, somehow: a shade darker than he remembered. But when he was wrapped inside them, he was powerless. He would have done anything she asked of him. She preyed upon his old fears; she drained him of all hope.

All the while, she seemed to take such joy from his memories. She sparked with a strange power, as she wallowed in them. Once, he turned to her, and the woman was gone, replaced with a flickering light. It had a kind of elemental force, and he could not look upon it for long.

He never knew a memory could hurt so much. He never knew a good memory could be woven into something bad, or a bad memory made harder to bear. But she showed him it was so.

Strangest of all were the memories that were not his own. Could he even be certain they *were* memories, or were they the creations of her imagination? They were terrible, whatever they were; she could lift things from them, and make them real. *How much power does she have?*

And that was how the last Tactician in the Overland spent his days.

Chapter Six

'What is there, when there is nothing at all?'

Brandione opened his eyes. They had returned to the blackness.

The Queen was by his side, her three bodies suspended in the air, weightless and timeless. Her gowns had been replaced by rags. *Like Katrina Paprissi. Like the Strategist.*

'You are in mourning, your Majesty,' Brandione said.

Three heads turned to him. 'Yes. In this place, we are close to death. Can you not feel it? Can you not taste it on the air?'

Brandione sucked in a breath. 'Yes.'

The Queen nodded. 'Last Doubter.' She surrounded him, placing him in the middle of three ragged women. 'What is there, when there is nothing at all?'

Brandione looked around. 'There is nothing,' he said. 'Just an empty room.'

'But what if there is no room? What if there is no house, no land, no forest, no lake, no mountain, no stars, no moon, no sun, no birds, no people – what is there then?'

'Emptiness.'

'Emptiness,' the Queen whispered. She glanced around

the dark. 'Once, long before my birth, there was only emptiness. We cannot know for certain what that emptiness was when it was alone. It is one of the great questions, is it not? What was there, before creation?' She gestured at the void. 'This is my imagining.'

She stared into the blackness, and seemed to shudder.

'My people call it the Absence. It was not good, or evil, or anything in between. It simply *was*. Or perhaps, it was *not*.' She giggled, though there was no humour in it.

Brandione gazed into the depths. 'There is nothing here. Only a feeling of ... death.' He shook himself. 'Not death – a void. Only the living die.'

'Yes,' the Queen said. 'I never saw it in its original state. What a glory it surely was.'

For a moment, Brandione felt a surge of anger. Was this all there was to the story of mortals? Were they nothing more than flotsam, pushed along eternal waters?

The Queen sighed. 'This is the Great Absence, at the height of its glory. But it is not a memory. It is only my dream, my drawing, of what the Absence might have been like, long ago. Before the mortals came to be. Before *I* came to be.'

'I can't see anything. But I can feel it.'

'There is nothing to see. There is nothing at all, except eternity.'

There was a sound, from far away in the ether, lasting only a moment: a low moan.

The Queen turned her bodies away from Brandione, and lined up at his side. The smallest spark of blue had appeared, far away in the darkness.

'The Absence was alone for such a long time. It existed, but nothing was there. It lived, but it was death.'

The light in the distance began to grow. 'But something

happened to it,' the Queen said. 'The great emptiness, over the long ages of solitude, began to change. It developed ... a *mind*. It recognised itself as a *something*. The expanse was no longer empty: something was changing, in the dark.'

She sighed, and held her hands out, pointing at the blue light. It was still growing.

'The changes accelerated. The Absence grew more aware of itself. It realised, for the first time, that it was alone. And it became lonely.'

She burst into laughter.

'Can you imagine? It realises its existence, and it becomes *lonely*.' She laughed again, and the sounds were sucked out into the ungrateful void.

'And so it decided to create companions.'

Brandione realised, now, that they were travelling through the darkness; the light was not a light at all, but a planet, green and blue and wet and lush. New lights sparkled around it, and the darkness was no more: the deathly sensation dissipated and stars sprang up in the emptiness. A moon revolved around the planet, which spun around a blazing sun.

The moment disappeared, and they were somewhere else: a field, in the sunshine. A naked man and woman lay in the grass, their eyes closed, their hands intertwined. Their bodies were surrounded by the blackness – by the Absence. It spun around them like a spider building a web.

'What is happening to them?'

'They are being created,' the Dust Queen said. 'This is the beginning of the world. Or rather, it is how I imagine it to have been.'

The people stood, and it soon became clear they were not alone. Others rose across the field, the Absence crawling across them.

'The Absence was no longer alone,' the Dust Queen said. 'It had created these things, so different to itself. Intelligent creatures, in a world of life.'

The strands of Absence rose away from the people, and ascended to the sky, where they formed into a strange tapestry among the clouds. The people below stood utterly still, statues of flesh and bone.

'The Absence had changed. It was no longer a void, but a *god*.'

Brandione winced. That word had been on his mind a great deal of late, but it rankled to hear it said aloud.

'It loved these creatures,' the Queen said. 'It loved them so much that, for a moment, it thought of giving them immortality. But this was the wrong path, it knew. They *should* die. Only the Absence should suffer the curse of forever: the sadness of being alone. Its children would sparkle for just a moment, but they would burn with such a fury in the time that they had. Still, the Absence did not want their lives to be meaningless. Do you understand, Last Doubter? It wanted them to remember the past. In this, it was selfish. It wanted to remember for itself. It wanted to hold on to the past, all of it, like trinkets on a shelf. Not just the glories of the world, but all the petty jealousies, and the rages, and the little loves and broken hearts. It was then that the Absence made its terrible mistake.'

Small flames sparked in the sky, in the heart of the Absence, before drifting downwards towards the people. Each of the flames flickered before an eyeball, their brightness intensifying, and then disappeared.

'The Absence gave the mortals a powerful gift, which it took from within itself: the gift of memory.'

They had returned to the place of fleshless death: the heart of the Great Absence. In the distance, a white light sprung to life. It began to expand, sending out tendrils in different colours, sparking between green and blue and red and a thousand other shades. Brandione saw images in the maelstrom. He saw moments of his past, shards of memory: a young man in a military uniform; a barn aflame, somewhere in the West; a bloodied, emaciated soldier, marching ever onwards.

Three hands pointed to the light.

'Do you know what that is?'

A familiar sensation overcame Brandione, as he gazed at the burning mass of light.

'It is the Underland,' he said.

Three heads nodded. 'Yes. The Absence placed great powers in memories: a part of its very being. But it did not realise what it had done. The powers of memory became their *own* creature: a thing formed of all memories, of all the power the Absence had put in them, and the new powers they had developed themselves. It was a god, to use the old word again. The god of memory.'

There came a sound in the darkness: a great hiss.

'The Absence realised its error. In its loneliness, it had unleashed something it could not control: a rival, created by its own hand. It felt a great *agony*, and despised itself for what it had become: a creature with a mind and a heart, and so capable of mistakes. It wished to be alone again, to cast any notions of life from whatever passed for its mind, and to return creation – and itself – to emptiness. But it could never go back. How could the father of time return to timelessness? How could the bringer of life become lifeless again? Even if it succeeded in destroying all of its creations, it would never become what it once was. But it did not understand, or did not care. It vowed that it would destroy this new god, and the world it had created: the birds, the trees, the humans and their memories. Everything, everything, everything.'

Something was happening in the blackness. It was draining away, slowly forming into a new shape. A figure appeared in the emptiness: a thin giant, his featureless face, his limbs, his torso, all formed of the Absence. When Brandione looked at this man, he felt his life draining away: he sensed an immense pressure crushing his memories with its weight. He looked to the Dust Queen, and realised that even she felt that terrible sensation as she turned her heads away from the Absence. She was thinner than before: weaker.

'This is nothing but my imagination,' she whispered. 'But even here, I feel its power.'

The expanse around them now was formed of two things: the walking figure of Absence, and the Old Place, which sparkled into all the space the Absence left behind, eagerly taking his place, surrounding Brandione and the Queen in a crazed haze. But the Absence reached out a hand, and seized a tendril of the Old Place's light, dragging the vortex towards it.

'The war waged for many eras,' the Queen said, gesturing at the creatures before them. 'The Absence demanded that the god of memory submit, but the Old Place was not to be easily defeated.'

Far above them, the Absence had become a towering creature. It held all that remained of the Old Place in a mighty hand: the light of memory still shone, but it was nothing more than a pinprick of blue. The pinprick began to tremble in the hand of the Absence. The darkness opened its paw, and emitted a low moan as it gazed at the Old Place.

'What is happening?' asked Brandione.

When the Dust Queen spoke again, her voice had changed. It was the movement of the mountains; it was the thunder of the ocean.

'The Old Place was close to defeat,' the three mouths said. 'In desperation, it looked within itself. It reached into its heart, and it plucked out a weapon, formed from all the strength and terror and love and loss that afflicted the mortal mind. A being was born: a creature of memory, a thing that could fight the Absence in a way the Old Place never could.'

Three streaks of light burst forth from the Old Place, great blasts of shifting colours, tearing into the Absence like cannon fire. Brandione gazed at the light, and for a moment, a thousand faces appeared in the blaze. There was no question in his mind: this was the Dust Queen.

The Great Absence began to recede, and colour filled the space it left behind. The void became a fury of memory, a tempest of the past. Even when he closed his eyes, Brandione could not avoid it: a stream of images, of cherished thoughts and fearful recollections. He felt the power of memory, and he bowed his head before it.

'Memory is its own thing,' the Queen said. 'No one knows what a memory will do: no one knows what a memory can conjure. Memories can trick; memories can deceive; memories can overwhelm us. The Old Place is unknowable.'

The blackness was now gone, and the stench of death had vanished. All the strands of light – Old Place and Dust Queen – joined together once more, and began to shrink. Soon, the sky became the true night once again: stars pricked the darkness, and the world appeared before them, thrumming with life. The Old Place disappeared from view, but it was still there. Brandione could feel it: the home of memory.

'What happened to the Absence?'

But now he was somewhere else.

Wayward was lying on Brandione's bed in the magnificent tent the Queen had given him. The courtier wore a nightgown of the brightest gold, with ribbons of the same colour running through his hair. His eyes were closed, but Brandione knew he was awake.

'That is enough talk of the Absence,' Wayward said in a quiet voice. 'It hurts her to speak of it. You must have seen that.'

Brandione reached out to his desk, and rested a hand against it, his head bowed. He was unsteady: on his feet, and within himself. An old anger rose within: the rage of the powerless.

Wayward sat up on the bed.

'I see that you are angry, Last Doubter.'

Brandione breathed deeply. 'My old Provost at the College said I was always angry, and that my whole life was an attempt to smother it. But I couldn't stop it, he said, so it propelled me forward.'

'Interesting.' Wayward nodded, and seemed lost in contemplation.

'Were you there, in that place, Wayward? How can you be my guide, when I couldn't see you there?'

Wayward stood from the bed. 'She lets me look through her eyes. It's good for you to have a guide, is it not? Through all this?' He waved a hand at their surroundings.

Brandione nodded. 'Yes, I suppose.' The anger was subsiding. He heard a noise from outside the tent: a steady drumming on the sand. He looked at the doorway, and saw line after line of the sand soldiers, marching past, massed ranks of grey infantry in yellow cloaks.

'Your army,' Wayward said. 'Once, it was her army. Now it is yours. The army of the Last Doubter.'

Brandione turned back, to see that the courtier had taken a place next to a painting which stood on a plinth in the centre of the room. Brandione had not seen it before. Had he simply never noticed it? Or had Wayward conjured it from thin air?

The subject of the painting was instantly familiar to Brandione, as it would have been to any citizen of the Overland. It was the Operator, standing alone against a night sky, his arms spread wide. He was a youth, here, a young man with long black hair. He wore a red cloak: no sign of his strange garment of a thousand entrapped faces.

'Do you know him?' Wayward asked.

Brandione nodded. 'Of course. It is the Operator.'

Wayward smiled. 'Indeed. He is the answer to your question – what happened to the Absence? I will answer it, if I may.' He bowed. 'After the Queen defeated the Absence, it returned, many times. How could it be killed? It was the stuff of the universe, hmm? And so they fought and fought and fought. Over the ages, the Old Place created new weapons: creatures of memory, like the Queen. Jandell was one of them.'

'Jandell?'

Wayward laughed. 'That is his name, Last Doubter, or the one we have called him for long ages. They say that Jandell was taken from a pit of sadness, a place of despair, grim memories with a dark power. Oh, he was quite a weapon. And there were others, too.'

He pointed again at the painting. When Brandione looked

now he saw a woman with red hair, wearing a white mask and a green dress.

'I know her,' he whispered.

'Shirkra,' Wayward said. 'A strange creature, born from strange things. She calls herself the Mother of Chaos, though she is no mother. It's just a childish title she gives herself. Indeed, I believe she is a child, in many ways.'

Brandione nodded. 'All of them are memories.'

'Yes, yes, all of them are creatures of memory – perhaps not one memory, but many.' He cocked his head to the side. 'None of them – not Jandell, not Mother, not Shirkra – none of them are as powerful as the Queen. She is a thing of so many parts.' He nodded, and for a moment his eyes clouded up, and he was far away. 'Eventually, the Absence could resist these weapons no longer. That conflicted being – caught between its desire to return to emptiness, and the truth of its godliness – was broken and destroyed, its being shattered. They say Jandell kept one of the shards.' He shrugged.

'Are you one too?'

Wayward laughed. 'Oh, I am very young indeed, and never knew the Absence: I was born just ten millennia ago, after the Machinery was made. The Queen was lonely, you see, as she went to live in the Prison.' He snapped his fingers together. 'She wanted a companion. The older creatures, like her, can form beings of their own, as the Old Place formed them. I cannot tell what kind of memories made me – weak ones, I imagine.' He gave a modest little chuckle. 'There are many more like me. Pale imitations of the great ones.' He shrugged. 'Still, can't complain.'

He rushed forward to Brandione.

'Have I pleased you?' he asked. 'Have I answered your question?' He gazed into Brandione's eyes.

The Last Doubter nodded. 'Yes, yes ...' He patted Wayward on the shoulder. His anger had dissipated. Was he being manipulated? He did not believe so. There was something eager about Wayward: a desire to please others. *That's why he made a good companion for her, perhaps.*

'What's next?' Brandione asked.

Wayward smiled. 'What do you think, Last Doubter? You must go back to her. You are learning so much. All of it will be so useful to you in the game. Oh yes, you ...'

But his words faded into nothing, as the tent melted away.

Chapter Seven

'Ask me a question, Aranfal. Ask me a lovely question.'

They were in Aranfal's apartments. Shirkra was standing at the Watcher's collection, a trove of ancient artefacts he had taken over the years from Doubters' dens. She was examining a bronze statue, turning it over in her hands. It showed a little girl and boy, hand in hand: twins, to look at them. Aranfal had never liked those children, yet he could not bring himself to throw them away. He could never throw anything away.

'I have many questions, my lady.'

He was sitting in a leather chair beside his fireplace. It was late at night, and the room glowed with candlelight. Shirkra had been here when he arrived, an hour before, from the See House library. He went there often, these days, searching for answers to strange questions. But the answers never came.

She turned and smiled at him from beneath her mask. She was a strange thing, beautiful, but hard to look upon. She reminded him of a firestorm he had once seen in the West, a terrible conflagration that devoured a forest and two villages before they could stop it. He had watched it from a hillside, repelled and attracted at once. *Perhaps Aranfal was attracted, and Aran Fal was repelled.*

He was beginning to wonder if both those two men could live within him, together, for much longer.

'Where are we going?' he asked.

Shirkra shrugged. 'Where are any of us going?'

'I didn't mean it in a philosophical sense. Mother said you should take me ... wherever you are going.'

She giggled. 'You are so serious, Aranfal, so serious! We are going to see the Gamesman, of course. Where else would we go when a game is being prepared? He should already be hard at work, getting everything ready for us. Oh, but he is a tricky thing, the Gamesman. It's just his nature. We must make sure he is not being slothful, or trying to deceive us.'

She crossed the room, and took a chair by Aranfal's side.

'Ask me something else, my Aranfal.' She rolled the syllables of his name in her mouth like she could taste every corner of them. 'Ask me another question. I know you have many questions, hmm, I can *feel* them within your beautiful head.'

She reached out and tapped his forehead. The Watcher coughed.

'What is the game?'

Shirkra waved a hand impatiently. 'A thing of old. I don't know why the Queen wants to play it again, but I don't trust her, oh no, not at all.' She grinned. 'But you will find out all about the game, in time. Ask me something else.'

Aranfal thought for a moment. He was learning that the only way to get answers from Shirkra was to approach her from strange angles, and *never* from the front.

'Ruin will come with the One,' he said.

Shirkra cocked her head to the side and gave the Watcher a curious look. 'Ah. That is not a question, my love. I spent many long years hidden away from civilisation, oh yes, but even I can tell that this is not a question, oh no.'

Aranfal nodded. 'Is Mother the One?'

Shirkra laughed. 'Of course! Of course! You know all this already, my Aranfal, or at least you *should* know it by now! Yes, she has many names: the One, Mother, and others besides. Jandell thought he had killed her, long ago, and so he did not believe the Promise. Hmm? How could Ruin come with the One, when there is no One, hmm? That is what he thought. Oh, the arrogant fool!'

'But what is Ruin, my lady? The One has come. The Machinery has Selected her. But the world is carrying on as normal. The worst thing she has done is ... well, nothing at all. She hasn't done anything. She doesn't attempt to run the country. She doesn't try to *ruin* the country. People don't know what she wants, so they just go about their business. That's not really Ruin, in my book.'

Aranfal was reminded of all the days and nights he had spent in the Bowels of the See House, coaxing information from Doubters in whatever way he could. Sometimes violence was unnecessary. He would have laughed, if he could. *The very idea that I'm using my tricks on a creature like Shirkra.*

'But it's not done yet, Aranfal, it's not done yet! Haven't you paid attention, my love? Mother must find the Machinery first, hmm? It is broken, but still Ruin hasn't come – so it must be trapped inside. That's why she wants to please the *Queen.*' Shirkra turned her head an inch, and spat upon the floor.

Almost there.

'So Ruin is not among us?'

79

'Oh no, oh no! Of course not, no! Ruin will surely come, but it has not come yet. It remains in bonds.' She grinned at him. 'Of course, Ruin may have changed over the millennia. It might not be the same thing that we are all expecting. So I can't tell you *exactly* what it is, if that's what you're getting at, oh no, my dear Aranfal.'

Damn.

Shirkra smiled, and held him with her gaze. Aranfal saw his own past, marching before him in an endless stream: cold days on northern coasts; a journey to a black tower, where he became Aranfal; and so many tormented souls, languishing under his grip. All of that felt distant, now: the work of another man.

'Let me ask *you* a question, my Aranfal.' Her voice came from afar, like a whisper from another room. 'What are you, now that the Machinery has abandoned you? What are *any* of you, hmm? Nothing but bags of flesh: the makers of lovely memories.'

There was a knock on the door outside, and the spell was broken.

'I'll get it!' Shirkra cried. She leapt to her feet and vanished from the room.

Aranfal placed his head in his hands. She was right, of course. What were they, without the Machinery? *Aranfal or Aran Fal? Do others feel a change, too? Back to some ... past ...*

He felt himself drifting, but Shirkra's reappearance snapped him back to reality. Another Watcher was there, a chubby woman, her unkempt hair spilling out from behind a cat mask. She thrummed with some inner rhythm, tapping her feet on the floor.

'Good evening, Aleah,' Aranfal said. There was a tremor

in his voice.

Aleah nodded to him.

She does not bow to me, once the second of all the Watchers. Her ambition is clear. The institution needed people like her. In fact, it actively encouraged their development: competition kept the senior Watchers on their toes, and nurtured the growth of the newest crop. Still, there was something about Aleah that made Aranfal uneasy. She had adapted too smoothly to the new world, the world of Mother and Shirkra, a world without the Machinery, without leaders, without Brightling. *She relishes the changes. She sees opportunity in upheaval.*

'Come, Aranfal,' Shirkra said, throwing him his aquamarine cloak. 'We must go.' She turned to Aleah, and caught her in a sudden embrace. 'You will look after the tower until we return, my darling, oh yes. You will care for Mother. Hmm?'

'Yes, Madam Shirkra.' This time, she bowed.

As Aranfal left the room with Shirkra, Aleah smirked at him. But he did not care. *Take my position. Take whatever you want. None of it matters any more.*

Chapter Eight

As time wore on, Canning felt himself change.

He could never recall, in later days, exactly when it happened. Perhaps that was only natural, when the days and nights were an endless cycle, watching Annya as she leapt and wallowing in so many other memories.

How best to describe the change that came over the one-time Tactician of Expansion? Perhaps it could be said that he developed a certain ... *capability*. He began to see his prison in a new light. When he was at that hated dock, he was trapped in a memory: his *own* memory, taken from him and twisted into something terrible. But over time, he became aware of the outline, the shape of the nightmare. He could see the edge of the memory. He could feel something there, an old, burning energy: the flickering light he had seen in Shirkra.

Over a long time – hours, days, months, who could tell – he felt himself develop a kind of separation from the nightmare. He could even tear himself away from it for periods of time, and return to his cell. He could feel the realness of the walls, before the memory overwhelmed him again.

He did not know how this had happened, but of one thing he was sure: Shirkra did not know about it. Once, she came

82

to him, and watched as the memory unfolded. She had thought him weak and humiliated. But she was wrong. He had been in the memory, but this time he had felt like an observer, rather than a victim. And she did not realise.

He thought she would work it out soon. But until she did, he held a kind of minor power over her. It was the first time he had really held a power over anyone, in truth, which was saying something for a former Tactician of the Overland.

And that was how he escaped.

Shirkra came one night while he slept on the cold ground, placing a hand on his shoulder and turning him over.

'Come,' she said. The door of the cell was open.

The former Tactician dreaded what this could mean, but he followed her nonetheless, staring at the train of the green dress as it was dragged across the stone and the dirt. It felt like they were descending deeper into the Bowels of the See House, though that seemed scarcely possible. *How deep can one building be?*

But on they went. After some time, the lines and form of the building gave way to damp rocks and pools of stagnant water, the trappings of a subterranean cave. The fineries of civilisation – if the See House had any – were now far behind.

'Where are we?' he asked into the gloom. He did not expect a response, and none came.

Will you ever leave this place? Perhaps not. Where would you go, anyway? There is no stall, any more, no Annya and no market. There is nothing for you, anywhere, nothing but the white mask and the memories and the cold stones.

The surroundings changed again. The cave became a corridor, wide and grand, illuminated by torches that sent out a flickering purple glow. It seemed to be a kind of museum, with shelves all around, groaning under the weight of strange objects. There was a spiked ball on a chain, rusted and broken. There were statuettes of creatures Canning had never seen before: spotted animals with long necks, and grey titans with short horns. He lifted a heavy object, like a handcannon, but smooth, black, and small. Its lines were too clean, its edges too perfect. Where did it come from?

Paintings hung on the walls. There was the old Operator, unmistakable; Shirkra, unmasked, a thing of unsurpassed beauty; and others he did not recognise.

'This is not the See House,' he said.

Shirkra stopped and turned her gaze upon him, the eyes no longer green, but burning red in the mask. 'No, it is not. This is the Old Place. But what is the See House, if not a spark of the Old Place?'

She pointed to the end of the corridor, where a purple light glowed. Canning did not know what it was, or where it could have come from. But when he looked at it, he felt the past whispering to him.

Shirkra removed her mask, and turned the full glare of her beauty upon him.

'Beyond sits the future of the world, as Selected by your Machinery. We will visit her now. I advise you to show respect of the most abject kind.'

Canning nodded. Abject respect was not difficult for him.

Shirkra went first. Canning turned back and stole a last glance at the corridor; some unseen force was extinguishing the torches.

He was on a beach. The sand was black, as was the sky, and a red sun burned down on them. The sea roiled in anger, its water an iron grey. In the distance was a woman. She was far away, but he could still make out the shape of her body, the pale skin, the black hair, the purple rags.

'No,' he said. 'I cannot go to *her*. She is too much for me.'

Shirkra smiled at him, but there was no warmth there. 'She is too much for us all. She will eat the world, one day: her and Ruin. We are all here to serve.'

They walked along the beach, Shirkra holding Canning's elbow in an iron grip. As they went, the woman in the purple rags seemed to jolt towards them. Time and distance were different here, if they existed at all.

She was before them, then: the body of Katrina Paprissi, the Strategist, the One, Mother. She was utterly warped and changed from the girl that once followed Brightling around. The hair was still black, the skin still pale, but there the likeness ended. This creature was twice Katrina's height, as if the Apprentice had been somehow stretched. She was sprawled across a throne, a dark thing made from the Machinery knew what. There was no wind here, but the purple rags moved incessantly, curling and twisting around the Strategist's thin body. She watched him with a lazy curiosity, and he felt himself quail before those purple eyes.

'You are Canning, the last of the Tacticians.'

This voice was not that of Katrina Paprissi. It had a hard tone, and was strangely deep, with a clunking, clanking quality. It reminded Canning of the movement of some war machine he had been forced to assess in the old days.

He did not know what to say, so simply bowed.

Shirkra took a position behind the throne. She knelt down and lifted some black sand; holding it above the Strategist's head, she allowed it to drain away from her clenched fist.

The Strategist stuck out her tongue, and drank the blackness in, watching Canning all the while.

'I suppose that makes you my servant,' said Mother, when she had finished with the sand. 'I have only one Tactician left. One has gone from these lands; the others I threw to Chaos, along with any threat they could have posed. What madness my daughter brought to you all!' She smiled at Shirkra, who giggled. 'I thought of doing the same to you, Canning. Shirkra would have liked that. But my position is now secure. What purpose would it serve? Besides, I think I like you, Canning. You will be a useful servant.'

'We are all your servants, madam,' said Canning.

Shirkra laughed.

'No,' said the Strategist, raising a hand to Shirkra. 'Do not mock him. It is a kind thing he says.'

Canning looked from Shirkra to the Strategist. He sensed he was expected to say something else, but it was beyond his reach.

The Strategist stood, casting Shirkra in her shadow. The red sun retreated into black clouds, and the dark sea fled from the shore.

'Do you know who I am?'

Canning fell to his knees.

'Mother,' he whispered. 'The One.'

'Yes. Look at me.'

Canning looked up into the purple eyes.

'Do you know where the Machinery is? Is that the sort of thing Jandell told you people? Your Operator – you do know his true name, don't you?'

Canning nodded. He had heard it in Shirkra's nightmares.

'It might save me a lot of time if I knew where it was,' Mother continued. 'I could call off the game!' She laughed, and glanced at Shirkra. 'Would you like that, daughter?'

Shirkra nodded fiercely, and Mother turned back to Canning.

'I realise, even as I speak, that I am being foolish.' The voice had turned harsh and despairing.

'I do not know where the Machinery is,' Canning said. 'I have never even seen it. No one has, except for the Operator himself.'

'Look at me. Never look away from me.'

Canning met the Strategist's gaze. He could see his life there, broken into fragments, being sorted and sifted through by this woman: this force.

'You are a sad man.'

Canning nodded.

'You have seen much that has hurt you. How pathetic, that the last Tactician in the Overland should be such a wretch.'

'Yes, madam.'

'But there is more to you, Canning. I can *feel* it. You have a future, I think, though it may not be one you hoped for. I believe you will be useful in the game.'

'I don't know what that is, madam. But I will do what you wish.'

She laughed. 'Do what I wish! Ah, how long has it been since mortals said such things to me.' She sighed. 'I spent a long time as nothing, Canning. I was no more than memory, in the air. But how things change. I found a host that I love.' She gestured at her body. 'The Machinery has broken, and sent new powers to me. I can hear the other children of memory, scrabbling at my door, yearning to serve me once more. But in the dark days, only my daughter was there. Chaos was my only companion.'

She smiled at Shirkra.

'Now I have returned,' she said. 'And you all once again pledge to do as I wish. It is strange to me.'

Mother sat down again on her throne. The purple drained from her eyes, and suddenly Canning was staring into the face of Katrina Paprissi.

'You do not know where the broken Machinery is, Canning.'

'No, Mother, I do not.'

'I will find it. I will open it. Ruin will come.'

'I understand.'

Mother turned to Shirkra, and nodded.

They were back at the wall, and Annya was about to leap for the thousandth time.

Shirkra was by his side, whispering, the tip of her tongue brushing against his face.

'I could make this so much worse, Canning. I could infuse this memory with other things, little bits and pieces I have picked up over the millennia. This woman could perish still, but in so many other ways, ways you are simply incapable of imagining. I am Chaos. I am the detritus of nightmares, and the echo of daydreams. I can bring such things before your eyes that you would wish you had died in the Circus. I can take the very heart of a memory, a thousand of them, their deepest powers, and burn you in them forever.'

She looked at Annya.

'A pretty wretch. Why would anyone choose death, particularly those whose lives are finite?'

She was gone, then, leaving him with the memory.

Canning looked to Annya.

'I feel I am able to control this,' he said. She did not

respond. *Of course not. She is a nothing – a memory.*

He closed his eyes, and he saw it: a febrile power that crackled between a thousand colours, hues that came from another world. This was the essence of the memory, and it burned with greatness. He felt he could touch it. He reached out his hand ...

When he opened his eyes again, the memory was gone, and he was standing in his cell.

In the corner he saw some clothes: green trousers, a loose, dark shirt, well-worn boots. *Are they mine?* He removed the old smock, and got himself dressed. *Did I drag these from a memory?*

There was a sound behind. He turned to the door, where a Watcher stood: a young man, in a lizard mask, holding a plate of bread and meat.

'The Operator – I was told to give you some food.' The eyes behind the mask were wide. 'How did you – she said you were still ... are you free of her? How did you do it?'

Canning shook his head.

'Can you feel it?' he asked the Watcher. Something had happened to him. He could still sense the power of the memory. He could hold it in his mind. He could *use* it. The heart of the memory was his. He could feel what Shirkra felt: the magic of memories. He knew, somehow, how she did what she did.

'What are you doing?' the boy asked. 'I can't – what are you doing to me?'

The Watcher seemed ready to cry for help, but Canning stopped him with a thought and, with another, threw him to the ground.

'Where are you?' he asked the boy. Canning could feel

the edge of the memory that the Watcher had fallen into; he could see it sparkling, but when he tried to look more closely, it vanished from his grasp.

'You? I see you, grandmother. But why ...?'

The boy lost consciousness.

Imbued with a sense of power he had never felt before, the one-time Tactician walked through the door.

Chapter Nine

Brightling had been in many cells, but she had never been an inmate.

To be fair, it was not the kind of cell they had in the Bowels of the See House. It was a wide space, the walls covered with faded tapestries, depicting strange scenes. One of the images showed a short little man, climbing a rock and looking to the sky. *Squatstout?* It was difficult to tell. In the centre of the room was a table, laden with golden bowls of fruit and bread and cheese, a wooden jug of wine, and a glass. In the corner was a single bed.

She studied her surroundings carefully. Unsurprisingly, the room was sealed tight.

She took a seat at the table, spread some blue cheese over a piece of crusty bread, and contemplated her situation. Squatstout had overpowered the Operator – Jandell –

with little apparent difficulty. How had that happened? Even Squatstout had seemed surprised. Perhaps Jandell had lost his strength over the years, as Squatstout thought. *All those memories you could have taken.* Or perhaps he was like the rest of them: shattered by the end of the Machinery, and everything they had known.

Memories. She thought of the fire Jandell had shown her, and the food he kept on his ship. Memories were magic, he had said. What a quaint word, to come from something like him! Magic was the stuff of the market. Magic was the talk of Doubters. But she understood the power of memory, all right. She always had. She thought of Katrina. She thought of her old life, and the terrible things she had done to impress the Machinery, with Jandell as her guide. She did not feel guilt for any of it: that was how the world worked, back then. Still, the memories weighed on her. She would have liked to …

She sighed, and rubbed her head. Introspection did not come easily. Besides, she had other things to worry about, like getting out of this cell.

'I bet you're wondering how to get out of this cell.'

Squatstout had appeared at the table, smiling, as if he had always been there.

'Yes, of course,' she said, concealing her surprise. She took a bite out of her bread. 'It would be remiss of me not to.'

Squatstout chuckled, and helped himself to an apple, which he crunched loudly. 'I'm dying to know – what do you make of my little island? I believe it's the first place you've visited, outside your Overland, so I'd love to know; truly, I would love to know.'

Brightling shrugged. 'It's cold, and it's wet. It reminds me of my childhood.'

'Ah yes, in the mighty West of the Plateau.' Squatstout grinned savagely, displaying chunks of apple that had caught between his yellowing teeth. 'A beautiful place. I missed it, after Jandell sent me into exile. Though the Habitation suits me well; it is a little island, and so it will always be the same. I do not have to worry about nasty changes, like

Jandell has for ten thousand years. I can control it with ease. We have some food we can take from the island – birds and fish, mostly. The rest, I provide, though my people do not know it.'

He waved a hand, and a pair of oranges appeared in them. He grinned, and placed them on the table.

'But I do love your land. I enjoyed my time there recently, with Aranfal. Ah! And I saw Shirkra again, for the first time in an age, though she sprinted away from me!' His eyes creased. 'How insulting – as if she didn't like me. Still, perhaps she was shocked. She had just killed some Tacticians.' He chuckled. 'I believe you blamed the poor General.'

Brightling did not respond. The memory of those days weighed upon her, like so many others.

Squatstout clapped his hands. 'Oh, she is such a beauty, but she is strange. She always has been. It got so much worse when Jandell gave her that mask. It's a funny thing, that mask of hers. I can't tell what she sees, when she looks through it, but it is not good for her at all.' His eyes widened. 'I almost forgot! What a fool! Your mask!' He clicked his fingers. 'Let me see it! If it is what I think it is, it must be such a thing!'

Brightling froze. She felt the mask against her skin, burning into her. *I cannot give it to him.*

'Squatstout,' she said, leaning forward. 'Why do you throw people into the sea?'

The little man's eyes narrowed, but he did not respond.

'I have seen them, Squatstout: the bodies in the water. Their bones wash upon the north of the Overland.'

Squatstout slammed his fist on the table, and the plates jumped. The Watcher did not react.

'Do not speak of things you do not understand.' The cell

darkened; the shadows in the corners seemed to grow. Squatstout looked up, and his aspect was changed: he seemed younger, and vulnerable. 'I will let you in on a secret, Brightling, but you must not tell anyone.'

'Tell me, Squatstout.' She reached out and grasped his hand. *Instinct.* He did not pull away. 'Perhaps I can help you.'

Squatstout leaned forward, and fixed Brightling with a desperate gaze, before glancing again at the shadows.

'I hear a Voice.'

In a heartbeat Brightling was back in the old days, to a time she had pushed away, a time before Jaco had left the Overland and the Paprissis had fallen apart. She felt a shudder of pain. *Memories, memories, memories.*

'The Machinery spoke to Alexander Paprissi, Squatstout. Is it speaking to you?'

The Autocrat laughed.

'The Voice did not tell Alexander what it says to me, oh no.'

He glanced in the corners, then leaned forward furtively, and began to whisper.

'It is *not* the Machinery – not really.'

Brightling allowed the words to linger.

'If it was not the Machinery that spoke to Alexander, then what was it?'

'It is a creature of memory,' Squatstout whispered. 'It is the source of the Machinery's powers, though it is older by far, and it is manipulative. It is trapped within the Machinery, but even in its current form, it is powerful, so powerful – it can see beyond its prison. It could be watching us even now …' He glanced once more at the shadows. His breaths came in strange little pants.

94

'When Ruin comes, the Voice will be free!' He thumped his chest. 'But creatures like us need bodies, don't we, Brightling? We need to live inside *you*, if we are to be anything at all. It is searching for the Chosen, to be its host. Hmm? It is like Mother, you see. She was nothing but a whisper on the wind, for such a long time, until she found the perfect host. But the Voice is greater than her, oh yes. The Voice holds sway over her.'

Mother. He means Katrina, and whatever she has become. 'So this Voice wants to do to someone else what that thing has done to Katrina.' For the first time in an age, Brightling felt a swell of anger.

But Squatstout was not listening.

'Once I asked it, "what if you find the host before Ruin comes?" "Then I will make you hold them prisoner in the Old Place, until the day I am released". That is what it said to me.'

'Does it even know what it is looking for?'

Squatstout laughed.

'My Brightling, the Voice is beyond even my comprehension, oh yes. I give it people, you see, people from my Habitation, all the time, hoping one of them will satisfy it. But they never do. Not in ten thousand years! They have all been Unchosen! It makes me kill them, then. It hates the ones that displease it. I must throw them from the cliff.'

'Why do the people stay?'

Squatstout cocked his head to the side. 'Because they believe in me, Brightling. When I came here, ten millennia ago, they were savages. The Voice called me here, hmm? I gave these animals a civilisation.'

Brightling winced. There was something ruthless about Squatstout: he spoke of his worshippers like a farmer assessing his cattle.

'And they believe in the Voice. They want to make it happy. They worship me and the Voice, they worship us! They would never believe in another world – how could anything be better than living here, with us?' He laughed. 'Besides, where would they go? This rock is all they know.'

Squatstout leaned forward. 'I fled back here, Brightling, when I knew the One had really returned. The Voice *must* have a host now, hmm? And who knows, my Brightling. Perhaps *you* could be the Chosen! Perhaps that's what Jandell has seen in you all these years, though he had not the wit to know it!'

Brightling shook her head. 'You are mistaken. I would be a terrible choice.' She grinned. 'I'm not … harmonious.' Red lights of panic sparked within the former Tactician; she snuffed them out with a thought.

Squatstout clicked his fingers, and a Guard entered: the one with the golden beak. The strange head nodded at Brightling, and she frowned back at it.

'My Protector will take you to the Choosing, Brightling. Oh, how exciting! If you are Chosen by the Voice to be its host when Ruin comes – and it would not surprise me, you are so impressive – then I will sit at your side forever, and take orders from you! It will be wonderful!'

'But it would not be me then, would it, Squatstout?' She fought to keep her voice steady. 'I would be the puppet of one of your creatures. Like Katrina.'

'Puppet? Puppet! Oh, what a thing to say about the host of the One!'

He chuckled, and snatched up some fruit.

'Take her to the Choosing, Protector.'

The Protector was a strange presence.

There was a sense of power, there: power hard-earned, power that brought a kind of ease to the bearer. He was wearing a long black gown, like a scholar of the Overland, and the only weapon he carried was the wooden stick, unlike the pikes the other Guards possessed. He could have had other weapons, under the gown, but she did not think so. This man believed in one weapon, above all others: himself. She could have fought him. Perhaps she could have snapped him in two. But he knew she wouldn't try. He just *knew*.

This wasn't what made him strange. That was something else. He was ... *sad*. A sad soldier, but devoted to his master. *What manner of man is this?*

They were walking up a stone staircase, now, a corkscrew that wound through the Keep. They passed by open windows as they went, looking out onto balconies that had been built into the side of the cliffs. Below these stretched waters, on and on. *I could try to escape, but it's a long way down.*

And so she walked beside the Protector, thinking, thinking, thinking, and willing something to happen that would save her from whatever this Choosing had in store for her.

'Wait!'

Squatstout. He was far below, calling up at them with panic in his voice.

The Protector turned and looked down upon his master. 'Her mask!' Squatstout panted. 'I can't let her go down there with that mask! Who knows what will happen to it? I must have it!'

Brightling froze. She could have faced anything he threw at her, apart from this. *He cannot have my mask.*

The Protector turned his golden face to Brightling, and put out his hand. She looked down the stairs. Squatstout was climbing the stone corkscrew as quickly as his little legs would allow, his eyes focused on her all the while.

Brightling felt the mask. It sent a thrill through her, as always. *I have no choice.* She removed it, just as Squatstout reached them.

The Protector leaned forward to gain a better view of it, his beak almost touching the mask itself. Squatstout arrived in a fluster, eyes wide, tongue lolling at the side of his mouth.

'Let me see it, Brightling, let me see it!'

He reached out and snatched the mask from her. They had stopped by one of the windows. Cold daylight shone through on the dark material. It had assumed one of its most common forms: the face of a man, his features flat and hard. The eyeholes were narrowed in anger; there was a mouth, this time, and it had formed itself into an 'O' shape, as if roaring some soundless threat.

She loved this thing, but it frightened her. She wondered if Squatstout and the Protector saw it, too. How could a mask change? Perhaps it did not; perhaps the viewer changed when they looked upon it.

'It is ... my goodness, Brightling.' Squatstout held the mask up to the window. 'Aranfal told me about this thing, but I could scarcely believe his words. Do you know what it is?'

'The Operator made it.'

'Yes, Jandell made this himself. Only he could craft such a thing.' Squatstout's grin widened. 'He does love his masks, you know. He has always been a craftsman, of many different things, but masks are his favourites. He thinks a mask has two aspects: a side that conceals, and a side that reveals. This thing, though ... it is different. It is not of the Old Place.' He winced. 'It is weak, now. But I can still feel its power. It hates me! It despises memory, and all the creatures of memory! Oh, it would kill me, if it could! Tell me, when you wear it, what do you feel?'

'I feel that I am utterly empty,' Brightling said without thinking. 'But it is ... a strange emptiness. It is an emptiness that seeks to devour. It wants to make *everything* empty, but it will never be satisfied. When I have used it on Doubters ...'

Squatstout brought the mask close to his eye. 'You have almost destroyed them, I am sure. You have felt close to scraping out their minds.'

Brightling nodded.

Squatstout turned the mask over in his pudgy little hands. 'Long ago, we had an enemy, a creature older than any of us, and so very different. This mask is formed of a part of that enemy.' A puzzled look crossed the little man's face. 'The Absence, we called it. It is dead, now. And yet, still I feel it hurting me. Don't you feel it, Protector? Don't you feel it tugging at you? It is weak ... but it still has a power.'

Brightling turned to the window. She noticed, then, that the Protector's hand was on her arm, holding her in a tight grip. How long had it been there? She felt something rise within her. *Take your fucking hand off me.*

And the mask was on her face.

Squatstout's mouth hung open as he looked at her; he held his empty hands in the air. Brightling felt the mask crawl over her skin, sensed it changing, though she did not know what form it took.

'No!' Squatstout called, cringing away from it. 'How can ...'

Brightling spun, and knocked the Protector aside. She kicked out, and sent Squatstout down the staircase.

She found herself on the balcony. She found herself on
the edge.
She found herself falling, down to the water.

Chapter Ten

It was a typical morning on the Habitation: wet, cold, and stinking of fish. But it was far from a normal day.

Drayn woke at the usual time. She breakfasted with Mother and talked of trivialities, as if two Choosings within days of one another was something that happened all the time. Mother passed the seagull and buttered the bread; she put too much salt on her plate, and chided Drayn, as ever, for the girl's late-night adventures with Cranwyl. There was no talk of what might happen that day. No mention of the cliff's edge.

But at the end of the meal, as Drayn stood to leave, Mother took her by the hand, and looked at her. She reached out, brushed the hair from her daughter's eye, seemed momentarily puzzled, and turned back to her kippers.

Cranwyl and Drayn were standing at the main gate of the house. The Thonns lived on the Higher Third, almost at the peak of the Habitation, and from here one could stare out across much of the island below. The Endless Ocean stretched on forever, grey and vast and, until recently, empty.

'We can't stand here much longer, Drayn. They'll see we're

not there.'

'We still have a few minutes.'

Cranwyl smiled and put a hand on her shoulder, as if he were some wise old man.

'Look, we might not even get sent to the Courtyard this time.'

'Perhaps.'

'Come on. There's no getting away from it. We'll have to go eventually, and it may as well be now.'

He took her by the arm, but she pulled away.

'Listen, Cranwyl, I'll go when I bloody want. You go ahead if you like. We're in the Higher Third, by the Autocrat's nose; we're two seconds away.'

Cranwyl sighed. Drayn folded her arms and looked out to the water for moment longer. It actually was getting quite late.

'Right, let's go.'

The first stage of the Choosing took place just below the Lord Squatstout's Keep. The people walked before the Guards, trudging along for hour after hour, herded together like animals. The Guards assessed them through their masks, and picked those who would have to take their chances in the Courtyard. No one knew how they reached their decisions, except the Guards themselves. Those who got a nod had to go in.

A Guard nodded at Cranwyl and Drayn as they walked by.

'I thought we might get away with it this time,' Cranwyl whispered.

'I didn't,' said Drayn.

They walked through the gate. The Courtyard was a

strange name for this place, but it was what Squatstout called it, and that was enough for them. It was a sand-covered pit, surrounded by high stone walls, with a stage at the front where the Guards strutted, staring out from behind their horrible masks. She studied them carefully. *Something is missing. The Protector. Where is the Protector?*

Above the stage there hung the great bell, a thing of iron, unscarred over the millennia. It rang out at its loudest, now, shaking the ground with its terrible toll. Some of the lucky ones – the ones who got a head shake, not a nod – had taken positions on the walls above, staring down at the spectacle. Mother was among them, impassive and restrained.

'No sign yet of the Autocrat,' said Cranwyl.

Drayn nodded. She noticed her foot was tapping on the ground. *A sign of nerves.* That's what Dad called it. She planted it hard on the ground. *There's no point in being afraid. You fall, or you don't. Then you get Chosen, or you don't. What happens, happens.* She believed all this; she believed it in her head, at least.

At the back of the stage, a wooden door groaned open, and the crowd fell into total silence. There was a delay of a minute or so before he emerged: Lord Squatstout, their Autocrat. He smiled at his people with his usual radiance, but there was something amiss. Drayn could always tell when something was wrong; *everyone* could tell when something was wrong with the Autocrat. He seemed worried; even his clothes were unkempt. *What has happened to him? It must be these newcomers. He's been thrown off balance by them, and the second Choosing, like everyone else.*

'Inhabitants,' the lord said, 'this is our second Choosing in – what is it? Two days? Three days?' There was a catch in his voice: a nervous little tickle.

No one in the Courtyard answered. They knew better than to respond. The Guards watched them carefully, gripping their pikes.

'The Choosing is the heart of our world. Through it, we seek to satisfy the mighty Voice, which has spoken to me for millennia,' the Autocrat said. 'But more than this – the Voice keeps us safe. It plucks out the weeds in our midst, the stinking little grubs unworthy of its beneficence. Yet the recent Choosing was incomplete. We did not know that new people would come to our Habitation. We have recently welcomed my brother, the Lord Jandell, and his mortal companion. My brother is staying with me, now, in my Keep. His friend has agreed to take part in our Choosing; I have already sent her down below.'

That is not the truth. Drayn knew it, in the depth of her heart.

The crowd cheered, but the noise was quickly drowned out by a rumbling sound from below the Courtyard. Drayn took Cranwyl by the hand. 'Don't worry,' he said. 'You didn't fall the last time. There's no reason you would this time, either. Your mother's always said the Autocrat would keep you safe.'

The girl knew this was nonsense, no matter who said it. But it didn't seem to matter, now. 'What about you, Cranwyl? What would I do if you fell?'

Cranwyl smiled, and patted her hand.

Squatstout clapped, and the earth opened up.

The hands had come.

They were everywhere, tearing and pulling: pale, thin things that scrabbled and clutched at their legs. Drayn had seen them so many times, but still she feared them. Anyone who didn't was a liar.

She watched as a young boy was torn from his mother's side, the woman screaming at the ground. An old couple to Drayn's right were swept into the darkness, hand in hand. At the front, a bald man tried to fight them off, but everyone knew that was a joke. He went the same way as the rest of them: down into the swirling ground.

It was all over in moments, though it felt far longer. As the lucky ones dusted themselves off, Drayn realised how tightly she had been holding Cranwyl. She dropped her grip, but he did not seem to notice. Instead, he was looking at the ground.

Drayn took a deep breath and followed his gaze until she saw it: a single hand, just by his ankle, twisting in the dirt.

'Cranwyl!'

The earth opened again, and Cranwyl fell into the darkness. Drayn looked upwards in desperation, to Mother. She mouthed a word at the head of the House of Thonn: *Help*. Mother shrugged; there was nothing she could do. *And she wouldn't help anyway.*

Drayn turned back to the dirt, to find that the hands had vanished. An unfamiliar feeling stirred in her stomach. She thought of Cranwyl, and the times they had spent together. She thought of all the things he had done for her; the way he had helped her when ... *Don't think of it.* Fearful scenes crowded her mind, images of Cranwyl, alone in the dark, scrabbling for help, looking for her. She was the heir to the House of Thonn; she should feel no affection for anyone, least of all this servant.

But she did.

'Take me, too!'

There was a stirring in the crowd. She thought she heard a laugh. But she didn't care.

She stamped the ground.

'Take me!'

'The hands take the people they want,' said a Guard, walking towards her. 'Don't fucking tell the hands what to do.'

Drayn stamped the ground again. 'Take *me!*'

She did not know what she was doing. She threw herself on the sandy dirt, pounding it with her fists. She wept into the ground, and barely heard the sounds of the Courtyard: the relief of those who had not been thrown into the Choosing, and the laughter of those who had seen her. *If I could go, I'd find him. I know I would. I'd find him, and I'd—*

She felt a tap on her leg. She turned around.

There was one hand remaining in the Courtyard.

It took hold of her, and she was gone.

Chapter Eleven

The Centre was empty.

This was not strictly true. Aranfal was there, and Shirkra, making their way on horseback to the Machinery knew where. But they had not seen a soul since they left the See House. The doors of houses hung open. Carts had been discarded on the sides of the roads, their rotting contents scattered across the cobbles.

The people have gone into the West, or the North, or the Wite itself, perhaps. Anywhere to escape the See House.

Strange, but he had not noticed this on his previous trips outside the See House since Mother's Selection. Had the people fled all at once? Had they gone in dribs and drabs, and he was only noticing now? *Perhaps I did notice. Perhaps I have forgotten. Perhaps she took my memories from me. Oh, if only that were true. I have so many more to give her.*

'I'm not sure which feels safer,' Shirkra said. 'Travelling through a throng, or along empty streets.'

Aranfal glanced at his companion. She had concealed her identity as best she could, swathed in a hooded black cloak, her red hair tucked inside. She was not wearing her mask, so only her green eyes could give her away. But even these were different, somehow; they lacked their usual intensity. If anyone looked at her, they would think she was a normal woman. Aranfal found this rather unsettling.

'A crowd is safer by far,' he said. 'One can hide within a crowd.'

'An assassin can hide in a crowd as well.'

'Why would a creature like you fear an assassin?'

She grinned. 'Who said I was worried for *myself*?'

She shook her head, and turned her attention to the road.

They had come to Seller's Square. This was the last place Aranfal had spoken to Katrina – the old Katrina. He looked up to the rooftops where they had stood, and wondered if he could have done anything to stop her. No: it would have been impossible. *Mother was always going to come, no matter what anyone did.*

'Where are we going, Shirkra?'

'To find the Gamesman, of course. How could we have a game without the Gamesman?'

He sighed. Every answer only spawned more questions. He thought of his days with Squatstout, in the old world, before everything changed. *Is it my doom to wander with these monsters through the highways and byways of the Overland?* Once, he was a man to be feared. Now, he was nothing but a man: perhaps a fearful man, at that.

An inn came into view on the side of the road, its doors open.

'You will need food,' Shirkra said. 'You must be hungry.'

He said nothing, but the Operator was not wrong.

The last customers had left in a hurry.

Stools had been knocked over, lying on their sides on the dirty floor, beside the filthy tables. A candle on the side of the bar had burned down into a waxy pulp. All around were half-full glasses, the liquid congealed with sticky film and green mould.

'Why did they leave so quickly, I wonder?' Aranfal asked.

'The Gamesman,' Shirkra said. 'He always does this.'

Aranfal nodded, though he did not understand.

In the corner sat a portrait of the Operator, standing upright and regal, his cloak bunched in his right fist. The painting was torn, like it had been thrown down from the wall.

'Drink?'

Shirkra was already behind the bar, uncorking a green bottle of the Machinery knew what.

'Why not?' Aranfal had never been much of a drinker, and neither had Aran Fal. But he did not know who he was, now. Perhaps he was neither of those men: not the bright-eyed wanderer, and not the torturer. Nothing but …

He shook himself. *Introspection. A new curse. The Machinery went away, and made me into this.*

The Operator produced two grimy glasses, rubbing them semi-clean on her cloak before sloshing the liquid inside. It was a violent type of drink, by the looks of it, bright and aggressive.

Shirkra knocked back a glass, and grimaced.

'I didn't know you drank,' Aranfal said.

'I haven't for a while,' Shirkra replied. 'Perhaps a thousand years. Or was it yesterday?' She licked her teeth. 'I do not like this one. I don't know if it's gone bad, or if it's supposed to be this way. Perhaps I will drink the oceans of the world, one day.'

'That doesn't sound healthy.'

Aranfal drained his own glass. 'Delicious,' he lied, grinning at Shirkra with green lips.

'There's a kitchen back here,' the Operator said, turning in to a door behind the bar. Aranfal lost sight of her. After much rummaging, she returned with a handful of dusty crackers and a wheel of blue cheese.

'Is it supposed to be blue?' Aranfal asked.

'I think it's supposed to be blue, if that drink is supposed to be green. We will eat it. It will give me something to do, and it will keep you alive.'

'Good enough.'

They ate in silence for a long while, lighting candles as the world grew dark around them. Aranfal removed his raven mask from his cloak, and placed it at his side. It comforted him, somehow, to know that it was there.

Shirkra reached out and stroked the side of the mask. She took her own mask in her hand, and placed it beside the raven. It stared upwards, this strange likeness of her. The candlelight flickered across its surface, and for a moment it seemed to change into a different person: a man with narrow features, a man called Aranfal and Aran Fal, a torturer and a child.

The moment passed in a heartbeat.

'This is the mother,' Shirkra whispered, placing her left hand on her own mask. 'And this is the child.' She placed her right hand on the raven. 'Do you understand? Hmm?'

'No.'

Shirkra tutted. 'Your mask is nothing, compared to mine. And my mask is nothing, compared to the endless power of the Old Place.'

Something caught her attention, through the grime of the inn's windows.

'Did you see that? There was a light across the way.'

Aranfal looked where she was pointing. 'I don't see anything.'

Shirkra stood, putting on her mask. 'It looked like someone was carrying a lamp. Hmm. The Gamesman must have missed them.'

Aranfal sighed. He became the raven, and they left the inn together.

They entered the building quietly, and found themselves in a cold hallway, from which led a corridor. The marble floors were littered with weaponry of a surprisingly old-fashioned variety: no handcannon here, but rusted swords and blunt axes.

'This house has fallen on hard times, I fear,' Shirkra whispered. She grasped Aranfal by the arm. 'Over there. Did you see that?'

At the end of the corridor was a flickering light.

They moved forward wordlessly, pressed against the wall. The light had vanished.

'Where is it?' asked Aranfal.

'There.' She pointed down another corridor that broke off to their left, at the end of which was a dull glow, no longer flickering but still and steady. The Watcher and the Operator headed for it with silent steps before coming to an open doorway. Shirkra held Aranfal's hand tightly. She was enjoying herself; he could tell.

'Let's go,' Aranfal said.

'You are Watchers.'

The old man sat alone at a table, before a dinner of buttered potatoes and glazed ham. He was a distinguished kind of fellow, the type who only associated with certain

111

people from certain families. People like the Paprissis, before that family fell apart.

But this was no Paprissi. His skin was a copper hue, and his eyes were a startling green, sparkling in the light of the candles he had arranged along the table and the walls. A lamp burned before him; this was the source of the light. He must have been walking around his house with it, the fool.

The old man did not seem in the least surprised to see them. He pointed to his meal. 'Would you like some?'

Aranfal shook his head, but Shirkra snatched up a chunk of meat and tore it apart with her front teeth. To his credit, the man did not flinch.

'This has got to be the infamous Aranfal, second only to Brightling, or second to none, now, I suppose. Is that right? The raven mask rather gives the game away.'

The Watcher was well used to his notoriety.

'I'm not sure if I'm second to none, or the first among equals, or the bottom of the shit heap, these days, sir, pardon my language.'

'Hmm.' The old man stood. 'I am—'

'Irandus Illarus,' said Aranfal.

The man grinned. 'Indeed! So my reputation precedes me, too, I see.'

'Perhaps,' Aranfal replied. 'But I also know you own the land around here, so it was something of an educated guess.'

Irandus laughed, but without warmth. 'Indeed. I own the land. Or perhaps I *owned* the land.' He gave a mock frown. 'I'm not sure the new Strategist has much respect for title deeds.'

'I very much doubt it,' Shirkra shrugged. 'No respect at all!'

The old man sighed, and sat back in his chair. 'Still, can't complain. I have a roof over my head. The Machinery only knows what happened to the rest of them. I thought the Watchers took them at first, you know.'

'What are you talking about?' Aranfal was tiring of questions and mysteries and memories. 'Who took whom?'

'Everyone, dear boy! Didn't you see? They've all gone. Marched off into the night, never to be seen again. Strange business. I was hiding, I'm afraid to say. I think a few others managed to hide, too, though I've not seen anyone else around. I'd be surprised if they hadn't. Seems the obvious move.'

'Did you see anything?' Shirkra asked. 'What did the people look like, the ones who took everyone away?'

The man cringed. 'I did steal a glance or two, and ... hmm. How to say this? I didn't see people – I saw only one person. The same person, but many versions of him ... a young man, very handsome. Called himself the Gamesman.'

'Why didn't you go, hmm?' asked Shirkra. 'Oh, you should have gone too.' She glanced at the corners. 'Oh yes.'

Irandus stood and walked to a side panel, from which he removed a bottle of red Watchfold and three glasses. He filled them all, and handed one each to Aranfal and Shirkra, retaining the third. Shirkra threw her drink down her throat.

'It is excellent,' she whispered. 'Excellent!'

'It is, it is,' Irandus nodded, sitting down. 'You know, until very recently, I never would have been so uncivilised to actually *drink* this stuff.'

'Perish the thought,' Aranfal said.

'Indeed! In the old times, I would have kept this in my cellar until the end of my days, paying it little visits, stroking the dust from its exquisite little body. Now I have it with ham and potatoes.' He grimaced. 'I mean to say, ham and potatoes!'

He drank greedily, and smacked his lips.

'Irandus.' Aranfal allowed a sharp edge to enter his voice. He removed his mask, and gave the man a cold look. 'Tell us what happened. Tell us about this ... handsome Gamesman.'

Irandus clicked his tongue in his mouth. 'It's like I told you already, my boy. I didn't get a good look at him, but that's what's in my memory: people marching down the street, followed by this man.'

'How come you missed out, then?' asked Aranfal.

'Because I hid, as I told you.' There was a tone of patrician impatience in his voice. 'I'm really very good at hiding. The Gamesman could never have found me.'

'Handsome, you say?' Shirkra asked.

'Oh yes! Most exquisitely so!'

Shirkra snatched up Irandus's dinner knife.

'Handsome! Ha!'

'Now, wait a second,' said Irandus, staring at the knife. 'What are you doing?'

Shirkra giggled, and slammed the knife into the man's throat. She laughed as she did it, a shrieking cackle that echoed through the kitchen. But the strangest thing of all, stranger than all the many things Aranfal had witnessed in recent times, was the reaction of Irandus himself.

He was laughing, too.

Chapter Twelve

'Cranwyl?'

Drayn was lying on her back, in blackness.

'Cranwyl?'

No reply came. No voice in the dark.

What happened? The hands. The hands took her to the Choosing. She had asked for it. She had wanted to follow Cranwyl. She had often wondered what happened when the hands took you. *Well, now I'm going to find out. I'm part of the Choosing.* A sudden jolt of panic. *I'm going to die.*

There was nothing that could be done for her. She was dead already.

Why did I do it? She remembered a surge of emotion. A surge of *love*. Love for Cranwyl. *Mother wouldn't have let it happen. No. She would have kept her emotion in check.* Drayn imagined how Mother must have felt, seeing her girl dragged under the dirt, if she could feel anything. *She would have felt annoyed, that's all. Annoyed that the heir was gone.*

And for what? What had she accomplished, forcing her way down here? *At best, I'll die with Cranwyl at my side. That's all.*

Unless you are Chosen.

She nibbled at her bottom lip, wondering at the thought. *The Voice must have a body of its own.* They all knew it. Perhaps it could be her. Perhaps a part of her would live on, even when the Voice took her over. It was a chance, at least, in this mess she had made for herself.

'Are you there, Voice?' she called into the dark. 'I could definitely be your body, you know. You should see the things I can do. I bet no one like me has been here in ten thousand years.'

There was no response.

'Fancy picking me?'

That also failed. *No matter. Better off without it. I wouldn't be myself, if it chose me, no matter what I say to convince myself. I'll find another way out – with Cranwyl. Wherever he is, by the Autocrat's fist.*

She sighed, and hopped onto her feet.

I can't see a bloody thing. But that did not deter her. Not Drayn, who had crawled through the darkest woods since she was barely a child born. Not Drayn, who had hidden from Cranwyl in every crevice of her house. This was no concern.

Though it is very dark indeed.

Using all her best skills, Drayn walked slowly forward, arms extended, until her hands brushed against rock. She kept one hand on this wall and continued moving, alert for any signs of danger. She heard no sound.

Eventually she found a hole in the rock. It was narrow, though she had been through worse, and it seemed her best way out. Screwing up her courage, she squeezed inside. The walls closed in around her, but she gave that no mind, shimmying her way through the narrow space until she emerged at the end, into yet another cave.

There was a light here: a dull glow from a row of red torches. The space before her was vast and empty: as large as the entire Habitation, she would wager. Rocks reached up from the floor and down from the ceiling, nasty, jagged things that looked fit to impale anyone stupid enough to come near them. Pools of water glowed in the red light, and creatures moved within them, rippling through the stagnant liquid. A white-eyed lizard appeared at her side, sitting on a rock right by her head. It licked its lips, and was gone.

She looked to the back of the hall. *I am seeing things.*

It was a gigantic curtain, falling from the roof to the floor: a ragged thing, with hints of purple, fluttering gently in the heavy air. But that was not the strangest thing about it. That honour was reserved for the things that surrounded the curtain and crawled along its fabric, moving with a febrile energy, alive and intelligent.

Hands.

Drayn walked slowly to the curtain, keeping the hands in view at all times. Were these the things that had taken her here, brought them all to the Choosing for ten millennia? She peered beneath the material. The hands were pointing towards her now, snatching wildly. She did not feel afraid of them. Well, maybe a bit.

'I wouldn't get too close to them,' someone said.

There was no one there. *Could this be the Voice?*

'Where are you?' Drayn asked.

'Here.'

The speaker was behind the curtain.

'Are you the Voice?'

There came a snigger. 'No.'

'Well, you threw your voice just now, didn't you? How did you do that, by the Autocrat's belly?'

117

A face appeared beneath the curtain, and the hands moved away. It was a boy, a couple of years younger than her by the looks of him. He was pale, and had curls of black hair.

'How did you get here?' he asked.

'These things grabbed me for the Choosing,' she said, casting a vicious glance at the hands.

'And they took you here?'

'Yes.'

'Do you know where you are?'

'The Old Place.'

The boy nodded. 'Yes. Not the deepest part. But you are here.'

'If I'm not in deep, can I get out and go home?' She jabbed a thumb over her shoulder. 'Back down through the caves?'

The boy laughed. 'No, you can't get out of here. You'd just spend forever searching through the tunnels, I'm afraid. But you're welcome to try.'

Drayn shook her head. 'No,' she said, in the firmest tone she could muster. *There's only one way to find Cranwyl.* 'I want to take part in the Choosing.'

She moved forward an inch, and the hands went wild.

'Ah, ah!' cried the boy behind the curtain. 'You can't just walk into the deepest Old Place. The hands will tear you up.'

'Then why did they put me here? I'm supposed to take part in the Choosing.'

The boy blinked, and Drayn's own hands curled into hard little knots. 'How do I get through?'

The boy grinned at her. 'I can sort it out for you. But you have to promise me something.'

'What's that?'

'That you'll let me be your guide down here, through your

Choosing. I'm so bored, you see. There are others, too, who like to serve as guides – ones who've been here much longer than me. And they've all failed, haven't they? I'm better than them. The Voice actually spoke to me, a long time ago. Oh, it tricked me! I thought it was the Machinery itself, at the time, but I've learned *so* much more about it since then. I reckon I know it better than anyone. So you stick with me. OK?'

Drayn thought this over. *Can't see anything wrong with it. I'll need a guide, anyway.*

'Fair enough.'

The boy nodded, and disappeared. She heard noises beyond, the sound of hushed and hurried words, before his face reappeared.

'They'll let you through now.'

Drayn hesitated. The hands looked as hostile as ever.

'Honestly,' said the boy. 'I've no reason to lie to you. Look.'

He reached out and gently patted one of the hands. It did not stir.

'How do I know they'll be like that for me? How do I know they won't tear me limb from limb?'

The boy shrugged. 'You'll just have to trust me. I am your guide, after all.'

Drayn sighed, and screwed her eyes closed. *Heroes face trials in all the great stories.*

She crawled under the curtain, until she stood at the other side with the boy.

He smacked her on the shoulder.

'There! Told you I wouldn't betray you!'

She brushed his hand aside. 'Who are you? What are you doing down here, in this place?'

119

'Oh, I've been here for years. I'm part of the furniture now, to be honest. I couldn't live in the Overland any more.'

'The Overland? What is the Overland?'

'You don't know it? It's where the strangers are from.'

'The creature, and the woman, in the boat?'

The boy nodded.

'So you are from the same country as those people?' Drayn asked.

The boy shrugged. 'I once lived in the same place as them, but I haven't been there now for such a long time.' His shoulders slumped. 'I'll never go back again. Now I'm just a thing of memory, really, like everything else down here. But it doesn't matter. What's your name?'

She stuck out her hand. 'Drayn.'

'Drayn. That's a nice name.'

He took her hand and shook it vigorously.

'My name is Alexander Paprissi.'

Chapter Thirteen

Canning could not remember his escape.

That was not completely true. He remembered the events, he believed, in a kind of haphazard order. But he could no longer recall the sense of power that had flowed within him. *The stuff of memories itself.*

Now it was gone, and he was nothing more than Timmon Canning, standing at an iron gate, somewhere deep within the Bowels of the See House. Water flowed around his feet: some kind of sewer, perhaps. It didn't bother him. He had seen worse.

With an effort he did not know he was capable of, the former master of the Fortress of Expansion grasped the gate and jolted it forward by inches. It started to give way slightly, and he redoubled his efforts, until metal screeched against stone and the gate fell away.

He stumbled through into a narrow stream, where the effluent fell. He turned and looked up, and was surprised to find that the See House was a long way away, high on its perch upon the Priador. *How far under the earth do the Bowels go?*

He began to walk, then, and he did not stop during the

night, his fear of Shirkra overcoming his physical weakness. He left the coast far behind, going west on Greatgift. At first he kept to the shadows, and for a time he lost himself among the alleys and lanes that interweaved with the great thoroughfare of the Overland. But he soon realised this was unnecessary; there was no one on the streets. Not a soul stopped him as he went, and no Watcher followed him along the way. Not that he could tell, anyway.

So he walked openly on the avenue, into the West, through the domes and cobbles of the Centre. Time went by in fits and starts, and he could not tell how long he had walked. Once, he looked to the sky and saw the sun burning upon him like a yellow eye. But when he looked again it had been replaced with a pale moon, that unhealthy orb he had watched from the Fortress on so many nights.

He had no direction and no purpose. But as the streets faded into rough tracks, the buildings into shacks and hovels, it dawned on him that he had taken an old and familiar path. Eventually – he could not tell how long the journey had taken – it loomed before him, terrible and majestic: the Fortress of Expansion.

He walked on, up through its gates, a strange sense of affection flowering in his gut. *Home.* He had never looked upon the black pyramid with these eyes. It was never home; it was a prison. But now, something had changed. *And all it took was a little torture in the Bowels of the See House.*

He reached the great wooden doors of the Fortress. There were no soldiers to be seen, and the doors were locked shut; even the green lights had been extinguished. He had hated those baleful lights, once, but now he would have given anything to see them again.

Why have I come here? Perhaps he could find a way into the Fortress, and secrete himself among its hidden chambers. *But how long would it be before Shirkra or the Strategist found me, or one of their Watchers?*

'Where else would you go, if not here?'

Timmon Canning was not a brave man at the best of times. Now, as he stood alone at the base of a giant black fortress, was not the ideal occasion to hear strange voices in the dark.

He resisted the urge to soil himself, and slowly turned. *This is the end. They are Watchers. They will send me back to her, and I will live forever in a world of nightmares, with half-mad Annya for company.*

He turned, looked up, and found himself facing two small children.

They were a boy and a girl, identical twins by the look of them, with dark skin and long curls of black hair falling to their shoulders. They had the same striking blue eyes, like shards of glass that had been impaled into their skulls, and wore the same azure robes, clothing that was ancient before the Machinery. They held hands, and their faces were broken by mad grins.

'Hello,' Canning said.

'Hello,' echoed the boy.

'What is your name, boy?'

'Boy.'

'What?'

'My name is Boy.'

Canning nodded. He was used to being mocked, even by the young, but something told him this child was not making fun of him. He turned to the girl.

'In that case, you must be Girl.'

'Yes.'

'You are brother and sister.'

'Yes,' said Boy. Their voices were virtually identical, too.

'We have other brothers and sisters,' said Girl. 'But Boy and I are different. We are *more*.'

'More brotherly and sisterly?'

'Yes,' said Boy. 'We are the Duet.'

'The Duet,' agreed Girl.

Canning sighed. It dawned on him that, despite appearances, these children were very, very old indeed.

'You are like the rest of them,' he said. 'That's why you can see into my thoughts.'

Boy chuckled, and closed his eyes. 'I can taste your memories. They have a certain sadness, and it is so sweet.' He snapped his eyes open. 'But no. I do not need memories to read you. You looked lost, but without a destination.' He waved a hand at the pyramid. 'And so you came here. Perhaps you have a connection with this place.'

'You don't know who I am.'

'No. Who are you?' asked Girl.

'My name is unimportant,' Canning said.

'Unimportant,' Boy repeated. 'That is a fine name.'

'Yes,' said Girl. 'I like that.'

'Why are you here, Unimportant?'

Unimportant is as good a name for me as any.

'Your sister is Shirkra?'

'Yes,' the Duet said as one.

Canning nodded. 'Once, I ruled this place,' he said, jabbing a thumb at the Fortress of Expansion. 'I was Selected by the Machinery. Do you know the Machinery?'

Boy nodded. 'We know of it. But we were not there at its birth. We were in the South.'

'And Jandell kept us away, after that,' said Girl. 'So we only know dribs and drabs.'

'Dribs and drabs,' said Boy, nodding vigorously.

Canning nodded. 'Well, the Machinery is the heart of the world. It has made the Overland into the greatest state the Plateau has ever seen by Selecting its best and brightest as our leaders. Apart from me, of course. Sometimes it makes mistakes.'

'Where is the Machinery?' asked Boy. 'Do you know?'

'No. Anyway, it's broken, now, I think, and Ruin will come with the One. Well, the One is here, but no Ruin, as far as I can see.'

'Ruin?' Boy shook his head. 'Ruin is not here yet.'

'Oh no,' Girl said. 'You will all know when Ruin is here.'

'We feel it though,' whispered Boy. 'We feel it in the air.'

Canning nodded. Words gushed forth from his mouth, almost involuntarily. 'We have always been told that Ruin will come in the ten thousandth year, and that the One would bring it. Well, this is the ten thousandth year, and the Machinery has Selected a *terrible thing*. It seems the Prophecy was correct, and Ruin is coming, whether we like it or not.'

The Duet skipped forward, until they were just a pace from Canning.

'Who is this terrible thing it has Selected?' Boy asked.

Canning shrank back from their blue eyes. 'It is a woman,' he stammered. 'Once, she was Katrina Paprissi, an Apprentice to the Watchers. But she isn't Katrina now.'

'Do you know her name?'

'She calls herself Mother.'

The Duet glanced at one another, and turned back to Canning.

'You are correct, Unimportant,' said Boy. 'I can *feel* her.'

'We should go and see her!' Girl yelled. 'The three of us!' The children took each other by the hands and began to dance around.

'Please,' said Canning, coming to a terrible realisation. 'We cannot go to see her. I was held by her, and Shirkra, against my will. I don't want anything to do with them again.'

'You escaped from Shirkra?' said the Duet. 'You escaped from Shirkra and Mother?' Their eyes narrowed into icy little slits.

'I – no, look, it's not what you think—'

Girl turned to Boy. 'We should take him back to them. They will reward us, if we do!'

'Yes! Yes!'

'No!' cried Canning. 'I can go with you anywhere – just don't take me there.'

Boy grinned and lifted his hand. A red light grew around it, flickering like a flame. It continued to expand, thrumming with power, until he pulled his arm back and flung it forward. Canning tried to duck away from the light, but it was impossible. It ensnared him, and he fell backwards, wrapped within its cold embrace. Memories flooded his mind's eye for half a heartbeat, his own and others he did not recognise. There was no fighting this. It was that same power again, the power he had seen in the Bowels, the burning core of memories. This was different; it tasted of *them*, these ancient children. For a moment, he tried to conjure the abilities he had, back then, in the See House. But he could not. The Duet were focusing on him, and there was no defeating them.

He was nothing; he was Unimportant; he was Canning.

'We will go to Mother and Shirkra,' Boy said with a nod. 'You will come with us willingly, or you will suffer the most enduring and terrible pain. Is this understood?'

Canning nodded miserably within his cell of light.

'Good,' said Girl. 'Then we go.'

Chapter Fourteen

'The game, the game, the game.'

Brandione opened his eyes. He had returned to the black beach, with the red sun glaring down. The Queen was ahead of him. She was half-formed, the lower parts of her bodies falling away into dust. Her faces were hidden behind dark veils. At her side was the table Brandione had seen before, the great circle of dark green stone, surrounded by chairs.

'The game, the game, the game.' She said the words in a thudding mantra, the chant of some savage religion. 'The game, the game, the game.'

Brandione walked towards the table. As he went, the sun moved across the sky, keeping pace with him. Waves crashed rhythmically, far away.

The one-time General of the Overland joined the Dust Queen's side, and looked down upon the table, where the five figurines still stood: Aranfal, Canning, the young girl, the plump female Watcher, and himself. As before, the surface was a picture of confusion: strange images played upon it, twisting across the stone, tortured lines and twisted shapes. They meant nothing to him, but he felt a power when he looked on them. He was a gnat, staring at a tornado.

'The game, the game, the game.'

The Queen dissolved into dust. She reformed a moment later, sitting in three of the chairs.

'Who will you play against?' Brandione asked.

The Queen removed her veils. She was older now by far, her skin wan and stretched, her heads bald except for some thin strands of silver hair. Her eyes were small and watery, and she looked at him with unconcealed pain.

'What am I?' she asked. Her voice was the same, but tinged with sadness.

'The Dust Queen,' Brandione whispered.

The Queen waved three hands impatiently. 'But what *am* I?'

'You are a power. You are a force of nature.'

'I am memory. All of this comes from memory.' She gestured at the table. 'I play the game with other memories, *for* other memories.'

Figures appeared in the other chairs, ghostly creatures whose outlines fell away into shadow. There was Shirkra, the murderer of Tacticians, and the Machinery knew who else. Two children sat side by side, a boy and girl, alike in almost every way; they were strangely familiar to him. The Operator was there, too – or the one he had known as the Operator, back in the old days. Jandell – that was his name. He was young, here, his hair long and dark. And finally there was the new Strategist, the creature that had once been Katrina Paprissi; she stared at the board with vacant eyes.

'All of us spring from the power of memory,' the Queen said. She pointed a finger at the children. 'Here is the cruelty of youth.' She flicked a finger at Shirkra. 'There is ... a tormented soul, born from the strangeness of memories.'

She paused for a moment, placing her heads in her hands.

She sighed, and a breath of dust puffed through the air. She turned to Jandell. 'There is despair, and hope, all at once. A complex thing; a thing that can lead to cruelty or action.' Finally, she pointed at the Strategist. 'And that ... well. That is a thing of fearsome nurture: the clanswoman defending her children with a blunt stick.'

She stood from the table, and the other figures disappeared.

'Question,' she said, glancing at Brandione. 'You have a question.'

He nodded. 'What are you, your Majesty? What memories are you born from?'

The Queen smiled. 'Too many to know, too many to know. I am the first child of the Old Place; it poured its young heart into me as it sought to beat back the Absence. Perhaps I am born of babies' dreams, or the final wishes of the dead. Perhaps I am the earliest memory of the dawn. Perhaps I am the storm, the storm of memory itself ... I do not know. But I am old; I am old.'

She flickered, and the old women were replaced with the Dust Queen Brandione knew.

'All of us are formed of memory. Like memories, we are complex, and we change over time. We can do such things. We can wield memories like weapons; we can build towers from the past. But we are weaker than humanity, in so many ways. Because memories come from *you*: the Absence gave memories to mortals, and we are only the reflection of that power. We can pluck memories from you; we can scour the Old Place for them; but we cannot create them.'

'Surely you remember the past.'

'Yes, but our memories are shadows; they are things of nothing. What are they, but the memories of memories! Yours are ... the gift of the Absence. We *yearn* for them, always,

130

always. That is why the game is so important. It is more than a game. It is our search for the beginning of ourselves.'

Brandione pointed at the board, and its shifting symbols and shapes. 'These are memories.'

The Dust Queen nodded. 'These are the paths of the Old Place. It is a map. We watch it during the game. We watch our pawns, as they move through the Old Place.'

Pawns. 'That's me,' Brandione said. An old anger flickered within him. *I am a pawn to her.* 'And Aranfal. And Canning. We're pieces in your game.'

The Queen nodded. 'Yes. You are my piece. I saw you long, long ago: you are the Last Doubter. A soldier and a scholar.'

'I'm not any of those things.' He stared at the table, and his words came in a harsh whisper. 'And I'm not a fucking *pawn.*'

He glanced at the Queen, who smiled at him.

'Pawn is the wrong word,' she said, spreading her palms.

Brandione felt suddenly ridiculous, as he always did after his bursts of anger. That was why he had suppressed them, so long ago. Now, his fit of pique had made this ancient being apologise to him. *Ludicrous.*

Brandione looked to the board again. 'What must I do in this game?'

The Dust Queen clapped her hands, and in an instant transformed into three young girls, bouncing on their heels with excitement.

'It is glorious, Brandione! Your prize is the greatest thing in creation … a thing of such power!'

He nodded. 'If I know you now, your Majesty, that can mean only one thing – a memory.'

The three children jumped up and down. 'Not just *any*

memory – the greatest memory of all. A memory born from all the power of the Absence. It must be delicious, this memory. It must be a glory of the world.' She sighed. 'The First Memory of the Old Place. The earliest memory of humanity, from the beginning of time itself. A memory older than all of us – older than me. Imagine what power it must hold.'

The girls spun around, and transformed into three young women.

'You have played this game for a long time,' Brandione said.

'Forever!'

'Why don't you go yourself, instead of sending me?'

'Oh, it wouldn't stand for it. The Old Place won't let us. We can watch the game on our board, but we cannot search for the memory ourselves. Perhaps it loves mortals more than us. It loves its parents more than its children.'

'No one has found the First Memory?'

'No! Oh no! The Old Place guards it so well.'

'If you have never found it, then how can anyone win the game?'

For the briefest of moments, the Queen seemed uncomfortable.

'I am afraid, my Last Doubter, that the game is ... challenging. Victory is a matter of degrees. Often the pieces become lost forever in the Old Place, unseen even to the players at the board. Or sometimes the Old Place grows tired of them, and ...' She let the sentence drift away.

'So they all die, in the end. Or they disappear. The winner is the player whose piece survives the longest.'

The Dust Queen nodded. 'That has been the way of it, yes. But do not despair, my Last Doubter. I see such things in you ... I believe you will find the First Memory of the Old Place. You will take it, and you will use it.'

'Use it?'

'Yes, yes, of course! You are the Last Doubter. A soldier and a scholar. You will save us all.'

'Save you?'

'With the First Memory, of course! The others think it cannot be done. They think the Old Place will never *let it* be done. But you will find it, Brandione, and you will seize its powers, and you will stop Ruin!' She grinned.

Brandione shook his head. 'Impossible. This is all ... it is a dream.' He looked up at the red sun. It seemed to laugh at him. 'A man could not do such a thing.'

The Dust Queen tutted. 'Mortals have done great things before. The last time we played the game, a mortal started a war. A *real* war, a war in which humans could fight back. That was thanks to a man, my Last Doubter. That changed everything!'

'I do not understand.'

The Dust Queen snapped her fingers.

They were standing on the roof of a dark tower, in the middle of a kind of courtyard. The tower was formed of smooth, black stone.

'This is the See House,' Brandione said. The Dust Queen cast him a sideways glance from her three heads.

'No. Perhaps Jandell based the See House on this memory. This is an older thing by far.'

'We are in a memory.'

The Dust Queen nodded.

Brandione walked to the side of the tower and found himself gazing out upon a great city of spires and domes, formed of yellow stone. Glass glinted in the sunlight, and dark birds wheeled in the sky.

'Where are we?'

'It is long ago. Just before the last war with humanity. This is the very beginning of the conflict, though we did not know it at the time.'

Brandione turned to the courtyard. That same green table stood in the centre, surrounded by five chairs.

'Is this the Overland?'

'Do you recognise it as the Overland?'

'No, but I thought it might be the Centre, long ago.'

'It is not the Centre.'

There was a thudding sound at the far side of the court-yard: a bolt being pushed from a lock. A black door opened, and five creatures emerged. Brandione recognised the first two immediately: the Operator and Shirkra. The Operator seemed young here, too. His hair was long and dark, and his skin was unblemished. He wore a simple black cloak, with no faces upon it. Shirkra was just as he remembered, in the green dress and the white mask, that strange thing that seemed to shift expression the more one looked upon it.

Behind them came Squatstout, who was the same as ever, in his dirty hareskin cloak. Then came those two children, the boy and girl. They must have been seven or eight years old, to judge by their appearance. The boy wore a silk shirt and short trousers, while his sister was wrapped in a golden gown, its fabric covered with images of garish flowers.

'Are these all Operators?' he asked the Dust Queen.

The three heads nodded as one.

'Who are the children?'

'Boy and Girl. Together, they are the Duet.'

The five Operators each took a seat, with the children pulling their chairs close together.

'This isn't all of them, your Majesty, is it? Where is the Strategist?'

'Mother does not always play the game. Games, after all, are really meant for children.'

In the courtyard, Squatstout was speaking.

'Our sister, Shirkra, attacked the humans yesterday – she killed their leader on his own throne. Suffice it to say, the years of peace with the mortals are over.'

'It was the only choice,' Shirkra said. 'The only choice.'

Squatstout ignored her. 'I have spoken with Mother. She is *not happy*.' He cast a sharp glance at Shirkra. 'I think she should lock you up in a dark hole, sister, but it isn't up to me. I don't know why she … anyway, it does not matter. The point is this – Mother realises this society is at an end, and that it is time to build another. She knows that our brother, Jandell, and our sister, Shirkra, have … opposing visions of the future.' He grinned at Jandell, who stared at the table and did not reply. 'And so she suggests we play a game to resolve our differences.'

'But *what* is the prize?' Shirkra asked. She smiled widely, and clapped her little white hands together.

Squatstout nodded. 'That's the interesting part. The mortals are mustering against us as we speak, in whatever fashion they can, with their sticks and stones. They will be defeated, and humiliated, as they always are.' He sighed. 'The winner of the game will decide the future – whether we share this world in peace with the mortals, as we did until recently, or whether they are enslaved again.' He shrugged. 'Or something else entirely.'

There was silence for a moment. The twin boy and girl

exchanged glances, and burst into laughter. Jandell raised a hand to silence them.

'We cannot decide these things with a game. We must have peace.'

'Jandell! Bleak Jandell! You are too serious, my brother,' said Squatstout.

'The Empire has been our greatest success,' Jandell said. 'It should not end at all – and certainly not because *she* has thrown a fit.' He gestured at Shirkra.

'They all end the same way, Jandell,' said Shirkra. There was a note of sorrow in her voice. 'Mortal empires are like mortals themselves. Death is always hanging overhead, waiting for its moment. We should put the mortals under our boots, and use them as we wish.'

The girl called Girl laughed, and stood on her chair. 'We do not need a game. Shirkra is right. Let's put them back where they belong.'

'You and Boy can do that,' Squatstout said, 'if you win the game.'

The courtyard darkened, as if a great bird had flown across the sun. Something familiar was happening in the air above them. It was sand, twisting and turning in the breeze, cascading down beside the table, and forming *her*, that awesome creature of three faces and three glass crowns.

The Queen was dressed all in black, her long bodies casting dark shadows on the floor. She was taller than usual, stretched and fearsome.

She turned to face Girl, who giggled. *Giggled*.

'Your highness,' she said.

The other Operators turned their gazes away. They feared the Queen. *They are right to do so.*

'You are playing a game.'

'Yes, your Majesty,' said Squatstout. 'Do you want to play?'

The Dust Queen turned her heads to him. 'No.'

'Then you shouldn't be here,' said Shirkra. 'You should leave.'

'She's making sure we play by the rules,' Jandell said. 'And she likes to watch.'

The Dust Queen smiled at him, before gesturing at the table. 'The Gamesman has been here already, and the board is prepared. Each player will get one pawn, with Boy and Girl playing together, as usual. You have already chosen your pieces.'

At the table, Shirkra clapped her hands, and grinned manically beneath her mask.

The Dust Queen sighed. 'Each of you should have chosen his or her piece. Tell us their names. I hope you have selected well.'

Shirkra leapt to her feet and removed a wooden figurine from somewhere in her dress. It was a man, middle-aged, his moustachioed face twisted into a sneer.

'This is Kyrrinn, a great and clever warlord, who would have been Emperor, had the cards not been stacked against him. He is bitter and full of envy, and he will make a most wonderful pawn, most wonderful. He will find his way through the Old Place, and go further than anyone has before!'

She placed the figurine on the board, and grinned at them all again.

The Dust Queen turned to the Duet. The children smiled and lifted their hands to show a figurine clasped between them. It was formed of ivory, and depicted a thin young woman with an impoverished air.

'We were playing, the other day, and she told us off,' said Boy.

'She had such a commanding air!' said Girl. 'She reminded me of Mother, in days of old.'

The Dust Queen nodded. 'What is her name?'

The Duet laughed. 'We do not know.'

The Dust Queen sighed. 'Place it on the table.'

The Duet did as they were told.

Next she turned her gaze on Squatstout. The little man already had his figurine in his hand. It was formed of a gleaming black stone, and showed a small girl, no older than nine or ten.

'This is Senndra. I have observed her now for a year. She has the makings of a clever mortal, oh yes.'

He placed her on the table.

The Dust Queen nodded. 'Good pawns, all of them.' She turned to Jandell. 'And you, Jandell the Bleak. Who will represent you in the game?'

A strange look passed across the Operator's face: he seemed excited and apprehensive all at once. He reached into his cloak, and took from it a green stone that sparkled like Shirkra's dress. The stone was shaped into a young man, slender and grim-faced.

'This is Arandel, a man of the South.'

At the side of the courtyard, Brandione sucked in a breath.

'Yes, my Last Doubter,' said the real Dust Queen. 'The first Strategist of the Overland. Of course, none of us knew that, then. Not even me.'

'I see great things in this man,' said the Operator.

They had returned to the black sands, and the table.

'Arandel was a pawn in the game,' Brandione said. 'The

prophet of the Machinery.'

The Dust Queen smiled at him. 'Yes. A great human. The greatest, in fact. He learned something important in the Old Place. He learned how to fight us.'

'No. No human could do that.'

The Queen laughed. 'And why not? Memories come from you, do they not? Who better to wield their power?' She nodded. 'Aranfal learned the great art, and everything changed. The world was turned upside down. A *real* war began. Not like all the other wars, when the mortals were simply crushed. We were all dragged into it. We could not allow ourselves to be subjugated.'

'Subjugated?' Brandione's eyes widened.

The Queen smiled. 'Arandel and his disciples fought with such vigour, and such power. The gift of the Absence was *their* weapon, now, too. And in many ways, they were stronger than us.

'A stalemate developed: the humans, with their new powers, on one side, and we immortals on the other. But we knew it would not last. We were on the back foot. Seeing no other option, Jandell struck a secret bargain with Arandel; he would create the Machinery, to protect and glorify humanity, if only Arandel would agree to make peace. I joined Jandell; it was our only hope.' A pained expression crossed her eyes. 'We had to betray our brothers and sisters. They would not have supported us, had they known. We took them by surprise, with the mortals at our side. We destroyed them.'

She fell silent for a moment. 'Jandell and I built the Machinery together. But as we laboured, I saw it, in the depths of our creation. I saw the Promise, and I spoke the words. Jandell would not believe me.'

'Ruin will come with the One.'

The three heads nodded. 'But there was more. I saw something else. Another game, before the end. A game for me to win!' The Queen grinned. '*You* will be like Arandel, my Last Doubter, don't you see? In the depths of the Old Place, you will learn the power of the Operators – and what is more, you will grasp the First Memory, and seize a power beyond any of us! You will become the greatest creature in all of history – greater even than me!'

She was before him, then. The central figure grasped him by the shoulders.

'You will be the hero of the world. Ruin *will* come with the One – but you will stop Ruin!'

Brandione sighed, and closed his eyes. When he opened them again, the beach was fading away.

Chapter Fifteen

Brightling woke upon the waves.

She did not know how long she fell, or how long she spent in the water. She was far from the shore, but the Habitation still loomed overhead. It was night, and the moon hung low behind the great rock, gigantic and sickly yellow.

She moved her limbs, flexed her muscles; she could find no injuries. Her clothes were soaked through. How had she not drowned? She had never been a great swimmer, even in the western rivers of her childhood. *Perhaps I did it subconsciously. Perhaps the waters here are different. Perhaps I was just lucky.*

Perhaps it doesn't matter. I'm alive.

She stared up at the stars. The water was surprisingly warm, and its tides were gentle. She felt she could have stayed like that, floating into nothing, until she washed back up on the Overland, a new addition to the Bony Shore.

She turned in the water, and looked once more at the island. It gleamed with the lights of a hundred thousand torches, but something dark also sparkled in that place. The Operator was still there, weak and at the cold mercy of Squatstout. She would not abandon him, though she did not know what she could do to help. Still, she had no choice, if she wanted to live. And she very badly wanted to live.

My mask. She felt it under her sodden clothes, and relief washed over her. *How did it get there?* She loved the mask, but she feared it more. Still, it was her only weapon, now, against beings like Squatstout. She remembered how it had fascinated him; she remembered how it had hurt him.

She touched it again, made sure it was safe, and swam back to the Habitation.

She spent the night in a small cave, nestled in the side of the rock. She stripped off her clothes and hung them over the rocks at the entrance, allowing them to dry in the stiff breeze that blew in from the waters.

She curled in the corner of the cave, the former Tactician of the Overland, mistress of the See House. She curled her naked body into a ball, and she fell asleep beside her mask.

It was past dawn when she awoke. She stretched her protesting muscles and climbed to her feet, carrying the mask with her. She inspected her cloak, trousers and shirt, finding them damp but wearable. Her boots had seen better days, but no matter. Her spectacles were gone: irritating, but she didn't really need them anyway. But she wished she had her pipe.

Enough of that. I'm lucky to be alive.

She did not know what side of the Habitation she was on, or how far she was from Squatstout and his Protector, but she believed she was safe. There were no signs of life nearby, not even a fishing boat on the waters. She clambered down to the shore, taking her knife with her, and found some shelled creatures, tightly fastened to the rocks. She cut them out of their homes and swallowed them whole, fighting back an urge to retch.

She looked up and saw nothing but rock. She would have to climb if she was to have any hope of freeing the Operator. But it was no easy task. The Guards would be scouring the island for her. She would have to become invisible.

A part of her began to despair. She had found an empty patch of land, yet the island itself was teeming with life – there was no way to climb it without being seen. If she did not at least try, Jandell was surely dead. But if she did, she would likely be apprehended, and thrown down into the Choosing, whatever that was. *By the Machinery, I should allow myself to die.*

But a person did not become the greatest Watcher of the Overland by succumbing to dark thoughts – no, a Watcher thrived upon adversity. There had to be a way back to the top of the Habitation. There was *always* a way to achieve one's goals. She only had to work it out.

She returned to her cave, took her cloak and turned it inside out. She tore the remainder of her clothes into rags; she did not know if the mourning customs were the same in this place, but it didn't matter. She did not want to look like a mourner. She wanted to look like a beggar.

She wrapped the cloak around herself and bunched her hair up under the hood. She hid her mask away and hunched her back, staring at the ground with head bowed. She was sure that no one would even look at her, and those who did would never remember.

She searched the entrance to the cave, and found some protruding rocks. She sighed. It had been a long while since she had scaled something like this. She wasn't sure if she had *ever* scaled something like this.

She looked up the side of the Habitation, sighed again, and began to climb.

It was high, this hateful rock. She wondered, not for the first time, how she had survived the fall.

She had been climbing for hours when she saw the edge of a worn path, trodden into the side of the rock over the millennia. She peered at it for a long while, clinging to the stone with her red-raw hands. *A path means people. A path means danger. But a path also means not fucking climbing any more.*

She decided to take her chances. The path wound upwards on a gentle incline, so it would take her a long while to reach the top, if it even went all the way. She felt increasingly confident, however, that she would be able to immerse herself in the population of the island as she went.

After a while, she began to hear noises: the thrum of conversations. The path snaked around the rock a while longer, before vanishing. Ahead were squalid houses, barely deserving the title of shacks. *This is a good place for a beggar.* She slipped among the buildings.

She had entered a village square. There were pigs rooting in filth, and straw scattered on the ground. She hacked and coughed and hobbled her way across the square, under the noses of an elderly man and woman who barely glanced in her direction. They weren't the most difficult pair to trick, in fairness; they seemed barely sentient. She passed them undisturbed, and found herself on a wider, smoother path. Shops and inns pressed in from either side; it was the early afternoon, and the place was thronged. She took herself to the side of the road, and sat down, crossing her legs and leaning against the side of a rickety inn. There were small knots of people clustered around her, drinking ale and talking nonsense.

She pulled the hood down firmly, turned her gaze to the ground, and vanished against the building. She stayed that way for hours, and learned many things.

The island was broken into different territories called Thirds, though there were five of them - a messiness that rankled with her. This was the Second Third. Squatstout's tower was on the Higher Third, the most elevated part of the island. The remaining levels comprised the Lower Third, the Middle Third, and the Fourth Third. She would have to make her way through these before she could enter the Higher Third again. She did not relish the thought, but there was no choice: Jandell must still be there, in Squatstout's Keep.

There was much talk of the Choosing, too. She could not make out any real details, but she gathered she was lucky to have avoided it. There was mention of the Unchosen, and being thrown from the top of a cliff. It sounded like a twisted version of Selection.

But the most important information she gleaned concerned the nature and dispersal of power on this awful rock. That was what mattered in the world, Overland or Habitation or anywhere else. In this place, power belonged to Squatstout; he was the people's guide and their saviour. He enforced his authority through his Guards, those beaked creatures. It was unclear how many there were in total, but it had to be a sizeable force.

The people spoke of the Voice, too: they feared it, and loved it, all at once. That was why they stayed here,

Squatstout had said, despite all the things they suffered: they worshipped the Voice. *The Voice is the key. If it really is the same thing that spoke to Alexander Paprissi, then all of this began with it.*

When night came, and the inn became more boisterous, Brightling shifted to her feet and hobbled along the street, slowly winding her way along the main path upwards. She walked for a long while through the Second Third, suppressing her instinct to dash into the night. This was a fairly poor place, it seemed, a home of struggling artisans and fallen families. The people did not seem to have much in the way of wealth or possessions, yet there was a spark in the atmosphere, a suggestion of repressed energy. She wondered what the Lower Third was like.

As she went, she found her mind drifting to the future. She ran a finger along her mask and felt its dark power. The world she knew had been shattered; the Machinery was no more. But she could salvage something, could she not? Her mask could hurt these beings, it seemed. *She* could hurt them when she wore it. Perhaps she could even free Katrina from the creature that held her. She could destroy the thing that spoke to Alexander and caused so much suffering. She could stop them, and their Ruin, whatever that may be. They could rebuild the world. She could find some redemption for all the things she had done. *It can't be too late, can it?*

It had all been easy, so far. Perhaps that lulled her into lowering her defences. Perhaps she had grown rusty, over her long years at the top of the See House. Perhaps that was how the Guard surprised her.

'Everyone is looking for you.'

She turned quickly, but not quickly enough. Two gloved

hands pinned her arms against her sides, and the silver beak was an inch from her face. A black hat encircled the Guard's head, like a strange halo, and a metal club hung at his side. Brightling could not see the eyes in the sunken sockets of the mask, but she knew they were studying her very closely indeed.

'We all thought you were dead.'

It was odd to hear a voice coming from beneath that mask. This one had a soft, thrumming sound: the purring of a cat.

She quickly scanned her surroundings. The road was clear to either side, with no signs of civilisation. *Why wasn't I paying attention? Oh, the old me would not be pleased.*

She considered sticking with the innocent old beggar woman routine, but there seemed little point. It wouldn't get her very far with these creatures, if they were anything like the Watchers of the Overland.

'I'm not dead yet,' she said, breaking into a wide grin.

'No. I see that. I am glad. There may still be time for you to take part in the Choosing.'

'That means death.'

'Only for the Unchosen. We can't have them hanging around, stinking the place out and confusing things.'

'Is anyone ever Chosen?'

'Not so far,' said the Guard.

'Not so far in ten thousand years,' said Brightling.

'Indeed.'

Keep him talking. 'How does the island survive, when you keep chucking people off a cliff?'

The beak leaned in closer. 'There are more people here than you might expect, my lady. A few dozen deaths every now and again is not so much to absorb. The Lord

Squatstout told us about the land you are from. People dying left, right and centre, poisons and stabbings and so on, oh dear me.'

He tutted.

'I imagine that Squatstout can always just nip out and get more people anyway, if he likes. Take away their memories.' *All those memories you could have taken.*

The man shrugged. 'We do not speculate on the Autocrat's activities.'

They stood like that for a moment longer. Brightling wondered if there was a smile beneath the mask.

'How did you recognise me?'

'No one from here would travel this road at night,' the Guard said. He pointed at her head. 'And a strand of your lovely white hair is visible below your hood.' He leaned forward. 'I'm going to chain you now. Do not try and resist.'

Brightling nodded. 'Go on then. Be gentle.'

The Guard released his left hand and reached under his cape. For half a heartbeat she thought of striking him. But she resisted the temptation; he would surely be primed for just such a manoeuvre.

So she kept smiling as the Guard withdrew an iron chain, and tightened it around her wrists. He tied the other end to his belt, just below his chainmail.

'Don't try anything stupid, please,' he said. 'My support will be here imminently.'

Brightling nodded. The Guard began to walk, slowly. He let her set the pace, and slowed down when she seemed to lag behind. He was considerate of his prisoner. That was a mistake.

She tugged on the chain, just once, very lightly.

The Guard sighed. 'What is it? Please feel free to speak,

if you want my attention. You don't need to pull on the chain.'

She nodded. 'I wanted to ask you a question.'

'Go on.'

'Are you new to your job?'

There was silence for a moment.

'Why does it matter?'

Brightling nodded. 'You're new. I thought so. It explains a lot. For instance, when you're alone with a potential troublemaker – Doubters, we used to call them – it is quite unwise to attach yourself to your target. It literally gives them leverage.'

The man laughed, but there was a nervous twinge to it. 'Only if the target is stronger than you are. I very much doubt you are stronger than me.'

'Strength is a funny thing,' said Brightling. 'It isn't just about muscle.'

She made as if to pull on the chain, and the Guard tensed up, preparing for a tug of war. His inexperience was endearing. Instead of pulling, she leapt in the air, twisted her body, and kicked him on the back of his beaked head, where his neck should be. The Guard was strong and well armoured, but he stumbled forward. Brightling curled the chain around the man's neck, and by sheer luck – no, *instinct* – she found a space between the mask and the chainmail. The chain snapped inside this hole and she twisted, feeling him choke beneath her.

But once again, her rustiness got the better of her. She did not look behind. She did not see the other Guard appear, raise his weapon, and strike her on the back of the head.

She fell forward, her face thumping into the dirt. She turned, her head screaming in pain. It was the Protector,

149

with his golden beak, his wooden stick held straight out before him.

'I am his support,' the Protector said, as Brightling fell into blackness.

Chapter Sixteen

Irandus laughed and laughed.

His laughter rattled through the kitchen, across the pots and pans. It tapped against the windows, and it crawled across the ceiling. It was a strange kind of laughter: a soulless laughter from the grave.

Why is he laughing? Aranfal almost said. But it was no good asking questions, here. Not with Shirkra, and not with Irandus, the laughing man with the blade in his throat.

Eventually the laughter subsided, and Irandus's face paled. He touched his neck, and withdrew his bloodied hand, looking upon it with horror.

'Actually, this is quite sore.'

He slumped forward, his head on his arms.

'That was *very fun*!' Shirkra cried. She slammed a hand against the wooden table. 'Now wake up, and reveal yourself!'

Reveal yourself? For a moment, Aranfal wondered if he could escape this place. Shirkra was preoccupied with the man she had stabbed, which was perhaps to be expected. *I could make a run for it. I could.*

But no. She would find me, wherever I went.

151

Irandus lay perfectly still, and Aranfal was certain the man was dead. *How could he not be?* But the world had changed, and things worked differently now. Or perhaps it *hadn't* changed. Perhaps it was always the same, and he was only now opening his eyes. Maybe the truth was revealing itself to him, thanks to Shirkra, and Mother, and all the things they had wrought ...

There came a chuckle from the lifeless Irandus. The candles and the lamp puffed into nothingness, and the room was cast into darkness.

'Shirkra,' said a male voice.

It was the kind of voice Aranfal knew well from his days in the North: hard, but flickering with intelligence, the kind of wisdom that was hard-earned. It was not the voice of Irandus Illarus.

'Gamesman,' Shirkra said, her own voice sweeping through the darkness, harsh as ever, but cut through with something else: disdain.

'I have not seen you in an age,' said the male voice.

'Many ages of the world,' Shirkra said. 'Many ages for mortals. But not so many for us, no, not so many for us at all.'

'Perhaps, perhaps. Yet the years have weighed on you, Mother of Chaos, even if they were nothing more than a heartbeat. I remember how the game ended the last time you played ... a real war ... you did not win.'

The candles came back to life. Shirkra held her mask in her hands, stroking the edges. She was smiling, but it was uneasy.

The Gamesman sat in the seat that had once been occupied by Irandus Illarus, but that was where the similarities ended. He appeared to be young, though Aranfal knew that could not be true. He had shoulder-length hair, thin and blond. His skin was ruddy, and his eyes were a cold and watchful blue. He was dressed in a dark green gown, on which were painted strange images: people and beasts, a hundred different malformed triangles and squares, eyes that stared into nothing. His features were delicate, in a way that many thought handsome. Aranfal knew this, because Aran Fal had once been thought handsome, and the Gamesman looked like that young man.

A Progress board was spread on the table before him, the tiles set out as if for a game. But there were not enough pieces, and fewer tiles than normal.

'Have you played this?' the Gamesman asked, looking at Aranfal.

'Progress? Yes. But I do not know this version.'

'This is the Third Iteration. It is old now, for you people.'

Aranfal nodded. The Gamesman sighed, and closed the board with the pieces still inside.

'I have slept for a long time,' he said, turning his attention to Shirkra. 'I slept, and I dreamed of games. Sometimes though, Jandell would wake me. He would ask me about this game.' He held up the board. 'We would finesse it together, and he would pass our thoughts on to the mortals.'

'That is all you have been doing, hmm?' Shirkra asked, before breaking into laughter. 'In all this time, you have helped Jandell with Progress? Oh, a shame for you, a shame.'

The Gamesman nodded. He lifted a hand to stroke his chin, and Aranfal noticed the man's fingernails for the first time; they were long, and yellowing. 'I would have willed it otherwise. But it is never up to me, is it? I only create the games, that is all I do, that is all I will ever do.'

Shirkra turned to Aranfal. 'The Gamesman was one of

our favourite servants, Aranfal my love. He was created by Mother herself, very early on. There are hundreds like him, thousands and thousands: young things, but powerful still. The Gamesman was one of our most beloved. In days of old, we knew him as—'

The Gamesman rapped the table with his fingernails. 'No, Shirkra. Do not say that name. It is dead, now.'

Shirkra giggled. 'So serious, for a lover of games!'

She turned again to Aranfal. 'The Gamesman was a wonderful creature, wonderful. But all he wanted to do was play games. Hmm? We played with him, we played with him so much, but he would *cheat*.'

The Gamesman winced, and covered his eyes with his hands.

'Yes, yes, he would cheat so much! And so one day, Mother punished him. She said that he would never again be allowed to play any of our games. He could create them, oh yes – that was now his role. But he could not play the games he loved to play. Oh no. He could do little tricks, like the one you saw earlier, when he pretended to be another man. He can toy around with things like this.' She flicked a finger at the Progress board. 'But he can never play *our* games again. Ha!'

The Gamesman's eyes glistened. 'Now all I do is watch.' He placed his hands on the table, and gave Shirkra a hard look. 'I have begun preparations for the game. I was surprised that you wanted to play. I thought there would be no games again – not after last time.'

'This time is different. There are no powerful mortals now, oh no. And when it is over, Ruin will come with such a fury that none will be able to stand in the way.'

Shirkra leaned forward. 'Do you know what happened,

hmm, Gamesman? The Queen! She wants to play, and she has offered us such wonderful prizes, even if we *lose*. She will take us to the Machinery. Mother will turn its remnants to dust, and she will bring Ruin. At last!' Shirkra cocked her head to the side.

The Gamesman blinked. 'I am not sure—'

'Do you seek to deny Mother her wish?'

'No! No! Not at all, Shirkra.'

'Good. Because she has been kind to you. Things could have gone worse for you, you cheat.'

The Gamesman bowed his head. He unfolded the Progress board again and studied it for a long while, before extending a fingernail and shifting a piece from one square to another.

'I used to miss the games more than I do now, anyway,' he said in a quiet voice. His head snapped up, and he grinned at Aranfal and Shirkra in turn. 'Come. I will show you the board, and you can tell me if you are pleased. I hope that you are pleased with me.'

'As do I, Gamesman,' Shirkra said. 'As do I.'

The Gamesman grinned at Shirkra, but it was a false smile. He reached in the air, clicked his fingers, and once again, the room fell into darkness.

Chapter Seventeen

'What will you do when you see Mother again, oh Boy, my brother?'

'I will tell her of all the things we have seen these ten thousand years, oh Girl, my sister. I will tell her our tale in a heartbeat. What will you do?'

'Oh, I will just *smell* her, my brother. I will wrap myself in her arms and I will *smell* her.'

Canning had studied the Duet on their journey to the See House. The way they spoke frightened him. Hardly surprising: he was, after all, a coward. But this was different. They put him in mind of the worst aspects of childhood. All the cruelties of the young had flowered within them and sparkled in their eyes.

He was still held in the red ball: a prisoner of light. But it was something more besides. It was a thing of memory, humming with the same power he had felt in the Bowels. Was it the essence of memories? Did they look like *this,* at root, this cold and draining light? *Perhaps it is a memory itself*.

As he stared at its sides, he thought he saw things there, images from his past and a thousand others. He tried to feel that old power again; tried to grasp it by its edges. But it was useless. He was just Canning. He knew what awaited him now: Shirkra, and her Mother.

'Unimportant.'

He looked up. Boy and Girl were standing before the light, staring in at him. He wasn't sure which one had spoken.

'Yes, my lord and lady?'

Boy giggled. 'Lord and lady! Very nice, very nice. Oh, it is lovely to be worshipped again!'

Girl poked Boy in the side. 'Ask him! Ask him!' She turned away, looking coyly at the ground.

Boy laughed, and grinned at Canning. 'Sometimes my sister is so shy, Unimportant. I hope you don't mind.'

'No ... of course not, my lord, my lady, of course I don't mind.'

Boy bowed. 'She wonders, Unimportant, how you would like to die?'

Girl was leering at the former Tactician, her face pressed against the light.

Canning's mind raced through possible answers. 'I do not want to die,' was what he finally came up with.

Girl looked confused. 'But all of you people die! If I *knew* I was going to die, I would think of nothing else. I would plan my death, over and over again.'

'That would be a sad way to live.'

The Duet laughed together. 'You are a fine man to speak of sad lives!' cried Boy.

'A fine man indeed,' said Girl.

Canning raised his hands, palms spread open like the supplicant he had always been.

'Let me help you, please,' he said, his voice trembling. 'There must be something I could do. Please don't send me

157

back to them.'

There came the sound of footsteps, and the three of them turned towards the noise. There was no one on the streets, these days, no one at all, so the footfalls echoed along Greatgift like shots from a handcannon.

That was strange. But stranger still was the reaction from Boy and Girl. The Duet fell forward, onto their knees, clutching at the sides of their heads.

'Sister!' Boy hissed. 'They have brought a strong one, tonight! The strongest in years!'

Girl did not reply. She seemed in a worse state than Boy, lying on her front, face down and weeping into the cobblestones.

The red light flickered and disappeared, and the former Tactician crashed to the ground. He yelped, and scrambled to his feet.

Three figures were approaching. At first, Canning took them for a group of drunks. Two men in hooded brown cloaks were dragging along a woman dressed in white. Her arms were thrown across the men's shoulders, and her head lolled wildly. For the briefest of moments, Canning caught a glimpse of her eyes, and saw that they were pale things, little ovals of bone.

Boy and Girl moaned as the three figures approached. For a second, Boy made eye contact with the strange, drunken woman, and he cried out like a wounded animal. Before long, however, the Duet were silent and still. Canning watched them for what felt like a long while: he was sure he could just make out something surrounding them, a kind of bubble of pale light. He thought he saw figures, there, moving across the surface. But soon they were gone.

The man on the left pulled his hood aside. He was middle-aged, perhaps as old as Canning, with a bald head and dark skin. His eyes darted wildly.

'They are down, but they won't be for long,' he said to the other man.

'No. We have to move, and get her out of here.' This man removed his own hood. He was rough looking, his raw white skin peppered with black stubble. His head was coated with a tight mass of black curls, which he had greased with a sweet-smelling oil. He was younger than his companion, perhaps in his mid-thirties.

The woman in the centre coughed violently, and vomited a dark line of blood. She was very young: a girl, really, no older than fifteen or sixteen. Her blonde hair was tied back with string, and she had a long nose, like the snout of an animal. Her skin was a sickly yellow.

The older man nodded at Canning.

'You should come with us. Right now. They'll kill you, if they find you. They'll kill you for years.' His accent was strange. It was not of the Plateau – Canning was sure of it.

'Kill me for years?' he whimpered. By the Machinery, he despised himself sometimes.

The other man pointed to one of the narrow side streets that veered south. 'Let's go.'

Canning glanced down at the Duet. They had begun to stir; it would not be long before they awoke.

He made up his mind in an instant, and followed the newcomers to the alleyway.

'You are not from the Overland,' Canning said.

They were sitting in the shadow of a decrepit mansion, a rambling old building of the type one often found between the Centre and the Far Below, suspended between a marvellous past and an impoverished present. The woman was still unconscious; the men had carried her between them, yet still managed to set a pace that was far beyond the former Tactician. He lost them on several occasions, and was ashamed to find them waiting for him round some distant corner. *Ah, shame: my old friend.*

The two men looked at one another, then back at Canning. 'No,' said the older man. 'This is our first time here.'

'We are from the South,' said the other man.

'There is nowhere south of the Overland, except the Wite,' Canning said. 'You're from the desert?'

'No,' said the older man. 'Our country lies beyond the desert. We call it the Wite, too – interesting, that we have the same name for it.'

'Yes,' Canning said. *Interesting and bizarre. Perhaps this is some new trick.*

'It is not a country we are from. It is a realm of disaster.'

It was the woman who spoke; Canning was startled to find her sitting up, leaning on her elbows. Her eyes had taken on a more human appearance, and her skin was now a healthier tone, though she still seemed weak. She had the same strange accent as the men, but there was a harsh edge to her voice; she was powerful, and she knew it.

'I am Controller Arlan,' the older man said. 'This is Controller Sanndro' – he gestured at the other man – 'and this lady is Raxx, a Manipulator of the Remnants.'

'They call themselves Controllers,' spat Raxx, 'as if that means something. But all they do is chaperone us. They are just bodyguards.'

'We dragged you away from death today,' said Sanndro with a smile. He did not seem surprised by her aggression. 'As we have done many times in the past.'

'Hmm. I'll give you that.' Raxx clambered to her feet, and placed a hand on Sanndro's head like it was a fence post. 'You are very good at dragging things.'

She laughed, and turned to Canning. 'What is your name?'

Unimportant. 'Timmon Canning. Just Canning, though. Everyone calls me Canning.'

'Canning. Very well, then. You were a help to us today, Canning, though I doubt you knew what you were doing. You distracted them.'

'I assure you, whatever I did was perfectly accidental.' He never found it sensible to talk himself up. In any case, it was the truth.

'Hmm. I'm sure you're right,' said Raxx. 'Anyway, no matter what you did, their thoughts were elsewhere when we came upon them, and for that I am grateful. It would not have been so easy, without you.'

It didn't look easy. 'Well, I owe you more thanks, I think, my lady. Those children were taking me back to their Mother.' *I can't believe I just said that.*

Raxx nodded. 'Perhaps they would have. Or perhaps they would have changed their minds, and done something else with you. The Duet are a capricious pair.'

'One thing they are *not*, though, is children,' said Sanndro. He scratched his stubble. 'There are few older than them.'

'They are Operators, like our one,' said Canning. 'And Shirkra. And Mother. They're all the same.'

'Yes, they are all one powerful, fucked-up family of merciless immortals,' Raxx said.

'But you can fight them.'

The three foreigners went silent, and exchanged glances.

'In a way,' said the girl. 'We have retained skills that were developed long ago, at the beginning of the war. We need them, where we are from.'

'Where the war never ended,' said Arlan. 'The Remnants.'

'The Duet have tormented us now for ten millennia,' said Raxx. 'We've never seen them come up here, though. The way used to be barred to all of us. We hoped we could capture them, you see – take them back to our land, where we're good at holding creatures like them. But I couldn't do it. I put them in a powerful memory, but I could feel it failing. They are too strong. We have to get away before they find us. We won't have surprise on our side any more.'

Raxx sighed, and rubbed her forehead. 'They must have sensed it – the machine, that's what you call it, isn't it? We know about the machine. Jandell made it long ago, and now it's broken. That's attracting them all like rats to grain.'

'Not the machine,' Canning whispered. He glanced into the shadows, half-expecting a Watcher to leap out upon him. 'The Machinery.'

'Whatever you call it, whatever happened took them here, and away from us.' Raxx grinned. 'Maybe we should have left them to it.'

'You shouldn't have tried to hold them in a memory, Manipulator,' said Sanndro. 'You could have hurt them badly, given them a little blast. You could have done more.'

Raxx jabbed a finger at him. 'Don't fucking try and tell me about Manipulating Autocrats, Sanndro. They've grown more powerful up here. I can feel it. We were lucky to get out of there alive.' She sighed. 'I apologise, my brother.' She placed a hand on his shoulder. 'I am exhausted.'

Sanndro smiled, and took her hand.

'We will leave this place, and return to the Remnants,' Raxx said. 'The Arch Manipulator will know what to do.' She pointed at Canning. 'You'll have to come with us. OK?'

162

Canning chuckled. 'Nothing could persuade me to stay here.'

She nodded. 'Then we go into the south and the east.'

'What is in the south-east, my lady?'

She gave him a quizzical look. 'Our ship, of course. You don't think we crossed the Wite on foot, do you?'

Arlan and Raxx gathered their things and turned away into the darkness. Sanndro appeared at Canning's side.

'You've not been on a ship before, have you, Overlander?'

Canning shook his head.

'They're bumpy things. Those with a weak constitution get sick easily.'

Sanndro laughed, and began to walk after his companions. Canning watched them for a moment in perfect misery.

Everything about me is weak.

Chapter Eighteen

'Your people call it the Old Place, then?'

Alexander Paprissi asked a lot of questions.

'Yes,' Drayn replied. 'What else would we call it?'

'We used to call it the Underland, where I come from. Though I suppose that's only because we lived in the Overland, and the Underland was below our feet. Or so we thought. I'm not sure where it is any more, truth be told.'

They were in a tunnel. There was only the palest of lights, coming from some unseen source. As they walked, Drayn thought of Cranwyl. Would she find him here? Or had he been taken to some other part of the Old Place, for the Voice to assess him alone? *Of course he has, you idiot. You forced your way down here for nothing.*

At long last they came to a stop. Alexander took her by the hand, and they ducked under an archway in the rock. Drayn fully expected another cave to open up before her, as damp and dreary as everything else she had seen in the Old Place. But her expectations were misguided.

They were in a garden, elegant and well-tended. Neat lines of blue and yellow flowers stood in rows upon the grass. There was no wind in this place, not even a breeze, so the flowers were eerily still. The sun was large in the sky, bigger by far than Drayn had ever seen it: a perfectly circular yellow ball that cast a sickly sweet light across the world.

In the centre of the garden was a courtyard, formed of silver tiles. Two wooden chairs sat on either side of a small iron table, upon which was a glass jug of an amber liquid and two ceramic mugs. There was food here, too: bowls of sausages, and chunks of fried bread.

'What is this place?' Drayn asked. 'How can this exist in a cave?'

Alexander grinned, and shrugged his shoulders. 'This is the Old Place. Things are different here.' He gestured at the sun in its cloudless sky. 'Have you ever seen a place and a day like this on your island?'

'No. There are hardly ever days like this on the Habitation, and there are no places like this.'

'That's a pity. I remember places like this in the Overland. But this is too perfect. And you can see the joins, if you look carefully. It's a memory, from another time, and memories are never just right, not even in the Underland.'

He pointed away from the courtyard, to the far distance, beyond fields of bright green grass. Drayn saw that the edges of the horizon were black and frazzled, throwing dark sparks into the sky.

'This is a strange place, Alexander.'

'Oh yes.'

The boy indicated to the chairs. They sat down opposite one another, and he filled their cups with the amber liquid. Drayn found she was suddenly thirsty. She drank deeply, and felt something warm bloom in the pit of her belly. Hunger followed, and she tore into the sausages and the bread.

'So your people really don't call this the Underland, then?'

the boy asked.

'No. You've already asked me that. Many times.'

'Hmm. And so you don't call your home the Overland?'

'My home is the Habitation.'

The thought of home sent a pang through Drayn.

'The Habitation,' said Alexander. 'That's a strange name. But then, so is the Overland.'

Drayn leaned back in her chair.

'So, Alexander. Let me ask *you* some questions. OK?'

'OK.'

'You say you're from this Overland. So you're not from the Old Place?'

'Correct.'

'But you seem quite relaxed down here.' She gestured at the unreal grass.

'Yes. It has taken me over, I am afraid. I'm not sure if I'm a boy, now, or just the memory of a boy. I don't think I could return, even if I wanted to.'

Drayn nodded. 'What took you here?'

'The Operator took me here. He is a brother to your Autocrat, or as close to a brother as those creatures get. He's the one that's now on your Habitation.'

'Why did he do that?'

Alexander gave a gentle smile. 'That's a long story, and a sad one, too.'

Drayn nodded.

'Tell me about the Choosing,' she said.

'I don't know much about it.'

That figures. My one ally is clueless.

'But,' Alexander continued, 'I am sure I can help you.'

'Help me?'

He leapt to his feet. 'Help you get Chosen, of course!

That's the only way out! And like I said – I *know* the Voice! I reckon you'll probably be presented with a puzzle or two, things of that nature. Well, I'll help!' He pounded his chest. 'I'm great at puzzles.'

'But you don't *know*? You don't really know anything about the Choosing?'

Alexander squinted. 'Well, not exactly. But if worst comes to worst, it's probably better to have me at your side than not, hmm? Keep you company? Hmm?'

Drayn nodded. *That seems fair.* 'Where do we begin?'

Alexander looked up at the strange sky. 'We are being watched, even now, by the Voice, though I don't think the Choosing has begun. Not properly, anyway.'

'You don't *think* it's begun? That's reassuring.'

The boy smiled.

'Well, I'm no expert. But you can trust me.'

Something in Drayn's gut told her this was true. 'I don't think I'm meant to be here,' she said, standing up.

'What do you mean? Of course you are. The hands wouldn't have taken you otherwise.'

'I … a friend of mine was taken. I asked to go, too, so I could follow him. I begged the Voice, and the hands. But I don't think it was a good idea. I don't think I'll find him in this place.'

Alexander shrugged. 'Who knows? You may find him, you may not. Perhaps you will be Chosen! And then you might even be able to save him before they throw him into the sea.'

Drayn felt suffocated. 'But I wouldn't be *me* then, would I? I'd be the Voice. I wouldn't care about Cranwyl at all.'

Alexander chuckled. 'Maybe a part of you would survive. Who knows? Why else would they want a host, if they didn't love the person that was there in the first place? But you shouldn't care about anyone else any more anyway. Not down here. Because no one cares about you.' He tapped his forehead. 'Except me. Perhaps.'

'Perhaps?'

'Perhaps.'

The sound of conversation came from across the fields of grass, muffled words just barely audible. Two men came into view; they seemed to leap forward in jolts, as if the land was shifting under their feet. They were quite different, these men, though they both looked older than the Autocrat himself. One was a tall character in a bedraggled suit, sporting a mop of unruly hair, while the other was a short, fat, round man. He reminded Drayn of a boulder she had seen once, on the edge of the Higher Third.

They approached, smiling broadly at Alexander.

'So!' cried the tall one. 'There he is. The Operator's friend. I haven't seen you in a while.'

'But we have met your sister, haven't we?' asked the shorter one. 'Yes, I'm sure we have.'

'You have, gentlemen, you have. But that part of the story is over now.' He walked to the men, and whispered something in their ears.

The tall man whistled through his teeth. 'Fancy that! The Strategist! An amazing development! You must be so proud of her. Still, we have seen a lot over the years, down here. I imagine this will all pass, too.'

'Yes indeed,' said the fat one. 'It will all pass, and we will return to our old stools, and we'll have a good drink.'

The two men laughed together, before the taller man turned his gaze on Drayn.

'And is this another sister of yours, then?'

Alexander shook his head. 'No, sir. This is Drayn, a child of the Habitation. She is taking part in the Choosing.'

'Oh!' said the tall one. 'That's a shame. Well, my girl, if we're to be the last creatures you ever meet, then you should know our names. I am Sharper, and my companion here is Sprig.'

'Are you Autocrats, like Squatstout?' Drayn asked.

The old men seemed surprised.

'Autocrats? Back to that, then? I thought it was Operators now.' Sharper sighed. He reached into the back pockets of his suit and removed a flask, from which he sipped. 'Let's have a drink.'

Sprig took the bottle from his friend, and took a deep draught.

'There is one thing that's bothering me,' Sprig said when he had finished. 'Why are we here?'

Alexander grinned. 'We need your help. In the Choosing.'

'Help?' Sprig cocked his head to the side, and gave the boy a quizzical look. 'What help is there to give? She is being assessed as we speak, the mortal. It doesn't matter where she is, here or there or everywhere. The Voice may be imprisoned, but it watches all.'

'But you can help, can't you? You know this place better than anyone. Tell us what she can do to impress the Voice.'

'Nothing,' said Sharper, in a serious tone. 'The Voice sees all. It can't be tricked or influenced.'

'No,' said Sprig. 'But she seems a nice girl.' He gestured at Drayn, then turned to Sharper. 'My friend, we do know some things about the Voice. We know the type of things it hates.'

He turned to Alexander.

'You are going with her?'

169

'Yes.'

'Then listen carefully. If she's trying to lie, and you can sense it, you have to stop her. It won't make much difference, in the end, but it's best that she doesn't anger the Voice. Sometimes it doesn't let them go, the Unchosen that anger it. Sometimes it keeps them here, and it hurts them.'

'I don't have anything to worry about, because I don't lie,' lied Drayn.

'No, well. Be that as it may,' said Sprig, 'most people don't *mean* to lie. But memories are memories, and sometimes people look at their own memories with liar's eyes and untruthful hearts, even if they don't mean to. The Voice *hates* that type of thing.'

The sky flickered, for a moment; the sun seemed to blink. They all looked up at it, the boy, the girl, and the two old men. Drayn felt a wave of coldness run through her.

'What's all this talk of memories?' She hoped her own voice was firm, but she knew that it was not.

Sprig and Sharper exchanged glances. 'That is what the Voice looks at, of course,' said Sharper.

'It digs inside you for them,' said Sprig.

The girl swallowed. For the briefest of moments, images of the past flashed before her mind's eye, things she had buried long ago. She pushed them away, back where they belonged.

'We have to go now,' said Sharper.

'We are needed, on our stools,' said Sprig.

'Wait!' Drayn cried. 'Have you seen a man down here? His name is Cranwyl! He's older than me, but he's not very old, and he's good, he's so good!'

But it was too late. The old men had turned their backs on Drayn and Alexander, and were on their way.

The sun began to sink, quicker than it should have, falling away beyond the horizon. When it disappeared, the courtyard vanished with it, and Drayn was somewhere else.

She was standing outside the house, on the Higher Third. The house she had grown up in. Thonn House.

She felt her breath catch in her throat. She turned, searching. Alexander was there, staring at the old building with wide eyes.

'So, we're in your memories!' he cried, glancing up at the sky. 'How much fun is this? It's like playing with new toys!'

Drayn turned back to the house. It stood alone, which was a rare thing in their cluttered land. It was built of a grey stone, and its roof was black and broken. The door was red, and it hung open.

Drayn knew when this was. The memory would not be suppressed. She had not been here for a long, long time.

'Do you like this? Walking through an old memory?' *Alexander, and his damned questions*. 'It must be nice, no? I wonder if it's just the same as you remember.'

'I try not to remember,' Drayn said, in a quiet voice. 'I am an expert at forgetting. I take memories, and I bury them.'

'Why would you do such a thing? Memories are art, Drayn.'

'Not all art is good, Alexander.' She sighed. 'Do I have to go inside?'

Alexander looked to the sky. It was night, and the stars were cool and crisp. 'Oh yes, Drayn. The Voice is watching you. The Voice is testing you.' The boy inclined his head slightly. 'Let's go in.'

Drayn walked to the door. She had not lied to Alexander.

She had learned how to do it, over the years. She had hidden away more memories than ... well, than she could remember. Life hadn't always been crawling through corridors with Cranwyl. Oh, no. Not at all.

But perhaps memories couldn't be destroyed, no matter how hard you tried. She entered the house, and she remembered everything.

'The House of Thonn is built on shadows. It has lived on shadows for ten millennia. But the thing about shadows is they wilt before the light, no matter how big they are. Do you follow me?'

The speaker was Uncle Simeon. He was a strange-looking man. He seemed old, at first glance, his face a yellow patchwork of wrinkles, but his head was crowned with the most luscious outcrop of youthful black hair. Cranwyl said Simeon had won the hair in a duel with a market magician. But Cranwyl said a lot of things.

Drayn's father was sitting on the same sofa as Simeon, while Mother was perched on a wooden chair. She had not changed over the years.

'What do you mean by that, Simeon?' Mother asked.

Father was not a blood member of the House of Thonn; he had gained his entry through marrying Mother. But still, Dad and Simeon looked strangely alike. Dad was much younger in appearance, but he had the same black hair, and the same clever-clever eyes. Mother always said that part of the reason she loved Dad was because he reminded her of Simeon. Drayn had found that a bit strange.

'I live on the Higher Third, like you,' Simeon said. He had a slithery kind of voice. 'I sit at the Autocrat's side, when he wants my advice, and all the people of the island look upon me as a lord. But they're wrong, aren't they, my sister and brother? I am not a lord.' He jabbed a finger at Dad. 'Teron is the lord. He has brought his blood into our House, and he has taken our name, and he calls himself a lord, all because he has married Lyna.' He gestured at Mother.

Drayn and Alexander were standing at the back of the hall, between the doorway and the fireplace. She felt a tug on her sleeve, and turned to her companion.

'If this is your memory,' Alexander said, 'then where are you?'

Drayn nodded upwards, to the top of a flight of stairs. There, barely visible behind the bannister, sat a young girl, with wide brown eyes and long brown hair.

'Ah,' said Alexander.

'Both of you sit in Thonn House,' Simeon said. 'You sit here, or in one of our other holdings. But you *should not be sitting at the head of our House*. Isn't that right, sister?' He turned upon Mother. 'I was the first-born. You have lied to me, all our lives.'

A silence fell across the hall.

'What are you talking about?' Mother's voice was quieter.

'Did you know, Teron, that my sister raised me?' Simeon asked, turning his gaze on Drayn's father. 'Our Mother died in a Choosing, when we were very young, and our father threw himself off the rock after her. A rare occurrence, to lose both at once like that, but be that as it may, it happens even on the Higher Third.'

He sighed, and closed his eyes, as if succumbing to a memory, before he clicked back into the real world.

'Well, when that happened, we were very small indeed. Perhaps three or four. Who knows? For years our nanny took good care of us, hmm? She raised us like one of her own. I look back on that time with fond memories.

'But then, one day, nanny was gone. Lyna sent her packing. She'd decided she would run our House, and look after her little brother. Her little brother by one minute. Not a big age gap, I'm sure you'll agree. But one minute makes a big difference in our world. It meant she was the head of the House, didn't it? And I just went along with it. Stupid boy!'

He reached into his cloak, and withdrew a sheaf of parchments, which he tossed on a table before the sofa.

'Except, of course, you *weren't* born first, were you, Lyna?' He gestured at the papers. 'These are documents I found in our mother's rooms. I bet you thought you'd got all the evidence. But that's always been your problem; you're so arrogant. It seems that *I* was born first.'

'Anyone could have written those,' Lyna said.

'And used Mother's seal? And hidden them in her rooms? Come now. We could make them public if you like, and see who is believed.'

Simeon grinned, leaned back in the sofa, and opened his arms wide. 'I want to make this fair on everyone. I could have you taken by the Guards, you know, for tricking a rightful lord. But I don't want anything nasty like that to happen. Not at all. So you sign everything over to me, in the morning, and we can forget the whole thing. Anyone asks, we'll say you grew exhausted from all the trials and tribulations of heading a great House. That's easily believable. I'll even let the three of you live in one of the other houses, and I'll make sure you get the same allowance you have permitted me, all these years. Now you can't get any fairer than that.'

Simeon leaned forward, lifted a glass of wine, and took a long sip.

'We will think it over,' said Mother.

Simeon nodded. 'There's no need for things to get unpleasant.' He gave her a slight smile. 'I forgive you, sister.'

Mother did not respond. She stared ahead; her lips were pursed, and her eyes were blank. That was a look of anger on her. Drayn knew it well.

Uncle Simeon stood, and bowed twice, once to his sister and once to his brother-in-law.

'I will come back in the morning,' he said. He clapped his hands, and another man entered the room. It was a young man, with bushy brown hair and darting eyes.

It was Cranwyl.

Drayn's heart leapt, and she almost ran to him. But it was just a memory. *Not my Cranwyl.*

'My servant has overheard our conversation,' Simeon said. 'He has already sent word around the Habitation. Everyone knows what you've done, now. So don't get any ideas about hurting me when I visit tomorrow. If I were to slip off the edge of the cliff, the whole island would know who helped me on the way.'

Simeon walked over to Cranwyl, and pinched the young man's cheek.

'Cranwyl here is a smart boy, loyal and strong. He'll be with me tomorrow, too.'

Simeon looked up at the ceiling, and the younger Drayn shrank into a ball; her older counterpart remembered the sensation as if it was yesterday. But Simeon did not see her. He thudded out of the room, running a hand through his hair, as Cranwyl followed close behind.

Mother and Father waited for a long while before they spoke.

'You never told me,' Father said. There was no anger in

175

his tone. There was no emotion at all.

'No.'

'So it is true?'

'Yes.'

Father shrugged. 'It was a wise decision, by a young person. Simeon would have destroyed this House.'

'And you would never have married me.'

'I like to think that isn't true.'

'You like to think it, but you know the truth.'

'You remember what my parents were like.'

'I do.'

Silence reigned again for another while.

'We know what we must do, Teron,' Mother whispered. 'We cannot lose everything we have built.'

Father nodded, though he seemed hesitant. 'Yes. But you heard him. That boy has told half the island.'

Mother laughed. 'That's always been poor Simeon's problem. He trusts his servants too much.'

The memory ended, then, as the young girl at the top of the stairs retreated to her bedroom.

They had returned to the courtyard in the garden.

'I did not sense any Voice, Alexander,' Drayn said.

'Oh, it was there. It was there.'

The sun flickered, and they went to another part of the memory.

Chapter Nineteen

'There has been a mistake.'

Wayward did not seem to hear Brandione. He was sitting at the table in the great tent, toying with the braids in his hair. They were blood red, the same colour as his gown.

Brandione sat up in his bed, and looked at the courtier. Wayward was his only companion, these days; the Queen had not summoned him in a long time.

'Did you hear me, Wayward?'

The courtier remained silent for a moment. He kicked out his legs and rested his feet on the table, almost knocking over a carafe of wine. After some time he let out a whistling sigh.

'Yes, I heard you. But why would I respond? You have told me the same thing many times now, my friend. "I am not the Last Doubter. There has been a mistake." You are wrong. I have told you that you are wrong. Yet you will not listen to me.'

'You are angry with me.'

Wayward shrugged, staring at the rippling ceiling. 'I am not angry. I am not *anything*. Do you think your attitude surprises me?' He glanced at Brandione. 'The Queen has foreseen this. She has foreseen everything. She knows more of the past than any other being, save the Old Place itself. When the past is known, the future can be seen, too.'

'She knows what will happen, because of what occurred in the past? That can't be true.'

'Perhaps, perhaps. But there are lessons, in old memories, and all kinds of strange powers.'

There was a rustling at the door. Sand blew inside, and formed into the shape of a man. It was one of the sand soldiers, holding a plate of peeled oranges. Brandione turned away. He found it difficult to look upon these pale imitations of human beings. Wayward and the Queen were immortals, creatures formed from memory, they said. But there was life in them; they thought, and they spoke, and they plotted. The soldiers, though, had no spark of humanity. Their bodies and their clothes were formed of swirling sand, pale white or yellow, and they stared at the world with lidless eyes that had no pupils. There were differences between them; this one had a long, lean face, and a pointed moustache. But they were all the same in the only way that mattered. They reeked of death.

'You do not like them, Brandione,' Wayward whispered. 'You do not like them, and yet they are your army to command. A strange attitude, for such an accomplished military mind.'

My army to command. Brandione looked again at the soldier. 'When am I to command this army? In the game?'

Wayward shook his head. 'The game is for you to play alone. The army ...' He shrugged. 'I do not know. That is the truth. But the Queen has given it to you, and there is a purpose to everything she does.'

The soldier bowed, collapsed into dust, and vanished from

the tent.

'They are the Doubters,' Brandione said. He walked to the table, and took a seat at Wayward's side. 'I know it. They're the ones the Watchers sent to the Prison, over the ages.'

Wayward nodded. 'Of course. They were given to her, and she took their memories for herself. She took all of them: all of their pasts, everything they had even smelled or tasted. She can do that in a heartbeat, Brandione: drink a person clean.'

'Why does she leave anything behind? Why keep them, even in that form?'

'A reminder, perhaps. Besides, what good would an army be to you, if there were no soldiers?'

There was a moment of silence.

'You love her,' Brandione said. 'The Queen.'

Wayward coughed out a joyless laugh. 'Love her? Of course I love her.' He spread his arms wide. 'She is my creator. Often, I wonder, what kind of memory did I come from? I have such an array of emotions, Last Doubter – I can be as playful as a little dog, or melancholic. I can be thoughtful, and I can be trite. What manner of memory am I?'

'More than one, perhaps.'

Wayward nodded. 'More than one, perhaps. You are right.'

The courtier hopped up from his chair.

'Are you worried about the game?'

Brandione nodded.

'You should be,' Wayward replied, in a quiet voice. 'Shirkra will be represented, there, for a certainty, and Mother. If you weren't worried about facing such opponents, and the pawns that they have chosen, then you would be a stupid man, and you are far from a stupid man. You are a soldier—'

'And a scholar, yes.' He thumped the table, and Wayward started at the noise.

'You are angry,' Wayward whispered. 'You are an angry man, underneath it all.'

'Don't I have a right to be angry?'

Wayward nodded. 'Yes. Oh yes! Anger is fair, in this scenario.'

'The scenario in which I'm a pawn.'

'Oh Brandione, do not feel ill-treated. This is a great honour. You have been selected as a ... well, yes, a pawn. But you have been chosen by the Queen herself. She sees such things in you. She believes you will be victorious, in a way that no one ever has. You will stop Ruin!'

'And if I'm not victorious, the Old Place will kill me, or hide me away somewhere.'

'Oh! You should not dread this, Brandione. What an opportunity you have been given! A player in the first game for ten millennia – and the *Queen's* player, at that!'

The courtier clicked his fingers, and the room fell away.

They were at the bottom of a hollow tower. The ceiling was far above them, disappearing into nothing. The tower was filled with countless doors on every level; doors of every type, wood and iron and gold and silver.

'Where are we?'

'The Old Place, of course,' said Wayward. 'Or one aspect of it, at any rate.'

He gestured at the doors, stretching away around them and above them.

'Behind each door is a corridor. Each corridor leads to another, and among these are halls and chambers and hidden passageways.'

'It is a maze.'

'Yes.' He pointed at a door to Brandione's side. It was light blue in colour, with golden leaves painted into the frame.

'There are memories hidden within the maze. The maze *is* a memory.'

'The memories of the Old Place.'

Wayward nodded. 'This is a vision of the Old Place. It is my vision, I suppose.' He looked at the doors, almost longingly. 'We wallow in this place, in all the powers of ancient memory: the older the better. But the First Memory ... can you imagine the power it must contain?'

'Have you ever sent in a pawn?'

Wayward laughed. 'Of course not – I wasn't even alive when the game was last played. Besides, only the Old Ones play it. The family that fought the Absence.'

Wayward sighed, and shook his head. 'The point is this – you have been given a great honour. You have been selected as a pawn, by the Queen herself, to walk through this wondrous place. It is a glorious thing: your heart should swell with pride!'

Wayward clapped his hands, and they returned to the table in Brandione's tent.

One of the servants of dust was holding a plate of bread.

'What *are* you for?' Brandione asked the soldier. But the soldier did not respond.

She called to him that night, while Wayward slept.

She was standing outside his tent, her backs to him, beneath a silver pool of a moon. She wore three dresses of the same colour as the moonlight, lending her a spectral sheen, and she held her glass crowns in her three right hands.

She did not acknowledge Brandione's presence. Something had seized her attention, far ahead, and the three faces stared into the dark of the desert. Sand swirled around her feet, and danced around her crowns.

Brandione stood to her left, and looked out into the distance. He could see nothing there but darkness, vast and empty and cold.

'It is beginning,' the Queen said.

Brandione remained silent.

'The Gamesman is on the move,' the Queen continued. 'The board is being set. The players are gathering.'

'I can't see anything, your Majesty.'

The Queen hummed something, a sad little tune.

'My Queen, why have you given me an army when I cannot take it into the game?'

The heads turned to him. 'It is your army. You will know how to use it, when the time comes.'

He looked on the three women, and for a moment, he felt a surge of some strange emotion, pure and overpowering. It was not love: it was more than that. He wanted to worship her, as the savages once worshipped their gods. He wanted to be her Last Doubter, even if he did not truly believe it.

She is doing this to me ... she is toying with me. But he did not believe that. Not really. *You are doing it to yourself.*

'None can stand against you,' he said.

The Queen laughed. 'No. The others cannot defeat me now. But when Ruin comes, it will come with such a force, that not even I will be able to withstand it. That is why you *must* succeed. Only the First Memory can stop Ruin.'

Brandione nodded, and looked out into the darkness.

'I do not understand what is happening, your Majesty. But I will do whatever you need. I only ask – could you school me for the game? Could you tell me what to do?'

The Queen shook her heads. 'The journey is made by mortals. Anything I say would only confuse you, for I look at the Old Place with different eyes.'

Brandione sighed, and stared out at the distance. He thought back to his days as a soldier, on the eve of a battle. Everything was confused, and depressed, and fearful, back then. But there were often moments, when he stood alone, that a sense of clarity rose within him: an iron certainty.

He felt that now.

'Your Majesty,' he said, in a voice that sounded distant, even to him. 'It may sound strange, given ... everything. But I believe ... I think that we will win.'

The three heads nodded. 'So do I, my Last Doubter. So do I.'

In a heartbeat she was gone. Brandione reached out his hand, wondering if he could still feel her there, on the air. But there was nothing: only a memory.

Chapter Twenty

Brightling awoke on the side of a road, tied to a tree, one leg crossed over the other. Her ankles were shackled together, her hands were bound, and a rag had been stuffed in her mouth. The Protector had not blindfolded her, at least. *Small mercies.*

She glanced around. They were much higher on the Habitation, now; the night air here was cold and thin. She could just make out the edges of a great house behind her, a high building formed of bricks and shadows. The place reeked of wealth: they must now be on the Higher Third. Had the Protector carried her up here? *He must be strong.*

There was no sign of him. It was night, and the road was empty. *He can't have gone far. There's no way he'd risk losing me for a second time. I'd kill a Watcher who failed me twice.*

Sure enough, after a moment there came the sound of shuffling footsteps and the *thunk* of a stick rhythmically hitting the cobbles of the path. The Protector appeared from a darkened corner, carrying a skin of water.

'Ah,' he said through the golden mask, the beak swinging in her direction. 'Welcome to the world of the living.' He

184

pointed to the path. 'We're almost at the Lord Autocrat's Keep.'

Brightling nodded at her captor. Speaking wasn't really an option.

The Protector held up the water skin. 'There's a well nearby. You should drink. You'll be thirsty.'

He was correct. Brightling nodded at him again.

'I will have to remove your gag,' the Protector said. 'Please do not scream, or shout, or anything of that nature. No one will come to your aid; you will only annoy me, and that would not be wise. Is this understood?'

The prisoner gave another nod.

'Good.'

The Protector removed Brightling's gag, and she sucked in a deep breath.

'Thank you,' she rasped.

The Protector tilted the skin and poured some water down her throat. She drank it down greedily.

'You are a great woman,' the Protector said.

Brightling's eyes widened. 'I didn't expect a compliment from you, if I'm honest. I thought I'd be more likely to get another taste of that.' She nodded at his stick.

The Protector shrugged. 'Only if you make me use it. I have no reason to hurt you. I admire you a great deal. I marvelled at your escape; I cannot recall anyone ever escaping from the Keep. Yes, I feel I could learn a lot from you.' He lowered himself down onto his haunches, so that the beak almost touched Brightling's forehead. She flinched away from it. 'He wants that mask of yours. He is afraid of it, and fascinated by it, all at the same time.'

Brightling felt a pang of desperation. *Where is it? What have you done with it?*

The Protector patted his chest. 'Don't worry. I have kept it close to me: beside my heart.'

A dog barked in the gardens of the house to their side, and the Protector leapt to his feet.

'That was a dog,' he said.

'Indeed it was.'

'I know that house. There are no dogs there.'

There was a creaking sound, and a gate opened to Brightling's left. A small woman emerged. Brightling took her for a servant, at first glance. She had seen this type a thousand times before in the great houses of the Overland, and they were likely the same everywhere. The woman wore a heavy brown shawl, splattered with sauces and oils. She had a bonnet on her head, grey in the moonlight. Her figure was hidden beneath the folds of her clothing, but her face was ruddy, a face that had spent too many days and nights in steam-filled kitchens.

She was as innocuous as they came. That was what put Brightling on edge: that, and the dog. It was a giant of an animal, almost reaching the woman's shoulder. Its fur was grey and matted and two black eyes stared out above a long, sharp snout. Its teeth were exposed, and a growl rumbled from somewhere deep within.

The Protector seemed to sense something about this woman, too. He tensed, and tilted his staff slightly to the side.

'You do not live in that house,' he said. 'And neither does your hound.'

The dog's growling became louder. The beast looked at its mistress, who patted it lightly on the head.

'There, there,' the woman said to the animal.

The voice was just as Brightling would have expected,

homely and warm, redolent of cakes and cream.

She turned her focus on the Protector. 'What's all this then? Is this how we treat newcomers to our home?'

The Protector stiffened. 'My lady, return to wherever you came from, for that is not your home. Go on up the road, away from here, or down if you prefer. But leave us be.'

The Protector's voice seemed as calm as usual, but Brightling could hear something there: the slightest of tremors. He was afraid of this woman, and her dog. The Watcher understood; she felt it too.

'I will go,' the woman said, with a cheerful smile. 'But I am taking this foreigner with me.' She gave the Protector a shrewd look. 'You are Squatstout's most loyal servant, hmm. You have been for such a long, long time. I have listened to you many times.'

The Protector was quiet. No – it was more than that. He had been frozen where he stood.

The woman walked to the Protector, and knocked the staff from his hand. She reached into the folds of his cloak, and removed something, throwing it to Brightling. It was her mask. *Thank the Machinery.*

'Who are you?' Brightling asked.

'We'd better go,' the woman said, ignoring the question. 'My tricks won't last long with this one. We'd better get to my place quickly.'

The woman turned and started to walk back in the direction of the gate. The dog lolled along behind her, no longer growling.

'I am still chained,' Brightling said. But when she looked at her bonds, she saw they had been broken.

She grasped her mask, got to her feet, and followed the woman and her dog. She wondered, not for the first time, what the old Tactician Brightling would have made of this scene, back when the world was normal.

They did not enter the house.

There was a barn in the back of the garden. The woman went inside, before beckoning Brightling to follow.

There was a trapdoor built into the floor.

'That is a way to the Underland,' Brightling said. She had seen such doors before. They stank of that other realm.

The woman nodded. 'Squatstout won't find us, if we go through this door. It is the Old Place, but it is *my* corner of it. We can listen to him, but he cannot see us.'

'Who are you?'

'I am the Listener.' She put her ear to the door. 'Come. The way is clear.'

The woman pulled open the doorway, revealing a wooden ladder that descended into darkness.

The two women took to the ladder, the Listener going first.

'What about him?' Brightling asked, nodding at the grey dog, which stared mournfully at them.

'The hound will find his own way down.'

When they reached the rooms below, the dog was already there, panting at them. Brightling gave him a quizzical look, which the animal returned.

'Welcome, welcome,' the Listener said. 'Are you hungry? Or thirsty?'

Brightling shook her head, and examined her new surroundings. *I am in the Underland.* She was reminded of Jandell, the sense of warped power he exuded. Here, it was all around her, permeating her. She could feel her mask, gently burning.

They were in the first of what appeared to be a series of interlinking wood-panelled rooms. The ceiling was so low that she had to crouch, though it posed little difficulty to the Listener. There was a very faint light in the room, emanating from some hidden source. Brightling could barely make out her hand before her.

As her eyes adjusted to the gloom, however, she *could* see things that set the place apart. The room seemed only partly complete. The corners faded into a flickering light, like clouds sparkling with lightning.

'I've lit the place up, especially for you,' the Listener said. 'Normally I keep it very, very dark. It makes it easier to hear, you know. Oh, I have heard such things here, in the dark.'

Before them were a wooden table and two chairs. On the table was spread a mixture of food: fish and fowl and fruit.

'Take a seat,' the Listener said. She had procured a steaming kettle from somewhere, and was making two cups of scalding tea.

'I heard you arrive,' the Listener said, placing the tea before Brightling and perching herself on the other chair. She pulled open a deep drawer in the table, and removed a strange contraption: a silver, stick-like instrument, with a wide opening at the top. She placed the narrow end into her ear. 'I listened to you most carefully. You, and your immortal companion.'

The Listener closed her eyes, and gently shook her head. 'You were so loud, the pair of you, clattering around the place like great big animals. You should be more like Rustigen the Third, who is large, but does not make much sound, unless he wishes to be heard.'

Brightling felt a weight on her leg. Looking down, she saw the grey dog, its head resting heavily upon her, its eyes gazing up with an empty expression. Realisation dawned.

'Hello, Rustigen the Third,' she said to the dog. It licked its teeth in response.

'Do you have a name, beyond the Listener?' Brightling asked.

The woman gnawed at a dark red apple. 'I do not. There is no need. The Listener is my title, and also my name, and serves both purposes well. I have listened to so many names over the years. I have heard all of them, and I like mine the best.'

'What did you mean, when you spoke to the Protector – you said he had been Squatstout's servant for a long time. What did that mean?'

The Listener tapped her nose. 'I'm the Listener. I'm not the *Talker*. You wouldn't like *her* much, I can tell you.'

Brightling nodded. She had noticed some changes in the Listener from the servant woman she had first encountered. The voice was plummier, now, like a matriarch of one of those grand old families of the Centre: a Paprissi, even. Her face seemed narrower, its features sharper and more pronounced; she had removed her bonnet, and her hair was a wild mass of dark blonde curls. She had discarded the shawl, and wore a dress of black satin, finely wrought and patterned with images of ... *No*. Brightling studied the dress carefully. *It is*.

It was entirely covered with images of ears.

'You are an Operator,' said Brightling. 'Or an Autocrat. Or whatever name you people prefer to use.'

The Listener laughed in a surprisingly deep voice. 'I was born amid all the noise, in the early times. I think the Old

190

Place wanted someone to listen, to pay attention to all the sounds, all the cacophony of new memories being born. Do you know this term, the Old Place? It is what you call the Underland, I think, or so I have heard.'

Brightling nodded.

'So that is what I do,' the Listener said with a sigh. 'I follow the noises, or they follow me. Either way, I am never able to escape them.'

'Can you hear the Machinery?'

The woman smiled.

'It has broken, and Ruin is coming.'

Brightling nodded. *This woman is not a liar.*

'I keep an ear on Squatstout, more than anyone else,' the Listener whispered. 'You can learn a lot from what he gets up to. Squatstout hears a Voice, you know. It does not speak to many, this Voice.'

Brightling nodded. 'He told me of it.'

The Listener reached into her table again, and removed another instrument. This one was entirely black.

'I made this, so I could listen to it,' she said. '*But I cannot hear this Voice.* Do you understand? It speaks to *Squatstout*, but not *me.*'

She leaned forward and grasped Brightling's hand. 'I must hear it. Do you understand? I am the Listener; I must hear everything.'

The woman withdrew, and slumped back in her chair.

'Well, let me see it then,' she said.

There was no need to say more. Brightling nodded, and withdrew her mask. It had taken one of its most common forms: a man's face, his brows knitted in consternation, his mouth open and fierce. In the strange half-light of the Listener's rooms, the mask seemed to glow with a dark illumination of its own.

'I have listened to you since you arrived, and I have heard such interesting things,' the Listener said. 'The Lord Squatstout does not care about you, for a start, and neither does his Protector. They want *this*.' She rested a finger on the mask, but quickly pulled it away, as if it had caused her pain.

'The Operator – Jandell – gave that to me,' Brightling said.

The Listener nodded. 'Yes. It bears his mark. It is interesting that he gave it to you. He sensed you had the ability to use it, perhaps.'

'It hurts when I wear it.'

'That doesn't mean you can't use it, Brightling.' The Listener stroked the mask gently, and suddenly withdrew her hand again. 'I would love ... But no.' Suddenly the Listener smiled. 'I am not a thief.' She lifted the mask, and handed it to the Watcher. 'I will look after you.'

The Listener leaned back in her chair, and grinned.

Something had been bothering the former Tactician. 'How did you know my name?' she asked.

A laugh. 'Oh, come now, Brightling. I've heard it a million times before.'

Chapter Twenty-One

'You have not sailed before.'

Canning remained where he was, leaning over the side of the vessel. He wiped the vomit from his mouth before turning to face Arlan.

'You are very perceptive,' he said.

Arlan grinned. 'You are being sarcastic! That's good. It shows spirit.'

Canning rubbed his forehead. He did not feel spirited as he looked at his surroundings. He had seen ships before, the small vessels Overlanders were permitted to sail on their rivers and close to the coast. This was different: a swift, narrow thing that bumped over the waves at high speed, its sails billowing ferociously. It was the kind of thing he once imagined Jaco Paprissi sailing in, all those long years ago.

He was not built for it. *I don't know how anyone could be built for this.*

Two men charged past, hauling a length of rope. *Who are they, by the Machinery?* He had been introduced to the crew when he first clambered aboard, but he couldn't remember their names for the life of him. It had always been the same way. He was as forgetful as he was stupid.

Sanndro appeared at the far side of the deck, climbing up the narrow stairs. He seemed to know his way around the ship very well, or better than Arlan at any rate. He rubbed his stubble and barked an order at some unfortunate crew-member, who scuttled quickly away.

Sanndro spotted Arlan and Canning and made his way to them, adopting his customary scowl.

'So, Canning. What have you learned today?'

The one-time Tactician of the Overland lowered his gaze. Sanndro was always asking him the same question. He had been nice, at the start. Now, after getting to know Canning, he had nothing but contempt for him. He saw him as a waste of space, and wanted to humiliate him. Brightling had been the same. *Everyone is the same, in the end. They're right to be.*

'Nothing,' Canning said, in a quiet voice.

'Nothing,' Sanndro echoed. 'Weeks at sea, and nothing learned.' He pointed at the coast, and then at the sun. 'What does that tell you?'

This was a new one. Canning looked up at the burning mass of heat and light, searching for something different. 'It tells me ... it is going to be hot today.'

There was silence for a moment.

'It tells you – it *should* tell you – that we are going—'

'South,' said Arlan. He gave Sanndro a harsh look. 'That's enough now, Sanndro.'

Sanndro frowned, and nodded. 'Fair enough.' He did not sound convinced, and turned back to Canning. 'Raxx wants you.'

Canning sucked in a breath. He had not seen the Manipulator since they set sail. He didn't know what she wanted with him now, but surprises were rarely a good thing, in his long and sad experience.

There were several rooms on the underside of the ship (he had not learned the proper terms for them, despite Sanndro's angriest efforts). There was some kind of kitchen, where he ate by himself, in silence; a wide space in which most of them slept; another place where things were stored; and finally, behind a closed door, the quarters of Manipulator Raxx.

He stood at that door now.

'Come in, Canning.'

He entered, head bowed, eyes on the ground.

'It would be useful if you looked at me, when I spoke to you.'

Raxx was curled into a wicker chair, perhaps six feet from him. There was no sign of a bed. She seemed healthier than before. Her skin glowed with youthful vitality, and her eyes sparked with a new light. Her pale blonde hair hung loose, framing her face like a mane.

Canning held the Manipulator's gaze for a moment, then turned his attention back to the floor.

'Why do you hate yourself so much?' the Manipulator asked.

He looked at her again. He considered lying, but there was no point. He couldn't do that very well, either.

'Because of what I am.'

'And what is that? A man who was Selected by the machine, hmm?'

Canning cursed himself. He had told them who he was on the journey. He had told them so many things. He wished now that he had not. He did not know anything about these people.

'That means the machine saw something good in you, Canning. That is something to be proud of.'

'It may have made a mistake.'

The woman laughed. 'We know some things about your people. I have never heard the machine's decisions described as a mistake.'

Canning squirmed. 'I don't mean to criticise the Machinery, my lady. What I mean is, it can't have *meant* to Select me. Perhaps there was a different Canning it wanted. I've often thought my cousin may have been the one. Maybe the Watchers made a mistake, and got the wrong Canning.'

'Hmm. It doesn't sound likely, from what I've heard of your Machinery, and its Watchers. We picked up a lot, over the last few decades, about your home. Your Overland. But I never expected it to be so ... advanced. And beautiful. Yes, it is an advanced and beautiful place.'

They remained in silence for a moment. Canning heard some seabird croak outside the window, and the sound of the heavy waves. For half a heartbeat he wondered if he had fallen into a dream.

'Who are you, Manipulator Raxx? Where do you come from?'

Raxx smiled. 'Where to begin?' She chuckled. 'There was once a game. This game turned into a war. In your land, the war is over, for now; in ours, it never came to an end.' She sighed. 'We did not know much about your people, Canning, until very recently. We knew you were there, and some of your history – for it is *our* history, too – but Jandell kept the gates closed to us for millennia.'

She rubbed her head, and a wave of pain seemed to engulf her; she grasped her stomach and grimaced.

'You are still in pain from what you did back there,'

196

Canning said. 'I did not thank you, for saving me.'

Raxx waved a hand dismissively. 'This is just what happens when we Manipulate them. It takes a great deal out of us. And the Duet are *powerful*. There are others down there, too, tormenting us, but those two are the worst. We try our best to fight them, though we are far weaker now than the Manipulators of the past. It's amazing there are any Remnants left, though perhaps they prefer having us around.' She sighed. 'They would have killed me for sure, if we'd stuck around. I don't know why we even tried.' She locked eyes with him. 'You could have done it yourself, I think, with the right training. I can see it in you.'

Canning laughed. 'Madam, thank you, but you are mistaken.'

Even as he said this, a part of him remembered the Bowels of the See House, and the things he had done there.

'Don't doubt yourself,' Raxx said. 'And stop accusing everyone of making mistakes.'

Her face twisted in pain again, and she bent over. 'Get out now,' she stammered. 'Get some sleep. We will soon be in the Remnants.'

The air had changed.

It had been a week since Canning's encounter with Raxx, and he had spent most of it on the deck. It meant he could keep to himself, even in the night. He did not mind the cold, so long as he had a blanket to wrap himself up in.

Now, as he stared up at the gleaming stars, he could feel that things were different. He could smell it. The air had changed.

He stood up, and walked to the side of the ship, where he looked upon the dark shadows and mounds of the continent. Black birds flew before him, out above the white foam of the waves. *What do they eat, these creatures? Are they just following us, and picking at our detritus?*

A face appeared before him: Katrina Paprissi. No – it was not that girl. It was the One. Mother. The Strategist. *All of this started with her. All of it.* She peered at him through purple eyes, and for a moment it seemed as if she was about to speak. *Is this real? Or my imagination? Or are they the same thing?* Her gaze narrowed, and her mouth formed into a tight little circle …

'What are you looking at?'

Arlan was by his side.

'Nothing,' said Canning. It was true; the image had faded away.

Arlan nodded, and passed Canning a cup of wine. The one-time Tactician was grateful for it. He smiled at the Controller, and took a drink.

'Why do they call you a Controller?' he asked.

Arlan seemed taken aback.

'It's just a title, really,' he said. 'It makes us sound grander than we are. Chaperones would be better. We carry the Manipulators around, look after them, drag them away when they're exhausted. That's all. But it's still a good job.' He nodded at the land. 'I think we're the first people from the Remnants to go north in ten thousand years. That's worthwhile, isn't it?'

'You were chasing the Duet all the way north?'

'Hmm. We have heard about your Machinery. I think it's calling to them, now it's broken. Don't get me wrong; I'd rather they were far away, than down here tormenting us. But you have to keep an eye on them. If they *chose* to leave, it probably meant they were planning something worse for us down the track. That's the way they are.'

'And so you followed them.'

'And so we followed them, to try and catch them. But we couldn't do it, as you well know.'

'The Remnants sounds like a strange land.'

'Stranger than one whose leaders are picked by a machine?' Canning laughed. 'Perhaps not.'

Arlan smacked him hard on his back, and the former Tactician almost toppled over the edge.

'You shouldn't worry so much, Canning. You've had a hard life. I can tell. But you shouldn't concern yourself so much with the opinions of others.'

'They are right. Sanndro and the rest. All of them are right about me.'

'Sanndro! Don't worry about Sanndro. He's tired, and taking it out on you, not that it's any excuse.'

Arlan looked out to the sea again. 'Maybe the Remnants is the place for you. It can be a bit ... strange, but the people are nicer than in your Overland, it sounds to me. We have nothing, so we take nothing for granted, you know? All we do is fight.'

'Sounds glorious.'

The Controller laughed. 'It's not so bad, really, so long as you stay near a good Manipulator.'

Canning nodded. 'I've noticed something, tonight. The air feels different.'

Arlan shot him a glance. 'What do you mean by that?'

'I mean ... I don't know. It feels *heavier*, somehow. It's as if we've crossed a threshold, of some kind, into another place.'

Arlan sucked in a breath, so quietly that Canning wondered if he was hearing things.

'How interesting that you feel this way. I can never feel it myself. Sanndro claims to, but he's a liar, I think. Only Manipulator Raxx ever *really* feels it. That's why she's locked herself down below; she might claim she's still tired from the fight with the Duet, but I know better.'

'Feel what?'

'The Old Place. It is heavy, here. It sparkles in the very air. It makes Raxx sick, though she'd never admit it.'

'I must feel something else. I don't feel sick at all.'

'Hmm. Perhaps.' He smiled, though he seemed unsure. 'Well, I hope you enjoyed your trip on the ocean waves, my friend Canning, for it's almost at an end.'

Canning turned and looked in the direction Arlan pointed. Far ahead, along the coast, he could just make out a narrow, black, semicircular bridge, set between two huge rocks. Along the edge of the arch there sparkled a strange blue light.

'What is it?'

'That, my friend,' said Arlan, 'is the gateway to the Remnants.'

Canning pulled his blanket around him, and stared into the night.

Chapter Twenty-Two

Thonn House was desolate in the morning light. It was always the same.

Perhaps its physical isolation was the problem. Or maybe it was due to its elevated position, high up on the Habitation. Drayn never knew. But it was never a warm place.

'Here we are again,' said Alexander.

The boy could see it, too. Drayn could tell by the way he held himself. He knew what kind of place this was.

'I lived somewhere like this, once,' he said. 'Or the old me did. The Alexander who belonged in the Overland. Everyone wants to live somewhere like this, until they do.'

Drayn nodded. 'That's it exactly.'

Alexander looked up at the sky. 'This is the clearest memory I've ever seen in the Old Place. Usually it's all furry edges, or things are too perfect. Not here. I wonder why that is? Maybe you remember this place very well, and it's spilled over.'

'Yes. I remember it, though I thought I'd hidden it away.' She turned to the boy, her guide through this madness. 'Why is this happening to me, Alexander? I'd rather take my chances on the cliff edge.'

The boy raised a finger. 'Don't say things like that. Besides, there's no choice now. I'm here, you're here, the Voice is watching, and we have to go in there.'

He nodded at Thonn House.

'Yes,' Drayn sighed. 'I know. Let's go, then.'

They shuffled to the great door together, the boy as hesitant as the girl.

He has been through bad things himself, maybe. He doesn't want to see them again, even if they've nothing to do with him. Or maybe he doesn't care at all. Maybe he's just toying with me.

They went inside, along the myriad corridors of the creaking house. Drayn thought of all the times she had run through here, with Cranwyl at her side.

Where are you, my Cranwyl? What have they done with you?

'Here,' she said. They stood before a tall set of double black doors.

'Watch this,' said Alexander, before walking through the closed door. He poked his head through and grinned at her. 'We're just observers, here.'

Drayn nodded, and walked through the door, too, like a ghost.

All of them were standing in the middle of the Great Hall: Mother, Dad, and the younger version of herself. The dining tables had been pushed to the sides, and two long sofas sat incongruously in the centre of the space, with a wooden desk between them and a few chairs scattered around. The tall windows at the back spewed icy light down on the occupants, who were spectres, frozen in time.

The chandelier was there, with that rope hanging from it.

That rope.

'Remember: it's just a memory,' Alexander told the real Drayn.

She nodded. 'That's what I'm afraid of.'

The people of the memory came to life.

'When is he getting here?' asked Dad.

'Soon,' said Mother.

'And Cranwyl knows … everything?'

'He knows his role, yes. When things are done, he'll come and stay with us. He would like to live here very much.'

There came a sound of footsteps from a door at another side of the Hall.

'Simeon is coming,' Mother said.

Dad rested a hand on the shoulder of the young Drayn: the Drayn of the memory.

'We should let her go, Lyna.'

Mother shook her head. 'She's staying.' She turned her eyes on her daughter. 'It's not easy leading this House. It's time you knew that.'

Simeon emerged through the door at the back of the Hall. He had dressed as if this was a state occasion, which for him it probably was. He wore a red doublet, offset with the white fur of some beast, along with black trousers and heavy dark boots. His hair had been slicked back with the Autocrat knew what muck, and his cheeks seemed to glow with a new freshness. Drayn felt a pang of anger when she saw him. *He deserved what happened.* But no – this was the voice of Mother.

Cranwyl came behind, carrying a sheaf of papers under his arm. A sword hung from his side.

Simeon clapped his hands as he approached the small group. 'Well, here we are. The moment of justice.' He grinned at his sister. 'Lyna, I just wanted to say, I've been very impressed with your restraint. Cranwyl and his men were up all night, on patrol, waiting for your assassins. But they never came. And now, to find the doors of old Thonn House lying open for me … well, it's been wonderful.'

He raised his eyebrows. 'But then, everyone on the island knows what you've done, don't they? So you couldn't very well kill me. And you all rather *depend* on me now, don't you, as head of the House – you could be homeless at my word. So maybe I shouldn't be so grateful. That's always been one of my problems: I'm too trusting.'

If you only knew.

'Still, here we are. Cranwyl – the papers.'

The servant bowed, and spread the parchments on the desk between the sofas.

'This shouldn't take too long,' Simeon said. 'We'll get everything signed off, and all of us can get on with our lives.' He reached into a pocket and withdrew a quill, which he handed to Mother.

The woman took the quill, and sat down on a sofa. She opened the desk and withdrew a small pot of ink, before seeming to catch herself. 'This is a serious business,' she said, 'but there's no reason we can't be civil about it.' She placed the quill down and lifted a small bell from the table. 'We will have wine.'

She raised the bell, but Simeon stopped her with a motion.

'Don't be stupid, Lyna. I'm not drinking or eating anything in this house until you're long gone.'

Mother feigned shock. 'I'm hurt by your lack of trust, Simeon. Besides, you've got everything sewn up, haven't you? Old Cranwyl has told half the island of my shame.' She nodded at the servant, who stared coldly back at her.

Good old Cranwyl, always so smart. He'll get himself out of whatever mess he's in. Of course he will.

'Indeed so,' said Simeon. 'But it wouldn't be wise of me to take risks now, would it? We all know what kind of people you are.' He grinned at Dad. 'Apologies, Teron, I don't mean you.' He nodded at Drayn. 'Or you, my darling, for that matter. Neither of you deserved to get caught up in this. With *her.*'

Teron nodded at his brother-in-law, and moved away from the little group, to the side of the Great Hall, where he began to set a fire in the stone hearth.

'So,' Simeon clapped his hands, 'let's get on with it, then.'

Lyna shrugged. 'It looks like you've got me in an impossible situation.' She snatched up the quill, dipped it in the ink, and began to scrawl her name on the various papers. When she was done she placed the quill back on the table, and leaned back in the sofa.

Simeon stared at the papers for a moment, in silence. He clasped his hands behind his back, nervously twiddling his fingers together. The real Drayn watched the memory Drayn, remembering every moment. She had locked these events away, but things like this could not stay locked up forever.

Teron returned to the group, and glanced at the papers. His fire had sparked into furious life, and there was a sheen of sweat on his forehead.

'It is done, then,' said Drayn's uncle. He turned to Cranwyl. 'Finish the job.'

The servant nodded, and unsheathed his sword, a heavy, ugly blade. Drayn had not been afraid. This dance was playing to Mother's tune, like everything else in the House of Thonn.

The servant walked up to Teron, and held the blade at

the man's throat.

Simeon grinned at Lyna. 'I really don't trust you, you see, Lyna. I hope you're not offended. In fact, you should take it as a compliment.'

Mother stood, and dusted herself down. If she was disturbed by this turn of events, she did not look it.

'How would you like to do it then, Lyna? Girl first, so she doesn't have to see her parents' blood? Or could you not bear to see her die yourself? It's a tricky choice, but I leave it to you. The last decision you will make as head of the House of Thonn.'

The real Drayn looked at her younger self, at that calm face and steady hands as the girl stood motionless beside her father. *Would I be like that now?*

Lyna cleared her throat. 'I don't understand, Simeon.'

'Then you are a fool. It has always been this way in the House of Thonn.'

Mother raised a finger. 'That's not it. I mean, I don't understand the mechanics of your plan. Who is going to carry out these murders for you?'

Simeon hesitated, before nodding at Cranwyl. 'My servant, of course.'

Mother smiled. 'That is not your servant.'

Everything changed in a heartbeat. Cranwyl swapped Dad for Simeon, who made a strange, strangled little noise as the blade was pushed against his throat. Yes, that was it – a *squeal*. Drayn remembered hating him, in that moment. She hated him still.

'This is not how you die,' said Lyna. Her voice was quiet, but trilled with excitement. She turned to Teron. 'Do it.'

Dad ran to the side of the Hall and shouted an instruction. As he returned, the chandelier began to creak downwards.

'What is this, Lyna?' Simeon's eyes shifted from the chandelier to the sword. 'What the *fuck* are you doing? You've signed everything now! Cranwyl has told the island of your deceit!' He swung his eyes to the servant, whose face held a ghost of a smile. 'You did, didn't you, Cranwyl? You told them, for me?' Pleading, now. 'You wouldn't let me down, would you, Cranwyl?'

'What does the blade tell you?' Cranwyl asked.

The chandelier stopped, perhaps four feet above their heads. The rope swung from it; it had been knotted into a loop.

Cranwyl hauled Simeon directly underneath the rope. Father grabbed it, and was about to put it around the struggling man's throat, when Mother spoke.

'No. Let Drayn do it.'

She turned to her daughter, whose face had blanched.

'It is in moments like this that the House of Thonn sustains itself over the millennia. If you are to lead it, one day ...' She did not finish the sentence.

'Did you kill that man?' It was the first time Alexander had spoken in a while, and it made the real Drayn jump. 'Did you really do it? I bet the Voice would like it, if you did.'

She did not answer. She turned back to the scene in the Hall, where the girl in the memory was climbing on a chair, taking the noose from her father, and placing it around her uncle's throat. Simeon looked at her, but he did not move; Cranwyl held him tightly. Cranwyl would always protect Drayn. Cranwyl would always keep her safe.

'You did it!' Alexander cried, almost triumphantly.

Drayn's father returned to the back of the hall, as Simeon

scrabbled at the rope. Teron called to the servants beyond the door, and the chandelier began to rise.

They came to another memory.

It was the same day, but evening now. The Drayn of the memory was alone in her bedroom, staring out of the window. She would have stared forever, if it hadn't been for Cranwyl.

'Your mother sent me up.'

He was standing in her doorway with a plate of food.

Drayn nodded to a table by her bed, and Cranwyl laid the food there. He walked to Drayn's side.

'You know, that's just the way of it among the great Houses. Your mum was right.'

'Mother. Don't call her mum.'

'I apologise.'

They stood in silence for a moment.

'I know, by the way,' Drayn said, in a quiet voice. 'But I never chose this.'

Cranwyl nodded. 'It is too serious. You are a child.' He seemed to think of something. 'When something nasty happens, all you have to do is hide it away,' he said. 'Do you understand? Only really clever people can do it, and *you* are really clever.'

The young girl furrowed her eyebrows. 'I just ... stop thinking about it?'

'Yes. You hide it away so deep that even *you* can't find it. Do you understand?'

The girl bit her bottom lip, and nodded.

'Good. Now, are there any decent places to play in this house?'

Drayn gave him a suspicious look. She had never played with anyone before.

'I'm sure we can find decent places to play,' Cranwyl said.

And then, as if it were nothing, he gave her a tap on the head.

'You're it.'

The servant turned, and charged out of Drayn's quarters. She remained still for a moment, before bustling after him, laughing wildly.

'You just ... forgot?' Alexander asked the real Drayn. 'That's impressive. Not everyone can just forget.'

The girl nodded. 'Yes. I thought I had, anyway. It got harder later, when I had to forget ... other things.'

The memory faded, and another bloomed to life.

209

Chapter Twenty-Three

The light returned, and Aranfal was somewhere else.

It was night, and the moon gazed down. The wind howled around them, suggesting they were in some elevated place. Rocks and masonry were all around. *The remains of some great building?*

Ah.

It was the Circus, the great stadium on Primary Hill, built on the very spot where the Operator had first appeared to Arandel ten thousand years before, bringing with him the gift of the Machinery. *If that ever even happened.* Aranfal had not been here since the Selection, when Katrina became Mother and she and Shirkra had torn the building to pieces. Why would he come back? No one did, any more. This was a desolate place.

They were high up in the ruins of the structure, where the Tacticians of the Overland had once sat, gazing over their subjects. All of them dead, now, except for Canning, the poor fool. *And Brightling. She's gone, but she lives. She'll come back for us one day.*

He pushed the thought away. It was perhaps best not to think treacherous thoughts when surrounded by creatures like Shirkra, beings so powerful they could twist your memories into a torture chamber.

'What are we doing here?' he asked.

Shirkra and the Gamesman were standing together. She was wearing her mask, and had thrown an arm across his shoulder. The Gamesman did not seem entirely comfortable.

'We are here to see what the Gamesman has wrought, of course!' Shirkra cried. She turned to Aranfal. 'He's been so busy!' The eyes sparkled beneath the mask. 'Do you know why the Centre was empty of people, Aranfal? Hmm? Have you guessed the reason?'

'No.' *But I fear for them.*

'Don't look so worried!' Shirkra laughed. 'They're quite safe. The Gamesman is a gentle soul, you see. He told us the truth, earlier, when he pretended to be Illarus. He really did shoo them all out of the Centre. Oh yes, he really did. They've fled all over the place, now, to wherever they think is safe. Who cares though, hmm? Once Ruin comes, it doesn't matter where they're hiding. Ruin will find them.'

'Why did he get rid of them all?'

The Gamesman gave a nervous smile, and gently freed himself of Shirkra's arm.

'I hope it is to your satisfaction, my lady,' he said.

He raised an arm into the sky, and tapped his fingernails together. Nothing happened at first. But after a while, Aranfal became aware of a great, grinding noise; the rubble of the Circus began to tremble, and the ground under the Watcher's feet started to shake. Something flashed across the sky, a purple light, and then *she* was there, just for a second, Mother herself, imposed upon the moon.

The broken marble beneath them began to shift, and Aranfal found himself pitching this way and that, barely able to stay on his feet. Great dusty heaps came together, merging into new forms, terrible shapes in the darkness. The walls of the building, much of which had been shattered in the Selection of Katrina Paprissi, grew once more, curving upwards, so that the great Circus of the Overland was once again complete.

But this was not the building that Jandell had created ten thousand years before. This was something else entirely. Torches burned along the sides, and Aranfal saw that the marble of the walls and the seats was now a purple hue: the colour of the Strategist. Once, four great statues of the Operator – Jandell – had stood at points along the walls. Now, statues of Mother took their place. These were giant, larger even than those of Jandell, monstrous things, painted in vivid colours, so that the purple of the rags was a startling contrast with the paleness of her skin and the black of her hair. As with the old statues of Jandell, each representation of the Strategist was different to the next. In one, she stood tall and erect, her arms in the air and her face pointing to the sky. In another, she was hunched over, facing directly into the bowl of the great stadium; she wore her mask, the white rat, and her purple eyes flickered beneath. In the third statue, she seemed melancholic; her shoulders were slumped, and she held her mask lankly at her side. And finally, she was the victorious Strategist that had long been prophesied, the One who would bring Ruin; she wore her mask with pride, staring down at the Circus with anger flashing in her eyes. She held a short blade in one hand, and raised the other into a fist.

Aranfal turned his attention to the Circus itself. This was where the people of the Overland had come, in older days, to witness the Selections. The Portal to the Machinery sat

212

in the centre of the floor; a terrible flame would erupt from it, bringing with it the names of those lucky enough to be elevated to the greatest of all glories. In the new Circus, the Portal remained, but at its side was a giant table, its stout legs driven firmly into the ground. It looked to Aranfal like a massive Progress board. When the Watcher looked down at it, its surface seemed to shift; the squares became circles and hexagons, and the colours switched from black to white and back again.

Eight chairs had been set up around the board, formed of a dark wood, almost growing from the ground of the Circus, twisted and sprouting black leaves.

'Eight chairs,' said Shirkra. 'One for Mother. One for me. Three for the Queen.' She turned to the Gamesman and scrutinised him. 'Who are the other players?'

The Gamesman shrugged. 'I cannot tell, as you well know, Madam Shirkra.' He swept an arm across the Circus. 'But do you like it? Are you pleased with me?'

Shirkra turned on the Gamesman with a dark smile. 'I could not be happier, my love, I could not be happier. Placing the board by that Portal of Jandell's – a triumph! What a way to humiliate him!'

'What is this place?'

The Gamesman and Shirkra twisted their necks to stare at Aranfal. The Watcher had not meant to speak; the words had just tumbled out. *By the Machinery, you must get a grip on Aran Fal, and become Aranfal again.*

'This is the Circus, of course,' Shirkra said, pacing towards him. 'But a new version. *Our* version.' Her green eyes flashed. 'It is greater than it ever was, don't you think?'

The Watcher turned back to the board. 'What is the game?'

Shirkra laughed. She gripped Aranfal by the shoulder, and

suddenly they were standing at the table, staring at the board. The Watcher was only able to look at it for moments at a time; the shapes and patterns that moved across its surface were too strange for him to comprehend, a tapestry of weirdness.

'What is the game?' he asked again.

'This is not the game. This is just the board, on which we *watch* the game.'

'But what *is* it?' Aranfal looked up to the heights of the Circus, where he could just make out the Gamesman, standing alone, a vision of sadness. 'What has the Gamesman made?'

Shirkra put her arm around the Watcher, and forced him to stare at the board. Acting on some inner impulse, Aranfal took his raven mask from his cloak and placed it on his face. He looked once more at the maelstrom and, for just a moment, he thought he saw his own face, reflected there in the chaos.

'This is a map of the Old Place,' Shirkra whispered. 'Like the Old Place, it moves in strange ways. Like the Old Place, only *we* can begin to understand it – and even we know only some of its mysteries, oh yes.'

Shirkra walked to one of the chairs, on the far side of the table. She pulled it out and sat down, sighing with pleasure.

'This is where I will sit, hmm? I will sit here, when we play.'

Aranfal went to her side. 'How is the game played?'

Shirkra chuckled. 'We are creatures of memory, Aranfal the torturer; we love memories beyond all things. And the Old Place is formed of them – in its very bones! We send our pieces there, in the game, to go through the memories it holds, searching for the very first one – the oldest one of all! Oh, we would give *anything*, we Operators, to know the First Memory of the Old Place – can you imagine what that might be? Can you imagine the *power* such an ancient memory must hold?'

Aranfal shook his head.

'No. Of course not. How could you? And yet, neither can we. The Old Place did not like it when we looked, so now we send mortals to search for us. The Old Place tolerates them; it loves them. But it is a dangerous journey, you must realise. The Old Place is memory, and memory is capricious. It often turns against our pawns, and … well, it does not treat them kindly, oh no, not kindly at all.'

Aranfal felt a growing sense of danger.

'How does the game actually *work*?'

Shirkra looked up at him, and a wicked grin was visible beneath the mask.

'Each of the players chooses a pawn to work on our behalf – to enter the Old Place, and search for us, with their beady little eyes, look look look for the First Memory! We watch their progress here, on the table.'

The unwelcome sensation bloomed in Aranfal's belly.

'How is the game won?' he asked.

'Why, isn't it obvious? Whoever's pawn finds the First Memory of the Old Place is immediately declared the winner!'

'But you haven't found it yet, have you?'

'Hmm, well, no, that is true, Watcher, that is true, ha ha. Whoever owns the longest-living pawn is the winner. Before the Old Place can stand them no longer, and takes them away to only it knows where. Or worse. Ha!'

The Watcher looked around, and saw that the seats in the Circus were filling up. Thousands of spectators were entering the great stadium, ghostly figures, men and women, boys and girls.

'How have they … they are so quiet …'

'They are like us,' the Gamesman said, now at Shirkra's side. 'No – they are like me. Younger immortals, following the older ones like animals. Some are weak, and some are strong, but most of them are cruel.'

'That's why he made the people leave the Centre!' Shirkra cried. 'He always does that, he always does! He is so soft, so soft, yes! He wanted them to run away before the audience arrived. He worries about the humans – he does not trust the immortals, his own brethren!'

'I understand,' Aranfal said.

'Yes, of course you understand, Aranfal, of course you do!' Shirkra was leering at him. 'You are so very, very clever! That is why you will do well, I feel.'

Oh no.

'What do you mean?'

Shirkra reached into her gown, and withdrew a small figurine. Aranfal crouched down and studied it for a moment. It was a perfect likeness of himself, carved in glass.

'This is one of the pieces,' the female Operator said.

Aranfal sighed, and he meant it. 'Then I am your pawn. That's why I'm important to you all. I'm just a pawn in this game.'

'Oh no, oh no!' Shirkra reached into her gown again, and withdrew another figurine. This one showed a young woman, plump, with unkempt hair. It was Aleah, the Watcher who had nipped at his heels all these years.

Good. At least she might die, too.

'*This* is my pawn. She is *wonderful.*'

'Then who—'

And she was among them: Mother. She smiled at Aranfal,

the smile of Katrina Paprissi: the smile of the face he had known and despised for so, so long.

She lifted him with one arm, and held him above her head.

'You are *my* pawn, torturer.'

With a flick of her arm, she tossed Aranfal into the Portal. The crowd cheered.

Chapter Twenty-Four

The Listener liked having a guest.

There were many rooms in her house, and she took Brightling on a frantic tour, carrying her strange black instrument with her as she went. Some of the rooms were oddly familiar to the former Tactician: receptions like she had known in the See House; small closets and bedrooms, similar in many ways to the sparse chambers she had slept in all her life. Others, though, were different, and somehow jarring, filled with objects unlike anything she had seen before.

Eventually they came to a large and airy space, the ceiling a dark blue and sprinkled with silver specks, like the sky at night. The Listener threw herself down and stared upwards. Brightling looked too, and for a moment it seemed she really was looking at a night sky: the moon glowered down at her amid the stars, and a comet streaked past her vision. But the image disappeared, and she found herself gazing once again at an ordinary ceiling.

'Are we still inside, Listener? For a moment ...'

The Listener leapt up and fixed Brightling with a quizzical look.

'For a moment what? What did you see?'

Brightling paused. 'It seemed that we were outside, my lady.'

The Listener cocked her head to the side.

'That is what *I* see, when I am here. This is a strange place. Funny, that you can see with the eyes of an immortal.'

'Not all the time. Only now, and only for a moment.'

The Listener threw her head back and laughed.

'Only for a moment! Oh, if you knew our age, you mortal thing, you would know what a moment is to us! Still, seeing the true glory of the Old Place for a moment is better than never seeing it at all. Perhaps your time with Jandell and the pretty little mask he gave you has had an effect on you. Let us look upon this place together, as it truly should be seen.'

The Listener waved a hand, and the black ceiling became the night sky once more. But now the whole scene had been transformed. They were standing on a hill, its surface gleaming with wet grass. In the centre was a narrow platform, a kind of needle, thrusting high above them. A staircase wound its way around the sides, up into the sky.

'Come,' the Listener said.

They climbed the staircase together. Brightling was reminded of the See House, and for a moment she felt absurdly gloomy, longing to return to her tower. She cast the notion aside. *My See House is gone forever.*

The top of the tower was a smooth, circular expanse, formed of a kind of grey slate. In the centre was a black wooden box. The Listener walked to it, beckoning Brightling to join her. She leaned over and snapped open the lid before reaching inside and removing another of her instruments. It was thin and black, like the one she held herself.

'This is a strange part of the Old Place, where I can hear many things,' the Listener said. 'But even in this place, I cannot hear the Voice.'

The Listener pressed her own instrument to her ear, and handed the other to Brightling. The former Tactician stared at it for a moment, running a finger along its surface, from the narrow point at one end to the wider opening that bloomed from the other side. She did not want to put this thing to her ear. She did not want to hear the things the Listener heard. She was certain she could not bear the weight. Perhaps the Listener knew this; perhaps she wanted to torment her mortal captive.

But Brightling put it to her ear all the same. The Listener stared into her eyes, holding her own instrument at a jaunty angle.

'Can you hear anything?'

Brightling listened carefully, but nothing came from the other end.

'No.'

The Listener sighed and nodded. 'I thought that perhaps that mask of yours would give you an ear. It is a powerful thing, that mask; I wondered if some of it had ... But no. I am a dreamer. Come – we will return to my chambers.'

She clicked her fingers, and they were once more in the Listener's quarters. A table had been spread with food, and a glass of wine had been placed next to a chair.

'This is for you, Brightling,' the Listener said.

Brightling took a seat, and began to eat. She realised, now, that she did not trust the Listener. There was something cruel about the woman, and her addiction to spying on all crea-tion. Still, the Watcher did not want to starve, and her belly told her that was possible, even in the Underland.

When Brightling had finished, the Listener took her to another room, a short walk down a low-ceilinged hallway.

A four-poster bed stood in the centre, covered with a black veil. A white nightgown hung at the side, along with a brown shirt and trousers and a pair of dark boots.

'Goodnight, Brightling,' the Listener said. 'I will return to my post, and listen again.'

The woman bowed, and left Brightling alone. The Watcher ignored the nightgown and changed into the clothes, pulling on the boots. She wrapped herself in her cloak, crawled into the bed, and against her better judgement, fell asleep.

She awoke to a crash.

Decades of experience sparked in the Watcher's muscles. She leapt from the bed, preparing to defend herself. But she knew, even in the second it took her to find her feet, that she was entirely alone.

It was gloomy in the room. A row of candles had been lit along the wall, and flickered strangely, as if in a breeze. *But no window is open. There are no windows.*

She studied the scene. No one had entered; the door was firmly shut. At the side, however, she saw the instrument. She could not remember bringing it with her when she came here. Had the Listener brought it? Or had it come of its own accord? Anything was possible in this place. *No. I must have taken it, and leaned it against the wall. It fell over. That explains the sound I heard.*

She lifted the instrument and examined it in the candlelight. It was strangely cool to the touch, and utterly black: in a way, it reminded her of her mask. The thought of the mask made her long for it. She removed it from its hiding place and studied it with that familiar blend of affection and fear. It was a woman, tonight, her features soft and delicate, the mouth firmly closed.

She held it next to the instrument, one of the items in each hand. At first, she thought she was seeing things. But no: the more she looked, the clearer it became. The instrument was trembling.

She did not know what compelled her to do it. Perhaps she just wanted to see what would happen. It didn't matter, in the end.

She lifted the instrument to her ear, and she listened.

Where did you get that mask?

Brightling threw the instrument down. She knew in a heartbeat what this was. This was the Voice the Listener had searched for all these years: the Voice that had spoken to Squatstout and to Alexander Paprissi. She was certain of it. It was old and tired, and its words were laced with pain; it wanted others to share in its suffering.

The instrument trembled again. Against her better judgement, she put it to her ear once more.

I know you! You are Brightling: the great fool.

'What do you mean?' She began to tremble.

You took Katrina Paprissi. You kept the One safe. What a service you performed!

This was the creature that was trapped within the Machinery, demanding Squatstout find it a host. How many millions had died – thrown off the edge of a cliff – in that endless search?

'You are nothing but a voice,' Brightling whispered. 'And I have something that you fear. I know what my mask is. I can hurt your kind when I wear it. I hurt Jandell and Squatstout, without even meaning to. Imagine what I will do to you. I will destroy you, and then I will find the thing that holds Katrina, and I will set her free.'

The door opened, and the Listener entered.

Keep away from me, the Voice said. **Keep away from me, keep away from the One, and you may live.**

The words were defiant, but Brightling sensed something else there. *Fear. Fear of me, and fear of my mask.*

'I heard a noise,' the Listener said. She looked at the Watcher, who still held the instrument to her ear. 'What are you doing?'

'Nothing.' Brightling threw the instrument on the ground.

'Were you listening? *Did you hear something?*'

Brightling shook her head. 'No.' Information was power, and she would keep hers to herself.

'Very well.' The Listener nodded, but did not seem convinced. 'I will come for you in the morning.'

She left the room. Brightling climbed into bed, her mask and the instrument in her arms, and stared at the veil until morning came, or whatever passed for morning in this place.

The Listener came with it.

'You lied to me in the night,' she said. She walked to the side of the bed and studied the Watcher. Brightling was not afraid. There was no anger in the Listener's eyes: just curiosity. The Listener twirled a blonde curl around her little finger. 'I have thought about what you said. I listen to everything, you know. No one has ears like mine. And I know you lied.'

She took the instrument from Brightling. 'What did you lie about, Brightling?' She held the instrument to her eye, and peered at it carefully. 'Why did you lie?'

Brightling rattled through her options. *The truth is likely as good as anything, in this place.* She climbed out of the bed.

'I'm sorry. I was afraid.'

223

'That is not the whole truth.'

Brightling sucked in a breath. 'I heard a voice.'

The Listener grasped Brightling by her shoulders. 'A *voice*? Was it *the* Voice? What did it say?'

'It ...' She thought of lying, but realised she needed the Listener's help to crawl through this maze. 'It is a ... darkness.' She held her mask in her hand. 'It is a thing of memory, isn't it?'

The Listener nodded. 'Of course, of course, we all are.'

'Then I have something that could hurt it.' She put on her mask. Through its eyes the Listener seemed small, and old indeed. Brightling was gratified to see fear, and pain, in her eyes. Brightling concentrated, as she had been trained to do as a Watcher, all those years. *The mask must become your second skin ... your inner eyes ...*

'Please, stop,' the Listener whispered.

Brightling nodded, and removed the mask.

'I will right the wrongs they have committed: the One, and Ruin. With this – the last part of the Absence.'

The Listener clicked her fingers, and they were once again on the tower upon the hill. It was daylight; a cold, pale sun glared down at them.

The Listener gestured at Brightling's mask. 'That thing – it has a power. But then, so does the Voice.'

Brightling nodded. 'I will destroy it.' Something was pushing her forward, down a dark and tangled path. *Instinct.* 'Just show me the way to the Voice. Show me to the Machinery.'

The Listener grinned. 'You don't need *me* to show you the way.' She looked down at the ground. 'They will take you where you need to go.'

Brightling glanced at the tower floor. She barely had time

to see the white hands, before they pulled her into darkness.

Chapter Twenty-Five

Brandione marched into the desert at the head of his army of dust.

The sands stretched on interminably. There was no wind here, but occasionally, he thought he saw movement in the emptiness: a swirl amid the dust. He wondered if *she* was out there, watching him, guiding the army on its march. But he dismissed the notion. He could always feel her, when she was nearby.

Wayward was at his side, buried under a mass of black robes.

'How long have we been here?' Brandione asked. The sands sucked up his words.

Wayward turned his head to him. 'Since the march began. We must march on, ever on, across the desert.'

'I remember we were in the tent, you and I. That was my life, wasn't it? The tent, and the Queen.'

'Life moves on.'

'I feel no heat. I have no thirst. How can that be? Is this even real?'

'Real? Am I real, Brandione? Is the Queen real?'

Brandione did not respond. He stopped walking, turned

his head, and looked back, to his endless troops. They trudged forward with a deadening rhythm, these pale creatures of sand, before coming to a halt. Their shapes and features shifted when he focused on them. In one moment, they were clearly crafted figures, a man with a fat face or a child with long hair. But in the next, they were barely visible amid the waves of sand.

'If you had to choose between being a soldier or a scholar, which would it be?'

Brandione turned back to Wayward.

'I made that choice when I joined the armies of the Overland.'

'Oh. I thought you would find the decision more agonising than that. I'm quite disappointed, truth be told.'

'I'm sorry to disappoint you.'

'No, you're not. Anyway, I don't believe you. You don't prefer being a soldier to a scholar, because you don't see a need to choose. You were an ambitious student. You read deeply of history, and it gave you a will to succeed beyond the dusty halls of the Administrators or the creaking shelves of the libraries. You feared you were a coward, brave only in debate, courageous only in his thoughts. You wanted to prove yourself, and you succeeded, so much so that you climbed to the top of the military tree, even though you inserted yourself at the lowliest possible position.'

Wayward grinned at Brandione.

'Sounds like you've figured me out,' the one-time General replied.

'Well, we've been thinking about you for thousands of years, my good man.'

'Then I am at a disadvantage.' He turned to the empty horizon. 'I would like to be with the Queen again. I have so much more to ask her.'

'You will see her when you see her,' Wayward said. 'She knows what you need.' He smiled. 'But it is almost upon us. We are nearing the board! We are nearing the game!'

Brandione saw nothing but the usual rolling sands.

'Wayward, I will not lie to you. I'm not ready for this game, whatever it may be. How do I find a memory? I feel like I need more help.'

'More help? Pah! Nothing can help you in the Old Place!'

Brandione sighed.

The courtier placed a hand on his shoulder. 'You are the Last Doubter. You are a soldier and a scholar. You will know what to do, in the end.' He chuckled. 'Besides – you cannot disappoint your audience.'

'What?'

Wayward gestured to the West. After a while, Brandione could just about make out shapes: figures, shadowing the path of the dust army.

'Who are they?'

'Immortals: weak ones, like me. They follow their betters like parasites, and live off their glory.'

Suddenly Wayward stopped talking. He looked to the horizon, and smiled.

'Do you know where you are yet?'

Brandione looked ahead. At first he saw nothing but the sands and the sky. After a while, though, something strange began to happen. Shapes began to form. The contours of buildings emerged, and great domes and glimmering spires shot up from the ground. For a moment, he wondered if he had gone mad, or if this was some effect of the desert: *mirages*, they were called. But no, that could not be possible. Wayward saw it, too.

'If I didn't know better,' Brandione said, 'I'd say that was the Centre of the Overland. But it can't be, can it? We haven't reached the southern settlements, let alone the Far Below.'

Wayward shrugged. 'The desert has taken us here, Brandione. The desert has taken us.'

Far ahead, a hill had appeared, rising above the rest of the city. On the top was a building, a monstrosity of marble with a purple hue. Great statues loomed up from the structure; they were too far away to make out the details, but Brandione knew what he was looking at.

'They have rebuilt the Circus,' he said. 'But this time, it has been made for the Strategist.' He looked at Wayward. 'That's where we're going, isn't it?'

Wayward nodded. 'From now on, you will be alone. I will stay here, with the dead.' He gestured at the army.

Brandione felt suddenly cold. 'What is the point of the army, if it cannot come with me?'

Wayward reached out, and touched the Last Doubter's face. 'The Queen knows what she has done, and we all must follow the Queen.'

Brandione turned back to the Circus. The sand had melted away below him, and he found himself standing on a stone path, snaking its way forward to the Primary Hill.

He looked once more at Wayward and his useless army of dust, and started walking to the Circus, to whatever awaited him there.

Chapter Twenty-Six

'You are finding all of this difficult, Drayn.'

The girl looked at Alexander, startled. She felt as if she had been woken from a dream.

'I put things away, you see. I try to get rid of them, so I don't have to think about them again. You're making me relive them.'

'Not me, Drayn.' Alexander wore a serious expression. 'This hasn't got anything to do with me.'

They were in the grounds of the great house. It was said there was not much land on the Habitation, and that the Thonns owned half of it. Drayn wasn't sure of that. But as she looked around the garden, she thought it might be true. The house itself seemed far from where they stood, just at the edge of the woods that clustered around the back of the property. In front of the trees was a wide stretch of water that the Thonns called the pond, though it was more of a lake, really.

Drayn and Alexander were standing between the woods and the pond. The trees were dark, and chirped with life.

'I don't recognise this memory, Alexander.'

The boy shrugged. 'We may be seeing it from a different

angle than you remember.'

'How can that be? If this is my memory, wouldn't we see it just exactly as I remember?'

'Not necessarily. Memories are their own things, especially in the Old Place.' He looked up at the sky, and his attention seemed fixed on a distant point. Drayn followed the direction of his gaze, until she saw it: a kind of tear in the fabric of the great blue expanse, crackling with a black energy.

'What is that?'

Alexander sighed. 'Memories are such funny, terrible things.'

There was a flurry of noise, and Cranwyl burst out from the trees. *Not the real Cranwyl. Not my Cranwyl. Just a memory.* He ran *through* them, as if they were nothing more than puffs of air. Drayn didn't know why that still came as a surprise, down here, in a world where she could walk through memory.

Cranwyl hurried to the edge of the pond and turned back to the forest, wildly scanning the trees. Twigs and branches were caught in his hair, and his clothes were muddy.

'I remember this now,' Drayn said, smiling at Alexander. 'This is about a year after Simeon ... you know. It's the *only* time I caught Cranwyl. *Ever.*'

Alexander looked around him. 'I can't see you anywhere.'

'That's because you're looking in the wrong places. Like Cranwyl.'

At the edge of the water, just next to where Cranwyl was now crouching, there was the slightest of movements.

'Ah,' Alexander said.

The waters parted and Drayn leapt out, throwing herself upon Cranwyl with a blood-curdling scream. Cranwyl cried out, and the pair of them bowled forward onto the ground.

'At last!' shouted the Drayn from the memory, her knees on Cranwyl's chest. She was utterly sodden, her clothes a muddy mess. Still, she had won.

This was her happiest memory.

'That's not fair!' Cranwyl spluttered. 'No one said you could hide in the pond!'

'No one said I couldn't hide in the pond, either.'

'No, well, yeah, I suppose you have a point.' His eyes narrowed. 'How did you breathe? Are you magical?'

Drayn cried out in triumph, and raised her hand before her friend, displaying a round tube she had fashioned from a stick. Her little games with Cranwyl had given her such focus, back then. They were just what she had needed.

Cranwyl took her by the arms and gently pushed her away. 'Very clever. Very, very clever.' He stood, and wagged a finger at her. 'But you won't catch me out like that again. I'll put some bitey fish in the pond.'

'Bitey fish?'

'Hmm, yeah. You won't want to hide in there, when the bitey fish are in the water.'

There was a movement far ahead, at the house itself.

'Here she comes,' sighed the real Drayn. 'Here to spoil my five minutes of fun.'

Mother was smiling when she came to the pond, but that didn't mean much where she was concerned. Drayn and Cranwyl turned guiltily towards her, hands behind their backs, standing up straight and formal. The real Drayn watched this with disgust. *I never should have let her frighten me like I did.*

Mother's smile was a fleeting thing, as it often was.

'Drayn, you are wet.'

'Yes, Mother.'

Mother looked at Cranwyl. 'How did she get wet?'

'She hid from me in the pond, madam. And she caught me!'

Mother squinted.

'Well. That sounds like fun.' She turned her focus back to her daughter. 'It's almost time for dinner. Get into the house, and by the Autocrat's nose, clean yourself up.'

Drayn bowed. Mother nodded once to Cranwyl, turned, and walked back to the house.

'I never understand why she always comes for you herself,' Cranwyl said, when Mother was well out of earshot. 'Why doesn't she just send a servant?'

'She wants to keep an eye on me, that's why. She doesn't trust the servants. Except you, Cranwyl.'

Cranwyl nodded, and Drayn walked back to the house.

They were in the private dining room. It was small, at least in comparison with the Great Hall, and far more comfortable, to Drayn's mind anyway. The walls were lined with shelves that groaned under the weight of mementoes and trinkets, from miniature portraits of earlier Thonns to jewellery and statuettes. The floor was overlaid with a deep red rug, woven from the furs of some unknown beast; it was a haven for discarded food, this rug, but no one ever thought to remove it. The room was gently lit by discreetly placed candles, which gave the intimate surroundings a warm glow.

There was no chandelier.

In the centre was a circular wooden table, an old, battered thing that had been in the family for generations. The Drayn of the memory sat between Mother and Dad, attacking her plate of fish with gusto. Mother picked at her food, as ever, and Dad lay back in his chair, worrying at a goblet of wine.

He was drinking more. That was how the badness started.

'You seem happy today, Drayn,' Mother said.

They never mentioned Simeon in the House of Thonn. No one ever said that name again, or at least not within earshot of a Thonn or their servants. This was not the first time that an upstart member of a great House had disappeared. The people were not surprised, and they did not care.

So when Mother said that Drayn seemed happy, she meant it was the happiest the girl had looked since she put a noose around her uncle's neck.

'Yes,' Drayn said, spooning more fish into her mouth. She saw no need to elaborate.

'Cranwyl has been good for you,' Mother said.

Drayn shrugged.

'He has been good for you, Drayn, and he has been good for the House of Thonn. Servants like Cranwyl are hard to come by. We will keep him on forever, I dare say.'

Drayn met her mother's eye. For once, they agreed.

'He has helped me ... with my thoughts,' the girl said.

Mother nodded, and Dad snorted. The female Thonns turned their attention to him. He had been strange, since Simeon went away.

'Perhaps your father needs a Cranwyl of his own,' Mother said.

Dad laughed: a cold sound. 'That would be good, wouldn't it? A Cranwyl, to talk to in the night. Hmm.' He slurped at his wine, then slumped forward in his chair, picking some food up in his fingers. He missed his mouth, and it fell onto his chest.

Mother lifted a small, silver bell from the table and rang it, sending a gentle tinkling through the room. Two male servants appeared from nowhere.

'Take my husband to bed.'

The servants nodded, and hooked Dad up from his chair. He did not object. His head lolled backwards and forwards, and his eyes glazed over.

Mother watched them leave, gave a little shake of her head, and returned to her meal.

'Wine is no good,' she said after a while. 'Stay away from it.'

Drayn nodded. 'I will.'

Mother sighed. 'It's not just the wine, of course. He is still upset by Simeon.'

The dreaded name had been spoken.

'I know.'

Mother studied her daughter for a moment. 'What do you know, Drayn?' Her interest seemed genuine.

Drayn hesitated, before taking the plunge. 'I know he hasn't been the same, since it happened. It wasn't obvious at first. He seemed to think it was the right thing to do, like the rest of us. But he got quiet, after a while. He never used to be quiet. And then he started on the wine. He never used to drink so much wine. He said something to me, once, too, but I don't know—'

'What did he say?'

Drayn paused for a moment. 'He asked me if I was happy, and I said I was. Then he said that was unusual in the House of Thonn.'

Mother tutted. 'What a thing to say to your only child.' She gave Drayn a hard look. 'You shouldn't listen to him, you know. He's weak. I never saw it until now. He doesn't understand what things are like in the House. He's an outsider. You know, we used to marry our cousins – did you know that? Just to avoid bringing outsiders into the family. Only Thonns understand Thonns. This is a hard rock we live on, and the Houses survive by breeding hard people.'

Drayn nodded. 'I think you were right. Dad does need a Cranwyl.'

'What do you mean?'

'Cranwyl made me feel better. He taught me to take the memory, and put it into a box, and keep it closed away, if I couldn't just destroy it completely.'

Mother laughed. 'Cranwyl was right. But he didn't teach you that, darling. You're a Thonn. That's just the way we are.'

Drayn nodded. They sat together in silence, the figures from Drayn's memory, while the real girl and her companion from the Old Place drank in the scene before them. It faded, starting around the edges, until they were immersed in blackness.

The light slowly returned. They had now come to Drayn's bedroom.

The girl was wrapped up tightly under the blankets. Her window was uncovered, and moonlight streamed in upon her. Her eyes were open, and she stared up at the ceiling.

There came a knock at the door, and the memory Drayn sat up in bed.

'Come in.'

Dad entered. He was still drunk – he stank of wine – but he was more composed than before. He found a stool, and took a seat at his daughter's side.

'Sorry about earlier,' he said. 'I wanted to come, and say sorry about earlier.' He put a finger to his mouth. 'But don't tell Mother. You know, she's a bit annoyed about how I was. I'm sorry about that. About earlier.'

'It's all right.'

'It's not all right.' He shook his head and sighed, a deep and raggedy sound that came from somewhere deep inside. 'Sometimes, I wish the hands would just take me, so I could be Unchosen and be done with it.'

'Don't say that. Things will work out. We've just got to keep on with it.' *Mother's words. Mother's voice.*

Dad smiled. 'I'm not a Thonn. Not really. I suppose I thought I was, because I married into the family. But I'm not. *You* are, and it is my greatest mistake.'

'I'm a mistake?'

He drunkenly shook his head. 'No, of course not, by the Autocrat's fingers. But I should never have let her make you into one of them, never, never. When I saw you put that noose around Simeon's neck ... Ah! Maybe I could have taken you away, hmm? It's too late now though. The Thonns run the Habitation, them and the other Houses. No one cares about what they do.' Something flashed across his eyes. 'The Autocrat mustn't know about what she's done. He mustn't know. Otherwise, he would've stopped it, wouldn't he? The Autocrat is the only good thing in the world. He wouldn't let them do what they do, if he knew.'

Dad leaned forward, over his daughter, staring into her eyes.

'We should go and tell him, Drayn! It's not too late!'

'What are you doing?' asked a new voice.

Dad leapt to his feet and spun around, almost toppling over. Mother stood in the doorway. Dad looked at her for a moment, and without saying a word, left the room, brushing gently past her as he went.

Mother smiled at Drayn. 'Get some sleep.'

But Drayn did not sleep.

She stayed awake all night, listening to her father and Mother arguing. She left her room and descended the stairs, and stood outside the door of the Great Hall. She never knew why her parents had gone to that room. Perhaps the memory of Simeon dragged them there.

Alexander and the real Drayn stood alongside the memory girl, outside the door to the hall.

'Well, this is all very interesting,' Alexander said.

The sounds of an argument came from behind the door.

'... the Autocrat doesn't know? Doesn't know what's happening on his own island? The Autocrat knows everything, Teron ...'

'How can he know? I'm going to tell him, Lyna. He'll clear out the Houses for good, then. The Houses have stopped the right person being Chosen—'

'Nonsense. You're drunk, Teron. As usual.'

There was a thud of footsteps and the door swung open. Teron stormed past, without noticing his daughter.

Mother did not seem surprised to find Drayn at the door.

'I'll have a servant watch him tonight,' she whispered. 'He won't go anywhere. We'll let him sleep it off. In the morning, if he still wants to go and make fools of the House of Thonn, well, we can deal with it then. Now go to bed.'

The Drayn in the memory nodded. She knew what her Mother meant, and she knew what would happen next. The scene faded, and another day dawned in the memory world of the Old Place.

Chapter Twenty-Seven

Timmon Canning awoke to a different world.

It was strange; he could not remember falling asleep. But fall asleep he surely had, for he was now lying on a wide, soft bed. He sat up, stretching his arms and examining his surroundings. He was in a large, airy room. It was uncluttered, the only furniture being the bed and a chest of drawers. The floor and walls were formed of a creamy stone. A window lay open, allowing a gentle breeze to play across the thin, transparent curtains.

He yawned. *What happened?* He had no idea how he had come to be in this strange place. He was now wearing a pair of silver pyjamas, which he could not remember putting on, meaning some poor soul must have undressed him before putting him to bed. Still, he was not anxious, which was unusual for him. On the contrary, he felt rested and relaxed, perhaps more so than he had ever been since before his days as a Tactician.

The bed was soft and yielding, and for a brief moment he considered throwing himself back into the arms of sleep. But he felt too good for that. And curious, too: another odd emotion for him. *Where am I, by the Machinery?*

He rolled out of the bed and walked to the window to examine his surroundings. He appeared to be in a coastal town of some sort. His building seemed to be at the top of a hill. Below, white houses stretched to the edge of a sparkling blue sea, and dustless paths snaked their way through clusters of bleached dwellings. People walked by, all of them wearing hooded white gowns. Canning breathed in the salty air, and it cheered him. *I'll live in this place forever. I don't care if they try and kick me out; I'll find my way back in.*

After a long while he turned away from the window. He walked to the door of the room and peered outside, half-expecting the scene to be a terrible trick of Shirkra. But she was not there. An empty corridor greeted him, stretching off to his right: his room must have been at the very end. For a moment, he thought of turning back, and staring out of the window until someone came to get him. But something urged him on. He went out into the corridor, and began to walk.

He eventually came to a hall. It was a large space, rivalling the Map Room of the Overland in the Fortress of Expansion, but different in every other way. Where the Fortress was all shadows and flickering candles, this place was open and filled with sunlight. The hall was made of that same white stone. It put him in mind of the Arboretum in Memory Hall. It had that same light and airy feel, with trees and colourful plants lining the walls and scattered around the centre of the floor. The ceiling was shaped into a great dome, formed of what appeared to be crystal, or perhaps a kind of glass: the sun streamed through in a thousand colours, creating a kaleidoscopic effect.

There were only two people in the hall, as far as Canning could make out: a man and a woman, sitting on black chairs in the centre. They were so alike that Canning thought they must have been twins. For a heartbeat he wondered if they were *those* twins, the ones that Raxx had wounded, in a different manifestation. But surely not: those creatures were far away, and these two were very old, with white hair falling in rings to their shoulders. Their skin was pale, lighter than anything Canning had seen on the Plateau, even among the far northerners. They wore the same white gowns that everyone in this place seemed to favour; from a distance they looked like strange puffs of air, or clouds that had descended to the earth.

He felt calm as he approached them. His time in bed had been good for him, and he was strangely confident.

It was only as he closed in on the old couple that he noticed how still they were. He wondered if they could be statues, crafted by a master whose skills outshone anything they had on the Plateau. He looked around the hall once more, to see if anyone else was there. But it was just the three of them.

He leaned towards the woman. Her narrow face was a patchwork of lines, and her skin seemed thin and frail. Her unblinking eyes were a pale blue, and they were creased with pleasure.

Canning turned to the man. He was almost identical to the woman, but he seemed somehow stronger, more vital.

These people can't be real, can they? He took a last glance around the hall, then reached out his hand, inching it closer to the man's face.

'Oh, hello.'

Canning leapt back with such violence that he fell onto the ground.

The man stood and shook himself, before turning to the

woman and tapping her shoulder. She sparked into life, took a deep breath, and got to her feet. She reached out to the man and took him by the hand.

'How long were we under?' she asked.

The man shrugged. 'Not long. Too long. Who knows? But we're free now.' He turned to Canning. 'Who are you? Where did you come from?'

Canning stood, and jabbed a thumb over his shoulder, at the corridor.

'Back there. I just woke up. I've no idea how long I was asleep.'

'Back there?' asked the woman. She moved forward without appearing to walk. 'There's nothing back there.'

'What?' Canning turned around. The room before him was falling away, becoming a haze of spectral white.

He turned back to the old man and woman, who regarded him with a blend of sympathy and contempt.

'Where am I?' he asked. His sense of contentment had evaporated, replaced with a more familiar wave of fear.

The woman was directly before him. She no longer seemed frail.

'Do you really not know where you are, and what you are doing here?'

He shook his head.

'You have been betrayed,' said the man. 'This happens all the time when they want to test someone. They put you in a memory, with us, or one of our relations, depending on who they've caught. Just to see how you get along.'

'It rarely works out well,' said the woman.

'No, it very rarely works out well at all,' the man echoed. 'We may not be the Duet, but we are quite strong. Stronger than *you*, at any rate.'

Canning looked around again in desperation. The walls at his side had now faded into the whiteness, which was creeping around the room, eating it up, until the three of them were floating in a void.

'He is particularly weak,' said the man.

'I feel sorry for him,' said the woman.

'I do, too, my love. He has been thrown here, with us, without anyone to protect him.'

'But we should not feel guilty, I think. They have used us, too. We did not ask for this.'

'No, we did not ask for it, my love, you are quite correct.'

'It would be rude to turn it up. He is standing before us with his beautiful memories.'

'Yes, his sad and beautiful memories.'

'Yes, we should take them for ourselves, these memories; we can drink them and rejoice in them. They have a kind of melancholic power. Perhaps they would give us strength. Perhaps we could use them to free ourselves.'

'Yes, yes ...'

The white void crept up on the old man and woman, and began to crawl along their skin. It became one with them, seeping into them, tearing them apart, until nothing was left but void, and Canning was utterly alone in the nothingness.

'Come,' said a voice. He could not tell if it was the man or the woman or someone else that spoke. 'Allow yourself to float away, and you will not suffer. All you have to do is float away.'

The void wrapped itself around his body, pinning him to the spot. It probed him, tugging at his thoughts, playing with his memories. It would drain him, if he allowed it.

'You are Operators,' he said. 'This is an Operator trick.'

'This is no trick,' the old man said from nowhere and

everywhere. 'We want your memories. We could do such things with them.'

'We will leave the husk behind,' said the woman.

For a moment, Canning came close to relenting. But then a memory sparked in his mind. He cast himself back to his time as a prisoner, suffering under Shirkra.

He remembered how he had felt when she played with his memories.

He remembered how he used the power of memory to escape.

For once in his life, he had fought back.

Why could he not fight again?

Acting on some strange instinct, he closed his eyes, and turned his thoughts away from the void. He allowed his mind to drift away, though not towards the Operators: to another place, a place within himself. He could hear them speaking, whispering to him of his failures. They told him he would fail again. They said he could not hope to defeat them. But as they spoke, a new tone entered their voices. *Panic.*

They could not control him.

He opened his eyes. He was standing on solid ground, though it was not the white stone of the domed room. The old man and woman were before him, gazing at him in shock. The void was falling away, and a real place was emerging, a hard place of dark colours. But he did not look at it; he knew he had to remain focused.

'No,' said the man. 'How did you do that?'

Canning glanced at his hands, and saw that they were trembling. He clenched his fists together, and the remaining void drifted towards him. He saw things in it, faces from the past, so many millions of people, flickering into nothing.

He gathered it around his arm, like a rope, and threw it at the Operators. It moved slowly, like it was floating through treacle, but there was nothing they could do to escape.

They watched as it encircled them, and they fell backwards.

Suddenly Canning felt capable of anything. He felt himself within the void, entangled with the Operators. He felt himself holding them down. He could reach inside them, if he wished, and drink down their thoughts, all the memories they had collected over long centuries. He felt himself capable of *controlling* them ...

The man and woman were screaming, now, but he barely noticed. He was their master; they had tried to exploit him, and he had turned the tables on them. He felt a sense of real power, stronger even than his experience in the Bowels of the See House. He wanted them to suffer for what they had tried to do. All the rage of his lifetime swirled within him, gathering like a storm. He brought it before his mind's eye. He aimed it at the old man and woman. How long had they walked the world? How long had they tormented others? Their day was done. He was here, Timmon Canning, the vengeance of humanity—

'Enough.'

The void vanished from his grip. The old man and woman lay before him.

Canning gasped, and stumbled backwards. His gaze flickered across the room. This space was just as cavernous as that white, domed room, but it was black, metallic, and monotonous: it reminded him of the foundries of the Fortress, but without the flame and the noise. Even his clothing had changed, the pyjamas replaced with a dark green vest, black trousers and hard boots.

A platform ran across the room, connecting two levels

high above his head. Manipulator Raxx was standing there with a group of men and women that Canning did not recognise. They all wore the same white robes as Raxx. Some of them held their hands in the air, their eyes bone white; they whispered some words, and the old man and woman became still as statues once again.

'You see,' whispered Raxx. 'I *told* you there was something about him.'

'What was that all about, by the Machinery?'

Raxx had taken him away from the dark room, after gathering up the two Operators and sending them to the Machinery knew where. They were now in what he supposed was her study. It was a miniature version of the room they had come from, a space of dark metal. The monotony was somewhat relieved by a painting on the wall, depicting a young boy in white robes, with curly black hair and light brown skin. He was standing on a cliff on the edge of a crashing sea, his arms aloft, his eyes burning with that familiar white intensity.

'You're annoyed with me, Canning.' Raxx took a white chair, and gestured to Canning to sit on another.

'You're very perceptive. Why shouldn't I be annoyed? You tried to kill me.'

'I certainly did not. I would have intervened, if you needed me to.'

'I did need you to.'

'You did? You overpowered two immortals, alone. No one's ever done that in their first go. Not that I remember, anyway.' She smiled. 'Maybe it *wasn't* your first go. Have you battled one of them before?'

Canning ignored the question. 'I don't understand.' He

leaned forward, and placed his head in his hands. He felt suddenly exhausted. 'When I woke up ... I was in such a nice place, like I'd never seen before. Was that all just a lie? How did you fool me, like that? Are you an Operator, too?'

Raxx's eyes widened. 'What a lot of questions to answer!' She laughed. 'Yes, I'm afraid it was a lie – or a memory, which is often the same thing. This city does lie on a harbour, but it is not so pretty as that.' She gestured to a window.

Canning stood and walked to it. Below, there stretched a black and ruined shore. The only buildings he could see were hovels. It was daylight, but even the sun here was pale and insipid, peeking out occasionally from a boiling black mess of clouds. The few people he saw wore dark shawls, and hurried from building to building.

'To answer your second question, I did not trick you. You tricked yourself.' Raxx was at his side, looking out of the window. She seemed far older, then, than the teenager he had taken her for. 'You awoke in a memory, but you could have seen it for what it was, if you had tried. We built a space, in which you and those immortals could test one another, but where we could control them, if we needed to.'

She guided him back to the chairs.

'What is this place?' he asked.

'The Remnants,' she replied. 'All that remains of a broken Empire.'

'What Empire?'

Raxx sighed. 'A place of legend, now, to us, in our misery. A place of dreams. Once, it covered all of our continent, including your Plateau.'

'Impossible. How big could it have been?'

Raxx smiled. 'Very, is the answer. But the size was not important. What mattered were the inhabitants: mortals and immortals, sharing the world. Sharing other things, too: we let them play with our memories. We even let them take some memories away, within reason. In return, they helped us build our Empire, with all their knowledge of the past.'

'Why did it fail?' Canning narrowed his eyes. 'It sounds perfect.'

Raxx shrugged. 'It's not in their nature to share: not all of their natures, anyway. There have been so many different eras of the world, Canning. We know little about them. But you can be sure that we were slaves. To some of the Old Ones, that is the way it should have remained. One of them – a volatile creature – decided to bring an end to the Empire.'

'Shirkra,' Canning said.

For a moment, Raxx seemed curious. 'Yes. She launched an attack on us, and a war began. As you know, Canning, no human army could stand against even one of those things – not back then, anyway. But what would come *after* the war? Should life return to how it was – or should the mortals be enslaved? That was the great question facing the Old Ones, and it divided them deeply. So they decided to do what they had always done, in their arrogance – they would play a *game*, and the winner would decide what to do with us. In this game, the Old Ones used humans as pawns. *Pawns*. Unluckily for them, Jandell selected a very special human as his pawn – his name was Arandel.'

Canning gasped. 'The prophet of the Machinery.'

Raxx nodded. 'Arandel was unlike any other participant in the game, in all of history. He learned something, in the Old Place. He learned how to use the power of memory. He learned how to Manipulate the Operators, even the Old Ones: he could imprison them, or hurt them, or steal from them. A pawn no more.'

'How could he do that?'

Raxx's eyes widened. 'Memories were created long ago, by a god. It's an old word, but it's the only word that suffices. Its name was the Absence: it was a god, and a bit of its power lives on in them.' She held out her palm. 'Memories have a magic in them, Canning. You can hurt someone with a memory. You can learn from their memories. Or you can do other things ... deeper things. You can touch an ancient power.' A small, red flame appeared in her palm, and flickered for a moment, before she snapped it shut.

'Arandel escaped the game. He taught his technique to others: soon, the Operators were no longer playing a game, but fighting for their very survival. It was a war – and we almost won! But Arandel came to an arrangement with Jandell, who built the glorious Machinery for him. He became the first ruler of your country. That was the last contact we had with your people, until very recently.'

Canning was struggling to take this in. 'Why didn't the people here go with Arandel?'

She shrugged. 'Some of us didn't want to leave our home in the South. Others were happy to go, or to stay in the North, but not under the rule of your Machinery. They founded other countries, other nations. I believe you have now destroyed them all.'

Canning nodded. 'I'm afraid so.'

Raxx laughed. 'The Machinery is a wondrous thing indeed.' She rubbed her head, and sighed. 'But the war was not yet over. In fact, it is still being fought today. Two of the most powerful of the Operators remained here, in the South, with many other immortals – not so old, but powerful creatures nonetheless. We have fought them ever since. Sometimes we are able to Manipulate them, and we use their

knowledge to learn of wonderful things, things those creatures remember from older, greater civilisations: cannon and
the like. But at other times, they gain the upper hand, and
they torment us.'

'The Duet. They're the powerful ones.'

She nodded. 'Recently, they went north, as you know. We
chased them. And that's when we found you. I could feel
your abilities, even then. And so I brought you here, to test
you. I wanted to see if you could make a Manipulator. And
I have been very, very impressed.'

She reached down to her side, and produced two mugs,
handing one to Canning. He sniffed it, and screwed up his
nose at the bitter smell.

'This is one of the cities of the Remnants, our term for
the ruined South,' Raxx continued. 'The war here has lasted
for such a long time that the boundaries between the Old
Place and reality have been utterly compromised. It is hard
to tell where the realm of memory ends, and the real world
begins. The only humans who can survive here are the
Manipulators, and the people they protect. The two Autocrats
you confronted were weak. We can control them for long
periods. I doubt you could have got away with a full confron-
tation with the Duet, had you met them unawares.

'Tell me,' Raxx said, standing again and walking to the
painting on the wall. 'What do you see when you look at
this?'

'A boy, on the edge of a cliff.'

Raxx raised her eyebrows. 'Interesting. I see something
completely different. This painting is a creation of the Arch
Manipulator: he formed it from a memory.' She grinned.
'The Arch Manipulator is powerful indeed. You see only
what he wants you to see when you look upon this painting.'

'Who is the Arch Manipulator?'

Raxx clapped her hands together. 'Why don't we go and meet him? I know he will be dying to make your acquaintance. He will admire your natural strength.'

As they left the room, Canning felt weaker than he ever had before, and that was saying something.

Chapter Twenty-Eight

Aranfal opened his eyes.

It was as if a vast, dark beach had been overturned above the world. Everything was covered in black sand, shifting in strange patterns and stretching away into nothingness. The sun burned blood red, hanging like a wound in a sky that was as dark as the sand itself.

'What are the rules?' he said, though no one was there to hear him. 'How do I play the game?'

But no reply came.

The red sun burned in the dark sky, and there was nothing in the world but Aranfal the torturer and the black, black sand.

He sighed, pulled his cloak tight around his body, and began to walk.

Chapter Twenty-Nine

Brandione was once more on the black sands, under their red sun.

How did I get here? He remembered approaching the Circus. Inside, there had been faces, thousands of them, staring and laughing. *Who were they?* And then there was a pit. *No. Not a pit. A Portal.*

'You will not win.'

Brandione turned, and *she* was before him.

He had seen Katrina Paprissi in the flesh only once, and that was a fleeting glimpse during the siege of Northern Blown. Still, he knew immediately that she had been utterly changed. The woman before him was as tall as two people. Her skin was as pale as before, and her hair was still black, but her rags of mourning were now the purple of Strategists, and her eyes sparkled with the same colour. She held a mask in her right hand; as she stared at him, she lifted it to her face and put it on.

Without meaning to do so, Brandione closed his eyes, shutting out this image. But it did not matter; she was still there, in his vision, this beautiful, warped creature, hidden behind the face of a rat.

He opened his eyes again.

'The game will soon begin,' the Strategist said.

This could not be the voice of Katrina Paprissi. This voice was ancient; it was the waves of the Peripheral Sea, or the winds of the Wite. The Strategist smiled beneath her mask, and a ripple passed across the black sands.

'Has it not already begun?' said Brandione.

The Strategist shook her head. 'You are here, but the rules have not been explained. The Gamesman waits for you, far ahead.'

'Who?'

She laughed.

'Memories are strange things, you know. They are never how we remember them.' She chuckled. 'A memory can bring us warmth, or a memory can freeze us. A memory is a friend, and a memory is an enemy. A memory is a shield, and a memory is a dagger. There is such power in memories. They are born of the universe itself.'

She looked away from Brandione.

'You are the pawn of the Dust Queen, most ancient of all living beings. Two of your foes are already here. They are the Watcher Aleah, who plays for Shirkra, and my own pawn, the torturer Aranfal. Do you know him?'

Brandione felt a coldness in his stomach. 'I know him, yes. He will be hard to beat.' He meant it.

She approached him, and reached out a ragged arm. She touched his face with her fingers, very gently, and Brandione felt only coldness.

'You fear the Queen,' he whispered.

The Strategist laughed, and it echoed across the black sands. 'Do I fear the Queen of Dust? The creature of flowing memory? Everything fears her, my child, everything that ever was. But Ruin has grown stronger than her, and Ruin is coming. Nothing can stop it now. When the game is over, she will take me to the Machinery, and I will bring Ruin. She has promised me this, even if you win. Do you understand?'

'What if I find the First Memory?'

The Strategist twisted her body around his until they stood side by side. She put one arm around him, and swept the other across the black sands of the desert.

'You will not find it; the Old Place will *never* allow anyone to find it. The desert will engulf you, and add you to the sands.'

The sun burned purple for a heartbeat, and the Strategist was gone.

The Last Doubter pulled his cloak tight across his shoulders, and marched into the sands.

Chapter Thirty

It was the worst day of Drayn's life.

She was back at the house with Alexander, on the morning everything changed. They were in the main hallway of the building, standing beside a stone statue of Haddon Thonn, an early leader of their House. He always seemed like such a kind man. But that must have been a mistake.

He was a Thonn.

'This is your last memory, in the Choosing,' Alexander said.

Drayn nodded. She knew it would be. *If I'm Chosen or Unchosen, it'll be because of what the Voice sees here.* She wasn't sure she cared, any more. She couldn't forget now. She couldn't box the memory away again, even if Cranwyl was there to help her.

She'd have to remember what happened that day.

There was a movement ahead, and the doors of the small reception room creaked open. Dad came staggering out, red-faced, a bottle of something in his hand. He had been drinking all night. Drayn remembered that, now.

Mother and the younger Drayn came after him. There was something imperious about Mother, and never more so than at this moment. Here was the House of Thonn person-ified. She held something in her hands, but it was hidden under the folds of her scarlet gown. Drayn knew what it was.

There was no one else there. Not even Cranwyl. It wouldn't have mattered anyway. No one interfered in the affairs of the House of Thonn, if they knew anything about the House of Thonn. And everyone on the Habitation knew all about the House of Thonn.

Drayn studied her younger self with a sense of detachment. Who was that girl, on this day? Who was she now? Would the Voice admire her, or hate her?

'Teron. Where are you going?'

Mother's tone was deadening, and Dad felt it, even in his drunken state. He fell into silence, except for his ragged breaths, and stood staring at the floor for a few moments before turning to his wife and daughter.

'You can say what you want,' he said, his voice strangely clear, 'but I'm going to the Autocrat. I'm going to tell him what you've done. He'd never stand for it, if he only knew.'

Mother smiled. It was sweet, on the surface.

'Teron,' she said, pacing forward slowly. 'Are you insane? What is it you plan on telling the Autocrat?'

'About *you*,' Dad spat, jabbing a finger at the head of the House of Thonn. 'I'm going to tell him what you did to your own *brother*.'

Mother laughed. 'Teron, the Houses have run this island for ten thousand years. Do you truly think the Lord Autocrat is so blind that he doesn't know how things work?'

Dad stared at her with bulging eyes.

'And even if you're right,' Mother continued, coming closer, 'how will you explain your involvement in it all? You were there, weren't you? You didn't start to whinge about it all until recently. You're as much a murderer as the rest of us.'

Dad shook his head again. He seemed to be sobering up. Perhaps if they'd given him a little longer, he would have come to his senses. But they didn't. They couldn't. This was the House of Thonn.

'You are proposing to humiliate the House of Thonn, which one day your daughter will lead. Do you not love us, Teron? You mustn't, I think. You wouldn't embarrass us like this if you really did.'

'I'm doing this for Drayn.'

'You don't know what Drayn needs. You can't even look after yourself. What happened to you?'

Dad sighed, and his chest rattled. 'The House of Thonn happened to me.'

Mother drew her hands out from underneath her gown. She was holding a long dagger with a golden hilt. Drayn had never seen this blade before, and she would never see it again.

Dad nodded. He did not seem surprised. Drayn wondered, now, if this was what he had wanted all along. He was too much of a coward to kill himself, so he did the one thing that would guarantee his death at someone else's hand: he threatened the House of Thonn.

'At least send the girl outside,' Dad said. He sounded stronger.

Mother shook her head. 'I can't do that. It's like I said before – there are unpleasant things you must accept, if you're to lead this House.' She turned to Drayn, and smiled.

She kept smiling as the blade went in.

258

They stood there, in the hallway, Drayn and Alexander. The people from the memory were frozen. Father was slumped on the floor, blood blooming across his chest. Mother stood over him, and Drayn hovered in the background.

It spoke, then: a word that echoed across the Old Place, with all the weight of the ages.

Unchosen.

The memory vanished. Drayn and Alexander were in a wide and gloomy passageway.

'No,' Alexander said, looking around him. 'This can't be right.'

Drayn shrugged. 'No one gets Chosen, Alexander.' She pointed along the passageway, to where it vanished into shadow. 'I'll bet this leads to the cave, and I'll walk out with all the other Unchosen. With Cranwyl, maybe.' She grinned. 'I suppose the House will go to one of Simeon's children. That means he won, in the end.'

'No.' Alexander shook his head. His eyes were wide. 'I sensed something there – but no, it can't be.'

Drayn began to walk, but Alexander ran up behind her and grasped her arm.

'Did you *lie* to the Voice? Was that memory ... false?'

'Don't be stupid.'

Alexander's eyes widened. 'I know when people are lying to me. And I can *feel* it upon you – you have tricked the Voice!'

He looked to the ceiling. 'Did you hear that? She tricked you! That memory was false! You must test her again!'

Drayn grabbed Alexander by the shoulders. 'Shut *up*, Alexander!'

Alexander turned his gaze from the ceiling. 'How did you

do it? How did you put us in a false memory?'

Drayn bit her lip. 'I don't know.' It was the truth. She had not wanted to go there again, and so they went to another place.

Alexander leaned forward. 'What really happened?'

Drayn hesitated for a moment.

'I'm sorry,' she said.

An image filled her head, then, of her father slumping backwards, clutching at a blade. She stood before him, her eyes smiling. Her mother came up behind her, and placed her hands on the girl's shoulders, before leaning forward and plucking the dagger from Teron's stomach. *Good*, Mother had said. *You've done well. This is just the sort of thing you have to do, to lead the House of Thonn.*

Drayn pushed the memory away, though it was not like before. This time, she knew she would never be rid of it, no matter how hard she tried.

She turned to the passageway. At the end, she could just about make out a dull light.

'I have to go now, Alexander. To the edge of the cliff.'

The boy nodded. 'You are brave, Drayn Thonn. You remind me of my sister.'

Drayn smiled, then turned her back on Alexander Paprissi. She began to march towards the real world, and the edge of the cliff.

She did not feel afraid. She would see Cranwyl, now; she could feel it.

She was never afraid when she was with Cranwyl.

Chapter Thirty-One

The hands vanished, and Brightling got to her feet.

She was in a hallway. To her left was a coat stand, shaped like some strange bird, its wings outstretched, its beak hanging open. It was dark, but she could just about make out images on the tiles below her feet: masks, in the shape of a rat's head. *The image of our new ruler. I remember the day she got it from the hand of the Operator himself.*

She walked further inside the building, and as her eyes adjusted to the gloom, she gradually realised she was not alone. A desk ran along the wall at the back; a woman sat there, her features hidden behind a veil.

'What is this place?' Brightling asked.

'This is the Museum of Older Times.'

I know that name. Katrina went here the night she disappeared.

'What am I doing here?'

The woman laughed. 'How am I supposed to know?' There was something melancholic about her. 'You came to me; I did not go to you.'

There was movement above; Brightling had failed to discern the staircase in the gloom. *You're getting rusty.* Two old men appeared there, one tall and rangy, the other short and overweight. A light glowed in the room behind them, and lifted the darkness by a fraction.

'We weren't expecting anyone,' said the short one.

'No,' said the tall one. He grinned at Brightling. 'It's nice to have surprises.' His expression soured. 'You haven't been sent by the landlord, have you?'

Brightling shook her head.

'Good, good,' he said. 'In that case, you'd better come up and have a drink.'

Brightling walked to the staircase. 'Something about this is wrong,' she said, stopping on the third stair.

'Of course, of course,' said the short man. 'Something's always wrong somewhere. That's the beauty of the world.'

'No. I'm not supposed to go with you. I'm here ...'

'You're here for the Machinery.'

It was the woman who spoke. Brightling turned to her, and nodded. 'How did you know?'

The woman did not respond.

'Ah,' said the tall man. 'Then you are indeed going the wrong way. You do not want to go with us.' He nodded down at the veiled woman. 'The lady can tell you where to go.'

The two men bowed to Brightling, then turned their backs and vanished into the room beyond.

Brightling descended the stairs and stood before the desk. She realised she was holding her mask.

'You carry part of the Absence,' the woman said. 'You wear it as a mask.'

She stood from the desk, and walked to Brightling with a shuffling gait. 'Can I see it?'

Brightling hesitated. She turned the mask over in her hand.

It had formed itself into the face of an old man, his eyes wide with fear, his mouth a jagged hole.

The woman gazed at the mask, and winced. 'It is painful to look upon the Absence, even in this state. It is dead – I *know* it is dead. Yet this seems to live, somehow. I can feel it pawing at me. It's like a little kitten that thinks it's a tiger.' Her hand shot up to her mouth, stifling a laugh. 'I wonder, did the Voice sense it?'

Brightling nodded. 'Yes.'

'I am not surprised. Once, the Voice fought the Absence with a terrible fury. But this thing can do it no—'

Brightling did not know why she did it. Perhaps it was frustration. Perhaps she wanted to feel her old power again: to feel like she was in control.

She put the mask on, and stared at the veiled woman. She saw lights before her, twinkling in a haze. She felt things, the sensation of memory: she grasped at it, dragging it towards her. She tore a corner away from a memory, and she began to pick at it.

She relented when the screams came, and removed the mask.

The veiled woman had pushed herself against the wall. 'A vicious thing to do,' she whispered. 'I thought you were going to eat me all up.'

Brightling was trembling. 'The mask has a power. I am only beginning to understand it. No memory can stand before it.'

'You wish to destroy the Voice, hmm?' The woman shuffled forward. 'Oh, how delicious.'

She pointed to a door behind her desk. 'The Voice is down there, trapped within the Machinery. But that path is treacherous indeed. Once, I tried to go myself.' She pulled her veil up slightly, revealing a burned and ruined neck. 'I was punished.'

The door blew open, and there came a flash of flame beyond. It illuminated the veiled woman, and for an instant Brightling had an image of her: her hair long and black, her eyes bright and blue, her neck and face red and raw. But the door slammed shut, the image vanished with the flames, and the veiled woman stood before her once again.

'When I tried to go to the Machinery, it greeted me with fire,' the woman said. Her voice was like ashes. 'But before it threw me back, I saw such things there, in the darkness.' She turned to the doorway. 'Perhaps the Absence will protect you, if you go. Perhaps the fire will not come for you.'

Brightling approached the burned woman. 'I will go. I will destroy the Voice, and then the thing that holds Katrina, and any of the rest of them that try to stop me.'

The woman nodded. 'You will descend steps for a long time. It will be a strange journey for you.' She sighed. 'But you will find the thing you call the Machinery, if that is what you want. You will find it, and the Voice.'

Brightling nodded, opened the door, and stepped into the darkness.

Chapter Thirty-Two

Canning and Raxx took to a staircase, a metallic monstrosity that clanged with their footsteps. The former Tactician thought back to the steps of Memory Hall and all the other great buildings of the Overland, and of how they had exhausted him. He thought of how that *world* had exhausted him.

'This way,' said Raxx.

The Manipulator took Canning by the arm and led him off the staircase, into a dark place. Canning could see nothing, but he had learned to trust Raxx; she seemed to like him, strangely enough. There was a loud screeching sound, which he took for a metal door being pushed open, and Raxx grunted with effort.

'Come,' she said, 'the Arch Manipulator will be expecting us.'

They walked into another room, as dark as the one they had left behind. But the gloom lifted as they went. Their surroundings had utterly changed; the metal had disappeared, replaced with wooden beams and white stone. It was not unlike the dreamland he had woken up in before, though this was not that place.

They came to a golden doorway, with a guard standing at either side. For a moment it reminded Canning of the Cabinet Room of the Tacticians of the Overland, though he quickly dismissed the notion. The guards here were Manipulators, like Raxx. They had the same air about them. They nodded as she approached, and pulled open the golden doors.

Before them was a kind of gigantic observatory. The walls and the domed ceiling were entirely transparent, a gateway to the roiling sky. There was no sign now of the sun. The only natural illumination – if it was natural – came from the lightning that blazed its way through the darkness.

At the centre of the room was a narrow structure, formed of dark wood. It took Canning some time to recognise it as a staircase, winding upwards in a corkscrew.

'He is here!'

Canning looked up. The staircase, he saw, bloomed out into a wide platform. Standing at the edge was the boy he had seen in the painting, grinning down at the former Tactician. The child seemed even younger in person: curly-haired, with light brown skin and hopeful eyes, almost swamped by his white robes.

'The Arch Manipulator,' Raxx said.

The boy clapped his hands. 'Raxx, leave. Send him up to me. Off you go!'

Raxx pointed Canning in the direction of the staircase. She bowed to the boy and left the room.

Canning went to the staircase and began to climb. There was no rail, so he leaned in against the wall, willing himself not to look down. He felt some of his old fear return, and he hated himself for it. He reached the top and stepped out onto the wooden platform, exhaling a gasp of relief. The

Arch Manipulator burst into laughter.

'You are afraid, hmm? Imagine, a creature like you being afraid of a little climb!'

Canning bowed. 'I'm just that sort of creature, your highness.'

The Arch Manipulator frowned. 'But you shouldn't be, my friend, you shouldn't be. I know what you did to Kalana and Fyr, the young immortals we tested you with. That is true talent. Not just anyone can Manipulate like that. Oh, no.'

'Arch Manipulator,' the former Tactician said, falling to his knees. He did not know what else to do.

The boy laughed. 'Yes, I am the head of our order. You may call me Darrlan, though – not Arch Manipulator.' He pulled a face.

Canning stood. 'You are young to have achieved so much.'

'Am I? Hmm. Who says I achieved anything? I was born with the ability to Manipulate beyond anyone else in the Remnants. I took my position as my right. Is that an achievement?' He began to walk around the platform, gesticulating with his small hands as he went. 'In your country, the great ones are chosen by the Machinery, is that not so? It is much the same, I think. What did those people do to deserve their luck? What have they achieved, except for being themselves?'

Canning nodded. *What have they achieved, indeed?*

'And what have you really managed to do, in your Overland?' the boy went on. 'You've been much the same for ten thousand years, though you think yourselves advanced. You are only advanced in comparison with those other countries Jandell suffered to develop in the North. You are the tallest mushroom in a dark, damp forest. It is only in the last generation or so that your people have taken great leaps.'

267

The Arch Manipulator laughed. 'You ask how I know so much about your Overland.'

Canning raised his eyebrows. He had asked nothing.

'It's quite simple,' the boy went on. 'Communication. We knew things before, of course, and we learned bits and pieces over the millennia – but recent times, oh, they have been a goldmine! A man came here and sold us so much information, for paltry things like weapons and smokestuff. Jaco Paprissi, he was called. Funny name.'

Canning gasped. *So this is where he went. This is where we obtained our modern wonders.*

'Do you know what became of Jaco Paprissi, your highness? He vanished from the Overland long ago.'

Darrlan giggled. 'No, no. I never even met him, of course, what with not being alive and all. He came in my predecessor's time. But it doesn't matter. All that matters is the information he sold us. So interesting! Because, of course, in those days, we could not go into the North. Jandell had built his defences. We were left here, in our torn lands, locked in endless war.

'But something changed, recently. A new creature rules the North – Mother. She is not protective of her borders. There are no borders, in her mind.'

Canning felt he had learned more in the past five minutes than in all the preceding years of his life.

'How could Jaco Paprissi come here, if Jandell prevented it?'

The boy laughed. 'Jandell allowed Jaco to leave. He must have thought it would be good for your people. And he was right, in a way: it broadened your horizons. You were on a path to advancement, on your own terms. But I imagine he regretted it, in the end. There are bad things, as well as good,

268

in the outside world.'

'The Operators are the source of your superiority,' Canning said, wondering at his own presumptuousness. 'You mock the Overland for its backwardness, but you steal your own advances from the minds of Operators.'

The boy smiled, and spread his palms. 'You are, of course, correct, my Canning. We are all of us nothing but rats, scrabbling at the feet of giants. We steal what we can from them, and you bathe in Jandell's glory.' The Arch Manipulator sighed, and looked to the ceiling, to the nightmare outside his palace.

'Look at what we are left with, Canning, down here in the Remnants. A world of constant warfare. A world in which the Old Place and reality are in endless strife. This is a place of madness, where we cling to our lives in cities of steel.'

'I don't understand the things I can do,' Canning said. The words tumbled out of him. 'I first felt it back in the Overland, when one of them held me prisoner. She tormented me in a memory. I suffered for a long time. But after a while …'

'You felt detached from the memory. It no longer held any power over you. You could see its edges. You could sense its power, and you felt capable of using it for yourself.'

'Something like that.'

The Arch Manipulator nodded. 'It is obvious you have a natural talent, as Arandel did. Tell me – which Operator held you in a memory?'

Canning sighed. He did not like thinking back to that time. *Half-mad Annya, on the edge.*

'It was a woman.'

'Which woman? What did she look like?'

'She is hateful, and she goes by the name of Shirkra.'

The Arch Manipulator sucked in a breath. 'You escaped the Mother of Chaos?'

Canning waved a hand dismissively. 'I didn't hold her in a memory or anything like it. All I did was step outside her powers, and take a bit of ... *something* from the memory. I felt powerful, for a while. But it soon disappeared.'

'Canning, this is ... I have never heard of such a thing in a beginner.'

There came a sound of footsteps, heavy and quick, in the hall. Canning and the boy ran to the edge of the platform. Raxx was below, rushing towards them.

'Arch Manipulator – the Duet ...'

Darrlan ran to the stairs, barking instructions as he went. 'Summon the Inner and Middle Cores. Send Manipulators to the Gates. We have been foolish! We are not prepared—'

But he was interrupted.

The sound was like a cannon, echoing through the observatory with a deafening crack, forcing all within to cover their ears. Canning twisted around, looking for the source of the sound.

'Up there!' Raxx cried, pointing to the glass ceiling.

Canning turned, and saw them: Boy and Girl. The Duet. They were at the highest point of the great domed roof, on the outside, their eyes burning red. Each of them held a ball of flame in their right hands. As he looked at the fire, Canning saw *things* within it, images of times long past, a smiling man, a crying child, a bird in the sky ...

A terrible crack grew in the glass before them, snaking its way across the dome. The Duet began to laugh, and Canning could hear the sound, in his head, though that was not possible, surely it was impossible ...

The ceiling shattered, and glass rained down in the observatory. The Arch Manipulator cried out and collapsed onto
the platform. Canning spun around and saw Raxx below,
lying in a bloody pile, her body rent apart.

'Unimportant!' cried Girl. 'You went away from us!'

'Yes, sister! He went away from us!'

Canning turned around. Boy and Girl were standing before
him on the platform, grinning and toying with their strange
flames.

'We thought you were in the Overland,' he said. 'And my
name is Canning.'

Girl laughed. 'Of course we came back! They always get
us wrong, down here.'

'They don't understand us,' said Boy, shaking his head
vigorously. 'We are strange creatures, Unimportant. I mean,
Canning.'

'What did you find in the North?' He was determined to
keep the Duet talking, because behind them, on the platform
floor, the Arch Manipulator was stirring.

'Everything, Canning, everything!' cried Boy. 'All is
wonderful, all is good. Our relations are preparing for the
first game for ten millennia! They are gathering their pawns!'

The Arch Manipulator had got to his feet. His eyes were
blazing white, and he raised his hands towards the Duet.

Girl stepped forward towards Canning. 'We must win,
Canning. You understand? If we win, Mother will be so
proud!'

She was almost on top of him. She reached out with the
hand that held the flame. He felt it touch him, licking at
him. 'But we need a pawn, you see, Canning. We need a
really *good* pawn.'

'That pawn is you, Canning, in case you were wondering,'

said Boy, grinning at Canning through a gap-toothed mouth. 'You are a brilliant creation!'

In the background, the Arch Manipulator was muttering something. He seemed to be building towards a climax.

But it was too late. The Duet had already taken Canning away.

Chapter Thirty-Three

As Drayn walked through the tunnel, she thought about death and memories.

Death had been with her forever. That was always the way in the House of Thonn. Death pruned the tree. Death cut out the rot. Death kept the House alive, vigorous and healthy.

It was even true of the times they had suffered in the Choosings. It was *especially* true of the Choosings. If you weren't good enough to be Chosen, how could you hope to be of use to the House? That's what they said, anyway. It never made much sense to her.

Memories had saved Drayn. No, that wasn't it. Her ability to hide them away had saved her, for a while, at least. It was Cranwyl who had shown her the way, but it was Mother who saw the need. Perhaps that was why she had hired Cranwyl in the first place: not to betray Simeon, but to help a child hide from the truth.

Drayn did not dwell on Simeon's death, because she did not think of it: not until the Voice forced her to look again. As for ... she could not look upon that again. Not even the

273

Voice could make her see what had happened back then. She was strangely proud of this. The Voice was the most powerful thing in creation, and it was sending her to her death. Yet she had tricked it.

She had beaten it.

A dull light came from up ahead. She was suddenly conscious of walking over some kind of threshold, entering a different kind of reality. She had crossed from the Old Place to the Habitation. She heard the sound of dripping water, and she knew she was almost at the cave from which the Unchosen would emerge. *I am one of them. And hopefully Cranwyl is, too.*

She did not want her friend to be Chosen. Something told her, now, that being Chosen by the Voice was no kind of victory at all. Besides, it was not a bad death, the islanders always said. You were gone before you went over the cliff, they said. *The Guards stab you with their pikes, cut you through clean, and you only feel it for a second.*

But she knew that wasn't true. She had heard the screams, as the Unchosen fell to the Endless Ocean.

The tunnel came to a meandering end. She stood at the gateway to the cave, and for a moment felt a sense of giddy excitement.

Death is better than some memories.

She was afraid. She did not want to be. She tried to fight the fear; she pushed it down, deep within her. But it came, and she felt like it would smother her. *I don't want to die.*

'We'll get through this.'

She spun around, and there he was: Cranwyl, just the same as always. She buried herself into him.

274

'Let's go,' he said.

Hand in hand, they stepped through the gateway.

It reminded Drayn of the cave in the Old Place, where she had seen the great curtain of hands, and where she had first met Alexander. But this was unmistakeably the real world. She could see it in the great rocks that hung from the ceiling and sprouted from the floor. She could feel it in the water that dripped from the stone and gathered in cold, stagnant pools. She knew it in her heart. *This is where the Unchosen go.*

'It's bigger than I would have thought,' she said.

'Hmm,' said Cranwyl. He sounded strange: distant.

'What'd you see, down there?' she asked him.

'I don't want to talk about it.' He looked at her. 'Do you?'

She shook her head. 'Nope.'

As they walked forward, Drayn slowly became aware of other people. They emerged from the shadows along the walls, blinking in the dull light of the real world, perhaps a dozen: men, women, and children. They seemed confused, startled, helpless. *Is that how we look?* But she knew she was different. *I tricked the Voice.*

The people gathered together, though they did not communicate; they did not even make eye contact. They walked forward as a group, deeper into the cavern. As they went, the light grew brighter. Soon she could see the mouth of the cave. The flickering light that came from the opening was unnatural. *Torches. It is night.*

'Stop walking.'

The voice came from the lights.

'I said, stop walking.'

The group did as it was told.

'You are the Unchosen. You know what comes next. There's nothing you can do about it now. So don't try anything stupid.'

Figures appeared before them, monsters climbing out of the dark. *Guards.* They lumbered forward, holding their pikes, wearing their hats and their terrible masks, looking for all the world like dumb birds that had never learned to fly.

The Guards surrounded them. There were perhaps six of them, maybe seven.

'Move forward,' said one at the back.

Drayn turned slightly, and in the light of the torches she saw a gleam of gold. *The Protector.*

The group began to walk towards the mouth of the cave. Drayn heard sobbing, somewhere to her side. She didn't look to see who was crying. She didn't want to see.

But she did check that it wasn't Cranwyl. She couldn't have Cranwyl crying. Not her Cranwyl.

They came to the threshold, and walked out onto the top of the island.

Mother was not in the crowd.

Drayn did not know what made her so certain. There were thousands of people, baying for the blood of the Unchosen. What made her so confident Mother wasn't there, hidden away amid the throng?

But she knew it. She just knew it. And she was glad of it.

Something is different.

She looked towards the edge of the cliff. Lord Squatstout was there, below a torch, smiling at the Unchosen, his hands in the air.

Something is different, and it's him.

'People of my Habitation,' he said. 'What a sight you are to behold tonight!'

He did not use the ancient words. There was something fearsome about him: a kind of triumphant aggression. The crowd could sense it. They backed away from him, glancing at one another. This was not the Autocrat they knew.

Squatstout walked towards the people, and Cranwyl squeezed Drayn's hand. He'd always been a bit afraid of the Autocrat. So was she, truth be told. So was everyone.

'I am an old creature,' Squatstout said. Drayn could feel the oldness in his voice, a grinding sense of exhaustion. His appearance began to change; lines formed upon his skin and the strands of chestnut hair turned a spectral white. 'I am an old creature, from an old family.'

He bowed his head, and his body seemed to fold over, creaking painfully. But when he looked up again, he was refreshed: his skin was smooth, and his hair was as brown as it had ever been.

'It is not a happy family.' He frowned. 'Our own brother betrayed us. We trusted him – that was how he deceived us. We never thought he would hurt us. For that naivety, we can only blame ourselves.' He grinned, and his teeth were daggers. 'But the universe has a way of exacting revenge upon traitors, and it has handed this one to *me*.'

He raised a hand. There was a flash of white light, and the people cowered before the glare. When they looked back up, they saw something incredible.

A creature was there, suspended in the night air beyond the cliff, held within a ball of light that crackled with a thousand colours. Drayn could see faces in the light, miserable faces, screaming and crying. She sensed memories, there:

so many painful memories.

Drayn did not know the prisoner, but she could tell he was one of Squatstout's people. *This must be the one Mother was talking about.* He was naked, apart from a black rag, and his pale body was a patchwork of wounds. His hair was long and dark, and covered his face completely. He seemed to be asleep, or frozen. Drayn shivered when she looked at him. *What has the Lord Squatstout done?*

'His name is Jandell,' Squatstout boomed. He spat it out like a swear word from ancient times: Jan*dell*. 'He is my brother. Long ago, he betrayed us, in a war, and took the side of our enemies. He crushed us. He built a terrible thing, a powerful thing, and he handed it to our foes. This thing was called the Machinery.'

A murmur ran through the crowd. They did not like the sound of this Machinery.

Squatstout looked at his brother, hanging in the air above the cliff. For a moment, a pang of sympathy, perhaps even love, flashed across the Autocrat's eyes. But it vanished as quickly as it had come.

'My brother is arrogant,' Squatstout said. His voice was quieter now. It seemed he was speaking directly to this Jandell. 'He was told, at the very beginning, that his Machinery would break. It would break, and our Mother would return, and she would bring Ruin to the world, the beautiful Ruin we love so much. We all knew it was true: all of us except Jandell. While I have been nurturing my own strength, here on this island, he sat in the Old Place, or in his little mortal kingdom, lazy and dissolute. He is weaker than me, now, for the first time in our lives.'

Squatstout turned back to the crowd. 'Still his arrogance survived, even *after* the Machinery broke! It must have, for why else would he dare to come here, to me, after all he did? He, who threw me to the waters, all those years ago. If it had not been for the Voice, which guided me to this beloved place, I would have perished.'

'All hail the Voice,' the crowd murmured.

'He thought he could come here, and that I would help him,' Squatstout continued. 'He wants to know where Mother came from. He knows I have watched the world for ten thousand years, while he languished in his ignorance. But I will not help him. Oh, no. I will certainly not help *him*!'

Squatstout twisted, and turned his gaze upon Jandell. He began to mutter something. His words were quiet at first, but slowly became louder. '... So treacherous! But I have taken new power, from new memories. I feel their energy within me. You will see it now, my brother. I have waited to show you!'

The creature known as Squatstout began to change before their eyes. The outline of his body became hazy, and a flame flickered in his eyes. *He is a memory, too. All of this is memory.*

Squatstout rose up from the side of the cliff, to the gasps of the crowd: all except Drayn. As he went, his body changed again, becoming mangled and deformed. His legs fell away into black smoke, and his arms stretched outwards, his hands melting and reforming into long blades. He turned his face from the crowd to Jandell and back again; his eyes were dark, bloodied holes.

Our Lord is a monster from a dream: the poison of a nightmare.

The crowd hissed, and backed away from the edge of the cliff, even the Guards. The only exception was the Protector, who moved forward, to the edge, on to his master.

'This is a great moment,' Squatstout said in a pained, scratching voice. The creature floated towards his brother, almost entering the crackling haze, the daggers of his hands held aloft. 'It is the last day that Jandell the Bleak torments us.'

As Drayn looked at Jandell's strange prison, at the faces in the storm of colour, she knew what it was. She recognised this thing. *Can the others not see it?* It was a memory, too. No: it was a million memories, all of them twisted, all of them torn apart and sewn together.

She focused on one corner of the haze. She felt herself able to touch it, very gently, with her own thoughts. It noticed her; it responded to her. A thin, black tendril, so slight that no one else could see it, not even Lord Squatstout, untangled itself from the glittering orb and began to snake towards her. She could feel, rather than hear, a melancholic tune. It wrapped itself around her, like a cord, ensnaring her legs, then her torso, reaching ever upwards until it surrounded her head. It meant no harm, she knew. It was looking into her, wondering about her, speaking to her.

Fallen Girl, it said.

She did not respond. She did not know how. Instead, she took the tendril in her hand. She began to pull, lightly, afraid she might break it, though knowing in truth that it could never break, oh no, not this thing.

'What are you doing?'

She looked at Cranwyl, and smiled.

The creature that once was Squatstout had noticed her now, too. It turned to her, glaring at her, willing her to die. But it was too late for that.

She pulled it again. No: it pulled *her*.

Fallen Girl.

And then she was *inside* the haze, with the creature called Jandell. She saw Squatstout staring in at her, his eyes glowing slits.

'You can't get in here now.' She didn't know why she said it, but she knew it was the truth.

She turned to Jandell. He had woken. He was weak, his breathing swift and ragged, yet he looked at her with interest.

'So,' he said. 'You have come to me, within my prison. You must be very special.'

Drayn glanced around. 'What is this place?'

Jandell smiled. 'It is a thing of memory, formed of those I once tormented. Squatstout is using it to hurt me. I am weak.'

'I hate memories.'

'No. You love them. You can feel the power in them – the same power that we feel ourselves, a power from the beginning of time, from before the beginning of time. Our addiction for so many ages. You *are* a power. I once knew a man like you.' His face screwed up. 'Who are you? Where did you come from?'

'I'm Drayn. I fell into the Old Place. I was Unchosen. I came to the cliff's edge to die.'

'You fell,' Jandell whispered. His eyes widened. 'So that was true, as well.'

He gestured with his finger, and they were no longer floating above the water.

They had come to a tower: a long and crooked thing, pointing at the sky like a broken finger. For a moment they stood at the base of the structure. But now they were at the top, standing in a wide courtyard of dark stone. In the centre was a table, upon which was the board of some game. Jandell was there, another Jandell, young and strong, huddled beneath a heavy black cloak and staring at the table. At the other side was a woman. In truth, she had the appearance of three women, identical creatures, their features hazy and swirling, as if formed of sand. But Drayn knew this was just one being, one creature wearing three crowns of glass.

'You ask me to betray the others,' the woman said.

Her voice put Drayn in mind of the winds that shrieked around the peak of the Habitation.

The other Jandell bowed his head. 'If we do not, the war will carry on forever, or until one side is destroyed.'

The three heads smiled, but without joy. 'We take our powers from their memories. Now, they are able to use that power too. Of course they are: the memories belong to *them*.'

Jandell moved to speak, but the woman silenced him with three raised hands.

'Jandell the Bleak. I called you that, long ago, before your sisters and brothers were born, when you were the only child in your family. I saw, then, the things that you would do. I saw them.'

She bowed her heads, and behind her, the air began to shimmer.

'I will help you, Jandell, but not for the reasons you think. I will help you, because I am afraid. Do you understand? There are worse things in creation than you.'

Jandell nodded.

The creature of three bodies stood quite still. Something was taking form in the air behind her. A great bird appeared, stretching its dark wings out across the courtyard. *No. Not a bird. A cloak.* It billowed fiercely, its edges twisted and torn, though Drayn could feel no wind in this place.

'The Bleak Jandell,' said the woman. 'Speak my name.'

Jandell fell to his knees. 'Dust Queen.'

Drayn struggled to look at the woman now. Her features were almost hidden behind a twisting storm of sand, black and white and red, shifting into strange and unknowable patterns.

Drayn looked to her right, to the real Jandell. The wounds on his body were bleeding.

There was a rending sound in the air, a great clap of thunder, and the Dust Queen vanished into a whirlwind of sand. The great cloak sparked with a black light, and *faces* appeared in it, agonised faces, prisoners who wailed in their jail of cloth.

'This cloak of memory,' said the Dust Queen, though Drayn could not see her, 'is your punishment. It will hold you, and restrain you, and remind you of the things you have done in the long years since your creation. It will always be with you; even if you remove it from your body, it will be there, within your mind.'

Jandell looked up. 'I have tried to be good, your Majesty, for so long.' He glanced at the howling creatures in the material. 'Do not make me ... I cannot look at them forever ...'

'This is my price.'

Jandell nodded. 'If I wear this thing, you will assist me?'

Yes, said the storm.

The cloak flew forward and wrapped itself around the crouched form of Jandell. When he stood, the faces stared out from his body.

The Dust Queen reformed.

'Then it is done,' she said. 'I will help you, Jandell the Bleak. We will build a prison for our enemy. It will be more than a prison, though, much more.'

'I do not understand.'

'You will. It will be called ... the Machinery.' The Dust Queen raised her three right hands, and pointed into the air. 'I ask only one thing. When all is done, you will tolerate none who question what we have created; you will send these Doubters to me.'

Jandell nodded.

They had come to a dead place, where the land was black and blasted.

The Dust Queen and Jandell were standing on the edge of a pit, from which smoke poured. They were not alone. A red-haired woman lay on the ground, broken and bloodied, her green dress torn into rags; Drayn wondered if she was dead, until the woman coughed once, violently. Her eyes opened and closed, over and over; she was battling to stay conscious.

The Lord Squatstout was there, too, at Jandell's side. He stared into the pit with mournful eyes.

'It is done,' the Dust Queen said. 'It is held inside the Machinery.'

Squatstout's head snapped up, and he gave the three women a hard stare. 'Inside the ... inside the *what*?'

'The Machinery,' Jandell said. 'The price of peace.'

Squatstout's mouth hung open. 'You cannot be serious, my brother.'

Jandell nodded.

Squatstout stamped a foot on the blackened earth. 'The Duet are gone. You have killed our Mother, and poor Shirkra is on the edge of death. And you have cast our—'

'Do not call it that,' Jandell whispered, before nodding at the hole. 'It is nothing but Ruin.'

Squatstout shook his head. 'In the Machinery.' He walked to the edge, and stared down into the blackness. 'What part of the Old Place have you *put* it in? Will you know where to find it, you fool?'

Jandell shrugged. 'When I need to. It doesn't matter. The Machinery will speak to me alone.'

'Until it begins to break,' said the Dust Queen.

Jandell looked at the Queen.

'No,' he said. The confidence had drained from his voice. 'That cannot be. You *promised* me, your Majesty.'

The three heads smiled. 'You will have ten millennia of glory in your land. But then the Machinery will break, and it will Select *her,* Jandell. And after she is Selected ... Ruin will come with the One.'

Squatstout clapped his hands. 'Then Mother lives!'

The Dust Queen gave him a strange look, halfway between pity and confusion. 'All I know are the words I saw, in the darkness. But she may well be alive. She may even be in the air now, listening to us.' The Dust Queen chuckled, and somehow it was more disconcerting than if she had screamed.

She threw her three heads back, and began to speak to the sky.

'Ruin will come with the One.'

The Queen looked at Jandell, and spoke to him alone. 'I have seen other things, Jandell, in there.' She nodded at the pit. 'But I know you do not believe me. You trusted me to this point; you came to me for help. Still, you do not believe me now, because you do not want to. Know this: your arrogance will take you to the brink of death. Only one thing can save you. I tell you now, Jandell – when she comes, look within the Fallen Girl. She will be your redemption.'

She was gone, then. One moment she stood before them; in the next there was nothing but dust.

Squatstout turned to Jandell. 'The One lives, Jandell, and one day she will bring Ruin! It is not yet over.'

Jandell closed his eyes. 'No. The Queen is mistaken. The One is dead. I killed her, with my own hands.'

Squatstout laughed. 'Of course you didn't kill her. She is too strong for you. But I am weak. You are going to kill me.'

'No,' Jandell said. 'I am not.'

They were once more in their bubble, suspended above the cliff.

'The Queen told me about you, long ago,' Jandell said. 'I did not believe her. I did not believe her about anything, but I should have.' He nodded to himself. 'I have allowed myself to wither. But you are the Fallen Girl, and you will be my saviour.'

He reached out to her.

'May I …'

She nodded. She knew what he wanted. *Memories, memories, memories.*

A dark wind ran through Drayn, and there was no hiding her memories from this storm. She could feel Jandell, the contours of his power. He was weak, now; his being ached.

'You are strong,' Jandell said. Drayn opened her eyes. 'Your memories have great power, and they have given this power to me.'

The strange prison vanished, and Jandell and Drayn stood in the middle of the air, with nothing supporting them. There came a noise on the wind, a terrible howl, and in a moment the cloak reappeared; it wrapped itself around Jandell, and for half a heartbeat the faces in the cloth seemed to smile.

'What have you done ... my brother?' Squatstout had resumed his normal form, and was lowering himself back down onto the cliff edge. 'Of course you are so powerful, so powerful. You have tricked me again. How funny! We will laugh about this.'

'No,' Jandell said. His voice was a thing of iron. 'I have not tricked you. The Fallen Girl has given me strength.' His smile was a bleak thing. *The Bleak Jandell.* 'There is no more time for you. I allowed you to live, once. I came to you, for your help; you saw weakness, and sought to exploit it. You are a worthless thing.'

Jandell grew as he spoke, a creature stretched out of all natural proportion, his edges shrouded in smoke, his eyes burning coals.

'No, my brother! No!'

'Yes, Squatstout. You had the chance to live again. All you could do was come to an island, and push mortals from the rocks.'

Jandell and Drayn glided downwards, towards the cliff.

'No! You don't understand, Jandell! It wasn't me ... I was *told* to do it, by the Voice! You know who the Voice is, you know!'

'Silence. You will not speak again.'

As they landed on the ground, Jandell gave a little flick of his finger, and Squatstout's mouth was sewn closed. The Autocrat grunted desperately, but Jandell did not hear him.

He would not hear him.

'You will tell me where Mother went after the war.' He looked to Drayn and he smiled, before turning back to Squatstout. 'I will look inside you, for your words are only lies.'

An edge of the cloak snaked out, and wrapped itself around Squatstout. The Autocrat groaned, and began to mouth an endless, wordless plea. But there was no pity for him, as the cloak embraced him, burning into his skin. There was no pity for him from Jandell, or Drayn, or all the people on the cliff.

'I have seen enough,' Jandell said.

He smiled at Squatstout, and clicked his fingers. The cloak tore itself from Squatstout and hung in the air for a moment, before the faces came. They floated away from their prison, heads with no bodies, grinning cuttings of immortal cloth.

'What are you doing, my brother? Come. Please. Together, we have—'

But his words were not enough. The faces scowled at him, and surged forward, their jaws hanging open. *Memories, devouring a memory.*

As Drayn watched the death of the Autocrat, she felt afraid. Not of Jandell, or his cloak. She was afraid of herself, and the power she had given him.

The faces were sated, and the Lord Squatstout was dead, but the people still stood on the cliff. They stood on the cliff for what seemed an age, all of them together, staring into history, staring into nothing at all.

A glint of gold in the corner of her eye seized Drayn's attention. She turned, and saw that the Protector was standing at the very edge. He looked at Drayn through his golden mask, and nodded, before walking into the emptiness.

She ran to the side, and looked down.

The Protector had not fallen into the water. He was floating above it, drifting away, out across the ocean.

Chapter Thirty-Four

Brightling wondered if the flames would come when she walked through the doorway. But there was only darkness, and the Voice.

It is you.

'Yes.'

Realising she was at the top of a staircase, she took a step downwards. She thought of the world that was gone, the world she had done more than anyone to protect. She was drifting. All of them were untethered, floating to whatever was next: a paradise or a nightmare, or something else entirely.

You can see nothing. You will not get far.

The Voice was right; she was lost. But then she felt the mask burning in her hand. There came a hiss in the dark.

Why have you come here? What do you hope to achieve?

'I have come to destroy you.'

Why? You do not even know what I am.

Brightling took another step.

'You are a monster. All of you are.' *Perhaps even Jandell.*

Monsters? Not monsters, Brightling. The Machinery was built by two of us, and it could not work without me: its

prisoner. How can you say 'monster'?

The certainties of her old world were peeling away. A new clarity was emerging.

'You have made us into your playthings,' said the one-time Tactician. 'People died for you, so many of them, while you looked for a host. And Katrina ...'

Has become something more. She is at one with THE One. She is a glory!

'She is a victim.'

Going by some instinct, she put the mask on. Suddenly, she could see the world around her: a staircase, winding downwards in a corkscrew, illuminated by a green light that swooned drunkenly, like the bottom of a river.

That mask is a strange thing, the Voice said after a moment. **It is a thing of power. And a thing of death. The ultimate death. The death of memories.**

Brightling nodded. 'It is *your* death. You, and the thing that holds Katrina. And any other member of your family who tries to exploit us again.'

There was silence for a time.

You should turn back.

Brightling heard a door open, somewhere behind her.

I allow you to leave. You are descending to your death; I offer you life.

Brightling smiled. She had heard begging before – many times – but never from a thing so powerful as this.

'I'm coming for you. And I'm coming for the Strategist, when I'm done.'

You are a fool. Ruin is coming; nothing can stop that now.

The mask burned against Brightling's skin.

'What are you? What is your name?'

I am a poor creature, who did nothing but love his family. For that, I was imprisoned.

There was a great sigh in the darkness. **All of you owe me so much. All these long millennia, you have benefited from my powers. The Machinery could never have worked without me.**

Brightling leaned out a foot, but withdrew it.

'Are you the Voice that spoke to Alexander Paprissi?'

Yes. What events I unleashed! Madness in Jandell, a family destroyed, and the One placed where she belonged – with you.

Brightling closed her eyes. *Do not listen.*

She began to tremble. 'You will die soon.'

The Voice laughed. **Turn around. Turn around, and save yourself.**

The Watcher took another step.

'Not until you are destroyed, and the One is dead, and Katrina is free. I am coming for both of you.'

Ruin is coming. You cannot destroy me.

Brightling sucked in a breath. *Ruin is coming. You cannot destroy me.*

'Who are you?'

There came a laugh, old and knowing.

Ruin is not a concept, Brightling. Ruin is alive.

I am Ruin.

And I am coming.

Chapter Thirty-Five

'Where are we?'

A grey light filled the world, turning swiftly to gold and red as the sun spilled over the horizon. Canning saw that he was sitting on the branch of a mighty oak, high up in the tree. A vast forest stretched away from him in every direction, dark and silent. Far ahead there was a mountain, a silvery outcrop of rock. All of it was somehow unreal. The mountain seemed to smile ...

'We have taken you to a quiet place.'

Canning snapped his head around. At the other end of the branch sat the Duet, Boy on top of Girl, her arms wrapped around him.

'This is long ago,' said Boy.

'Very long ago,' Girl agreed.

Canning turned back to the forest. It seemed to fill half a continent. No animal sounds came from the darkness; it was only trees, and shadows.

'This is a memory,' Canning said with a nod.

'Yes,' Girl said. She untangled herself from Boy and crawled to Canning's side, tucking herself in close to him, and laying her head on his soft shoulder. 'This is one of our favourites.'

She gestured at the forest.

'We come here, when we seek solitude,' Boy said. He sat up, and crossed his legs. He had a contemplative air that Canning had not noticed before. 'You are the first mortal to see this beautiful memory in many, many ages.'

Canning laughed. 'Such an honour, before you kill me.'

Boy's eyes widened in horror. 'You do us a disservice, Canning. We would never harm anyone in this place.'

'We have brought you here to talk, Canning,' Girl said, her voice muffled in Canning's shoulder.

'Yes, yes,' said Boy, nodding vigorously. 'We have brought you here to discuss the future, and your role in it.'

'My role is finished,' Canning said. 'It finished with the Overland.'

Boy waved his hand dismissively. 'Whatever you were before is of no importance. Don't you see?' He seemed frustrated, unable to convey the full strength of his convictions to the captured human. 'Don't you see your role in the game? You are our pawn, and with you we will win!'

Canning was no longer listening, but staring into the sky. The past seemed alive in this place. It reached out and seized him. *Always a victim. Always taken to places I did not want to go.* He thought of Amyllia Brightling, of the things she had done to him as she sought to impress the Machinery. He thought of the time he had spent in the cruel embrace of Operator Shirkra, where his own memories were twisted and used to torment him. He thought of the Duet, this Boy and Girl. He thought of Raxx, tricking him, throwing him into combat with Operators. He thought of her lying in a red and crumpled heap.

He thought of the Machinery, and his anger grew. *It was*

meant to be our saviour. It was meant to elevate us. But didn't it really subjugate us? What manner of people were we, to prostrate ourselves before something we never even saw?

He looked at Boy, who had leaned in close to him. Boy's lips were moving, though Canning could no longer hear his words. He turned his head to Girl, who fell away from his shoulder. Her eyes were round and moist.

He looked again at his surroundings, and he felt the memory before him. He could see its edges, its seams. He could feel the energy that coursed through it, an old, febrile power.

He knew where it had been sewn together, and he knew how to tear it apart.

'What are you doing?'

Boy and Girl were both in front of him now, staring at him with a blend of fascination and terror. *Which one of them spoke?*

'I am not a plaything,' he whispered. 'I will no longer fill any role, unless I choose it for myself. Do you understand?'

Boy spread his palms wide before the last Expansion Tactician of the Overland. 'No, Canning! You don't understand! We don't want to hurt you!'

'Not at all, no!' cried Girl. 'We need you, you are so important ...'

Canning closed his eyes, and all the contours of the memory became visible. He reached out with his mind, and he tugged at the edges. It came to him, then, like a piece of cloth. He twisted it in his imagination, folded it and tugged at it. He pushed with his mind, and he felt its life. He felt its power: an old thing, a magic of the ancient past.

He looked at the Duet. He smiled at them. He closed his

eyes once more, and he wrapped the memory around them.

When he opened his eyes he was back in the observatory.

He was on the ground, directly below the platform. Arlan and Sanndro were there, hunched over Raxx's corpse; they looked up when he appeared, eyes wide, mouths drooping open.

'Arch Manipulator,' Sanndro croaked. 'You'd better take a look at this.'

There was a burst of noise from above, and Darrlan appeared at the side of the platform. He sucked in a breath when he saw Canning.

'By the burned throne,' he said in a whisper, 'what have you done?'

Canning slowly turned his gaze from the Arch Manipulator, and looked to his side, to where Darrlan, Arlan and Sanndro were staring. For a moment, he could not believe what he was seeing. But that moment soon disappeared. He could *feel* his achievement. He knew it to be real.

The Duet were suspended in a flickering blue orb, a sphere of memory; as he looked upon it, he could see images, glimpses of that ancient forest. Boy and Girl were completely still, their surprised expressions held in a moment. They reminded Canning of an insect he had once seen, frozen in amber. But these were no insects. These were the tormentors of the Remnants, two of the greatest powers in creation. He looked to his hand, and saw a flickering beam of light, flowing from his clenched fist to the pulsating orb.

He realised, then, that he was holding the Duet. *Him*. He had trapped them in a memory.

'What do you feel?' the Arch Manipulator asked. The boy had descended his platform and was standing beside Canning, tapping a foot anxiously on the ground and glancing from the Duet to their gaoler.

'I feel ... their power,' Canning said. 'I feel like I could take things ... knowledge, memories ...'

'Good, good. You should—'

'There's more,' Canning said. 'I feel like I can use their power as a weapon ... no, not just a weapon ...' He was finding it difficult to breathe. 'I can use them to build, or to ...' Darkness, at the corner of his eyes. 'They are mine ...'

The darkness grew, and he fell inside it.

He awoke in bed. But this time, it was not a trick.

The Arch Manipulator was at his side, grinning, holding a crystal jug of a rose-coloured liquid and a golden cup. He filled the cup and thrust it at Canning.

'Drink, drink. You must be tired. I would be dead, I think. Ha!'

Canning drank gratefully. He glanced around the room, and saw nothing but dull, hard metal. *Definitely not a dream.*

'What happened?' His voice was raspy.

'You don't remember? You held the Duet against their will, and they couldn't escape! It was the most incredible feat I have ever seen!'

Canning coughed, and tasted something in his mouth. *Blood?*

'Hardly,' he said. 'I ended up knocking myself out.' A wave of panic came over him. 'Where are they now?'

'Still in the memory you put them in,' the Arch Manipulator beamed. 'They won't be free until you let them out.'

'A memory cannot do that.'

Darrlan cocked his head to the side. 'How can you, of all people, doubt the power of a memory? Memories were made by the Absence itself; they were its greatest gift, at the beginning of life.'

An image filled Canning's mind: the sky at night, without stars. This was the clay of the universe, from which everything else was formed. But there was a struggle, at the heart of this thing: a battle between life and emptiness.

'A memory can be a prison,' said Darrlan. 'A memory can be used for creation, or for knowledge. And a memory holds power – a memory holds *magic*, put there by the hand of the Absence itself!' Darrlan gestured with his own hand, and for just a moment the room filled with a cold fire.

His expression turned suddenly serious. 'We learned to use the power of memory long ago. But no one has ever done this to the Duet, Canning. We have chipped little memories away from them. We have learned things from them. Sometimes we have kept them imprisoned for a moment. But never like this. They are at our mercy!' He bowed his head. 'Or rather, they are at *your* mercy. They are conscious, now. They ask for you constantly. They think you will help them.' The boy's expression darkened. 'But they are not to be trusted. Do you understand?'

Canning nodded, and Darrlan sighed.

'We have waited for you for such a long time, you know. We have always known you would come, but I confess, I had begun to despair of ever finding you.'

'I don't understand.'

The Arch Manipulator clapped his hands. 'Come,' he said. 'I will show you.'

The boy helped Canning climb out of the bed and led him from the room, through a series of metallic corridors and walkways. Canning tried to keep track of their progress, but it was useless. Everything in the Remnants seemed to have been laid out according to some manic plan, or no plan at all, more likely.

They came to the end of a corridor, and the Arch Manipulator abruptly stopped.

'What you see in this room will change you,' he said. He spoke in a strange voice, far older than his years. 'I give you this warning now. There is no turning back, but you should be prepared.'

Canning nodded. *It can't be stranger than everything else that's happened.*

Darrlan leaned against the wall, and it fell away before him, revealing a secret door. He grasped Canning by the hand and led him inside.

This room was unlike anything Canning had seen in the Remnants. The floor was formed of a red carpet, and the walls were hung with heavy tapestries, depicting scenes that the former Tactician could not begin to understand: battles from the past, he believed, with white-eyed humans standing amid clouds of fire. There was a strange scent in the air, a kind of musk or perfume. Everything glowed with candlelight.

'This is all that remains of the great palace in which our ancestors once lived,' Darrlan whispered. 'The rest of the building was destroyed in the war, long ago, but this room remains. We have made it the centre of our world, and built our existence around it. No one may enter except the Arch Manipulators, and whomever we choose to invite.'

The boy beckoned Canning to enter, and the former Tactician walked carefully forward. He had that strange feeling again, of crossing from one threshold to another. Was this the Underland, or the Overland, or a mixture of both? Perhaps there was no difference. Perhaps he was crossing another line: one within himself. He certainly did not feel like the same man who had fled the See House, long ago. *Was that long ago? I can't tell any more.*

'Do you know who you are?'

Darrlan's words startled Canning from his thoughts. The older man turned to the boy, who was standing in the centre of the room beside a kind of plinth that had been covered with a heavy, black cloth. The boy's expression had changed; the vitality had vanished from his eyes, and he looked at Canning with the hard gaze of a far older man.

'I am Timmon Canning. I was a Tactician of the Overland, though it was not the right place for me. I sold fish in the market.'

'No,' Darrlan said. 'You are more than that. Far more. Though you are partly correct: you are not a Tactician of the Overland. Perhaps the Machinery saw your greatness, without understanding its purpose.'

Canning snorted. 'I have had some success, playing with memories, or whatever they are. But greatness?' He gave the boy a sceptical glance, but part of him wondered at his own words. He *did* feel different. *Stronger.*

The Arch Manipulator shook his head. He turned away from the plinth and began to pace the room.

'Our battles with the Duet have lasted for a long, long, time, Canning. They have not been without their victories. Great heroes and heroines have appeared: men and women who were able to beat down the Duet for a minute, two minutes, and *really* exploit them. The other, weaker, immortals have been easier to defeat. Our society has advanced in fits and starts, all depending on these moments. It's quite pathetic, really. We are the heirs to a broken Empire. Everything we have achieved, we stole from other beings.

'Apart from these moments, we have only been able to

defend ourselves. At that, we have been successful. The Duet have won terrible victories against us, and we have suffered. But so far, we have clung on in our little cities. Whether that is down to our talents, I do not know: more likely the Duet allow us to live, like cats toying with mice.'

The Arch Manipulator laughed, but there was no humour to it.

'Some of us are good Manipulators, and some of us are excellent Manipulators, but nobody has ever matched the abilities of Arandel. He could overpower any Old One. He could hold them in a memory, and use them as he wished. That is why Jandell made peace with him: because he could not defeat him.

'Many here see Arandel as a traitor. He should have ruined the immortals, they say. He should have stayed here, in the heart of the Empire; he should never have made a pact with the enemy, and built a new country in the North.

'But we Manipulators do not think this way, Canning. We understand why Arandel did what he did. War is not a glorious thing, and a war of memory is worst of all. Besides, who would want to live in a world without the immortals? Wouldn't something glorious die with them? In the old Empire, we all worked together – Jandell and the others would share their knowledge with the leaders of the mortals, knowledge they had accrued over their long lives. In return, mortals would allow the Operators to play with their memories. Wouldn't that be a good way to live, if we could return to it some day?'

Canning shrugged, and Darrlan grinned at him.

'It doesn't matter,' the boy went on. 'The past is gone. We must think of the present.' He walked back to the plinth, and placed his hand gingerly on the black cloth.

'Before Arandel built his country in the North, he spoke to those who wished to stay in the South. In fact, he *encouraged* them to stay. There would be need of an independent place, one day, he said. There would be a need for a country, separate from what he was doing with Jandell.'

He looked again at the plinth. 'The future, Canning, is in many ways nothing more than the endless repetition of the past. Don't you think?'

'I do not know.'

Darrlan smiled. 'Arandel was so powerful, Canning, that he could ... *see* things, in the power of memory. He had the power to glimpse the future, by looking to the past. He told us, before he left the South forever, that one day a powerful Manipulator would emerge in this wasted land: a Manipulator who would have the abilities of Arandel himself. A Manipulator capable of holding Operators for as long as he chose. The Great Manipulator – the one to lead us in the final struggle with the immortals.'

Darrlan grasped the cloth tight in his small fist. 'He *saw* this person, Canning. He saw him in his mind, and he left us a portrait. It is a strange thing. It is empty. But it will show us the face of the Great Manipulator, when the Great Manipulator arrives.'

No. Not again. Please, let me lead a normal life.

The Arch Manipulator gave a sharp pull, and the cloth fell away, revealing a wooden stand, upon which was a small canvas in a golden frame.

The canvas was blank.

Canning grinned, and sighed with relief. 'Well, there you are. No Great Manipulator here.'

But as he gazed upon the canvas, he saw it begin to change. Colour bloomed across the surface, swirling and twisting until the outlines of a face appeared, a chubby face, the face of a weakling, no, the face of someone who was *more* than a weakling, the face of a new man, a powerful man ...

The Arch Manipulator was on his knees.

'Canning, you are the Great Manipulator,' the boy said, his arms outstretched, his mouth a crooked smile. 'The King of the Remnants.'

Chapter Thirty-Six

'Ask me a question.'

Drayn pushed her hands into her pockets, and stared at her island as it faded away. They had left the great rock behind many hours before, yet still it was there: a stone monster of the sea, basking in the moonlight.

'You are a memory,' she said.

'That is not a question.'

Jandell had appeared at her side, wearing his strange cloak. Faces formed, and fell away, over and over, on that dark material. There was a strength to him that she had not seen before. His features were somehow thicker, more muscular.

'I am many memories,' Jandell said. 'I was born of the power of memory, like my brothers and sisters, in the distant past. We were made to fight a god: a conflicted god, caught between a timeless death and his new life as a creator.' He placed a hand on her shoulder.

She nodded, and turned back to the Habitation.

'Will you miss your family?' he asked.

Drayn thought of Mother, and shook her head. 'I never had much of a family. I had a House. And I won't miss my House at all.'

'There's nobody at all, back there, then, that you care for? No friends, even?'

Her mind filled with an image, for a moment, of a man who had always been by her side. She had not seen Cranwyl since the Choosing. She had gone away with Jandell, and never looked back. She had taken the memory of him, and she had locked it away.

'No.'

'You have not asked where we are going,' Jandell said.

They were on the deck of the ship again. It was morning, and the water glowed. Drayn wondered how the vessel propelled itself forward. She had never been on such a thing before, not even the fishing vessels they used near the Habitation. But even she knew there was something strange about this boat. It was a dream; they were travelling forward on the back of a dream.

'You told me before,' she said. 'Into the East.'

Jandell nodded. 'Yes. But you haven't asked me anything about it.' He grinned. He appeared youthful, but there was something about him that spoke of a terrible weariness.

'I don't mind where we go,' she said. 'I trust you.'

Jandell bowed. 'Of course. You are the Fallen Girl.'

'How did you know that? How did you know it was me?'

Jandell sighed. 'I am the first spoiled youth of creation, Drayn. My parents gave me all the love in the universe, and it made me into an arrogant thing. It has always been my bane.'

For a moment, a vision flashed across Drayn's mind of a decomposing corpse, its skin rotten and crawling with insects.

'I should have listened,' Jandell continued. 'I should have listened when the Dust Queen told me about the Machinery.

305

You were there: you heard what she said. She was right about everything.'

'Yes, but how did you know *I* was the Fallen Girl?'

'Because you fell.'

'Oh.'

Jandell laughed. 'You fell, but you returned. I looked inside you, and I found such memories, stored away, such powerful things. I touched them, only for a moment, and they gave me new power. I will grow stronger, now, with you at my side. You are a great … *person*. You will be a help to me: I know it. I need you.'

He turned to face the waters. 'We must find where Mother came from. There is more there. People who can help. I can *feel* it.'

'Who is Mother? And who is out there?'

'Mother is Mother, and I am her son. As for who is out there, I do not know. But they are there. I know it.'

'Was Squatstout her son, too? And the Protector?'

Jandell gave her a quizzical look. 'The Protector? That thing was made by Squatstout, I feel. Plucked from a memory, long ago, to serve as his companion.'

'What will happen to him? Will he die?'

'Die? He is a thing of memory. It is hard for a memory to ever die.'

'So Squatstout might not be dead, either.'

Jandell did not respond.

Time was irrelevant, on the waters, with Jandell. All they did was talk about days of old. He told her many things.

They often sat inside the ship itself, in a room like a great hall, where there always seemed to be a banquet. The food was strange. Drayn chewed on a piece of bread, and it tasted like a memory.

'What is the Machinery?' she asked him one evening.

He gave her a funny look. 'It is a broken thing,' he said, and a look of terrible sadness passed over his face, before he smiled. 'But all is not lost. Ruin has not yet come.'

She nodded, though she did not understand. 'Something is happening to you. I can feel it.'

Jandell put his head in his hands. 'I am in one of my moods,' he whispered. It was meant to be a light-hearted comment, but it had just the opposite effect.

'Do you have many moods?'

Jandell pulled his hands away, and gave her a curious look. 'I was born from a bleak place, you know, Fallen Girl. Sorrow made me, and for such a long time, I made more sorrow. I found such strength in those memories. But then I changed; I felt something new. What is the word ...'

Drayn closed her eyes. For the briefest of moments, she could feel Jandell's mind.

'Regret,' she said. 'Or guilt.'

She met his gaze.

'Yes,' Jandell said. 'It changed me. I began to look for new paths. I would do anything to avoid this feeling ... this *regret*. This *guilt*. I tried to make amends.' He laughed. 'How ridiculous.'

'No. It is good.'

He waved a hand. 'But I am still myself, Drayn Thonn. I will always be myself. There is no denying it. We built the Machinery to make things better, do you understand? But when it began to break, I became the old Jandell again; I became the Bleak Jandell, without even realising it, and I did terrible things. I thought I had no choice.' He smiled at her. 'I sense painful memories, beyond the waters. I feel them, where we are going. I must confront a moment from my past, and I must atone for it.'

He placed his head in his hands again, and spoke no more.

After days or weeks or months of sailing, they saw land. It was the first land Drayn had ever seen beyond the island. It stretched as far as her eye could see, right across the horizon, a jagged line of grey rocks.

'We will be there soon,' Jandell said.

And they were.

They came to an inlet. The ship dragged itself forward, onwards and onwards, until it ran up on the sand and seemed to sigh.

'Come,' Jandell said.

They climbed down from the vessel. The beach was wide and empty, overhung with outcrops of stone.

'This way,' Jandell said.

He led her up the beach, until they came to gently inclining grasslands. They climbed for an hour, perhaps more, until the land levelled off. On and on it went, into nothing, nothing but green grass studded with rocks, like black and white bones.

'This way,' Jandell said again, and led them forward.

'Do you see that?'

Drayn squinted, studying the horizon.

'No.'

'There,' Jandell said, taking her hand and pointing her finger. 'Over there.'

She looked again. 'It's a building.'

Jandell nodded. 'The outskirts of a town.'

They began to walk on, towards the building. But they did not get far.

'Halt,' came a voice from the ground.

People appeared all around them, dressed in green, their faces painted the same colour.

'Such disguises,' Jandell breathed.

One of the men stepped forward. He was old, his face a patchwork of wrinkles, his head a thatch of grey hairs. He had a long beard, and he carried a spear in his hand. He looked different from the others, somehow.

'I know you, Operator,' he said, in a strange voice from another land. 'Do you know me?'

Jandell walked to the man, and studied him carefully.

'Yes,' he said.

He fell to his knees.

'Forgive me.'

The old man turned to Drayn.

'Who are you?' she asked.

The old man looked from the girl, to Jandell, and back again.

'Tell her who I am, Operator.'

Jandell stood.

'His name is Jaco Paprissi,' whispered the creature in the cloak. 'I took his son away.'

Hilda came to work on towards the building, but the
old man got up.

They came awake from the ground.

Hilda paused and then stood, then glanced in a certain place.
They passed the same colour.

"Stop!" she replied, Heidell Hamhead.

One of the men marched forward and it was old. His face
was shiny, or it was smashed in a dash of grey under the
lamp. a long beard, and he carried a spear in his hand. It
looked different from the others. Someone—

"I know you, you were too long in a square. I see you from
another land. Do you know me?"

She all walked to the wall and stretched out, crying out.

"I?" he said.

He fell to his knees.

To the sky.

The old man rang through it.

"Who are you?" she asked.

The old man looked down. He gathered to his left, and back
came.

"all her who I am?" he cried.

"I?" I told her.

Hilda said it aloud. "Plump, we heard the creature in the
sky upon took his own sword.